DATE DUE

4-30-04			

Demco No. 62-0549

Slaying the Red Slayer

ALSO BY BOB GARLAND

DERFFLINGER

R.I.P. 37E

Slaying the Red Slayer

(Second Edition)

▼

The First Humboldt Prior Adventure

Bob Garland

Writers Club Press
San Jose New York Lincoln Shanghai

Slaying the Red Slayer (Second Edition)
The First Humboldt Prior Adventure

All Rights Reserved © 2001 by Robert F. Garland

No part of this book may be reproduced or transmitted in any form or by any means, graphic, electronic, or mechanical, including photocopying, recording, taping, or by any information storage retrieval system, without the permission in writing from the publisher.

Writers Club Press
an imprint of iUniverse.com, Inc.

For information address:
iUniverse.com, Inc.
5220 S 16th, Ste. 200
Lincoln, NE 68512
www.iuniverse.com

This story is entirely fictional. Any resemblance to actual persons, circumstances, or events is purely coincidental.

ISBN: 0-595-18101-5

Printed in the United States of America

To my late parents,

Anne Merrill Garland and Donald Field Garland.

Epigraph

In an advertisement for her novel, *Northanger Abbey*, the great Jane Austen wrote: "This little work was finished in the year 1803, and intended for immediate publication. It was disposed of to a bookseller, it was even advertised, and why the business proceeded no farther, the author has never been able to learn. That any bookseller should think it worth while to purchase what he did not think it worth while to publish seems extraordinary."

The same thing happened with the first edition of *Slaying the Red Slayer* in 1979. There are very probably no other similarities!

Notes

1. A program for a mainframe electronic computer of the 1960's consists of three sections, viz.:
Initialization
Processing or Production
Termination
2. The chapter subtitles are from the poem "Brahma," by Ralph Waldo Emerson

Initialization

Chapter 1—The Report

Storyteller's Note: I learned about the events told in the first chapter of this story long after the rest of it happened. However, the place to write of them is at the beginning, for this is how the story, in fact and in time, began. Various intelligence materials had to be declassified before I could use them. These materials make it possible to tell the story from two viewpoints. Mine and that of two Russian army officers who now seem almost as old friends. This second point of view reappears from time to time.

*   *   *

"Major Grusev, will you come in please?" Colonel Yalinin's voice rasped and crackled over the intercom. "I want to talk to you about that new report. The one on which you, yesterday, handed in a brief."

Major Grusev stretched and yawned. He was not particularly interested in discussing a rather odd report from a suspect North American agent. Instead he wanted to leave the office early and spend a little time with his family. This had been difficult lately. It was spring in Kuybyshev, and although spring fever is not supposed to affect a Soviet Intelligence Officer, it is remotely possible that the virus had penetrated even to the Soviet Central Data Processing and Cybernetics Intelligence Office.

To put it mildly, Colonel Yalinin hadn't sounded enthusiastic. That was customary. The note of irritation was what worried Alex Grusev. It was true that the report was unusual, even extraordinary. Both form and content varied from the rigid standards required of Soviet intelligence field personnel. The source was well placed, but the subject matter and circumstances were bizarre.

Then too, there was the matter of the brief. What to put in? Everything? Colonel Yalinin would refuse it. Bare facts? Colonel Yalinin wouldn't be interested. Grusev had settled for the circumstances of the discovery and an outline. Names had been largely omitted from the brief. So had the peculiar and clearly fictitious reference to a Soviet disaster during the Great Patriotic War.

What to do? Colonel Stephan could be avoided. It was only necessary to call back and say that new material cancelled the report. Grusev had done that before!

All the same, Alex was anxious to process the report. It seemed convincing. In any event, the important thing to do was to conclude it, cross-reference it, extract pertinent portions of it, and most importantly, file it. Major Grusev sighed. Outside, spring birds were competing successfully with the noise of an occasional army truck. It was not the afternoon for a long session with a chronic skeptic like Colonel Yalinin. Nonetheless, Major Grusev rose, stretched again, and walked into the next room.

"Good afternoon, Comrade Colonel."

"Good afternoon, Grusev."

Stepan Yalinin, Colonel of Intelligence (GRU), to give him for the first and last time his full title, had an office befitting his rank and importance. Pictures of Lenin and the current President of the Supreme Soviet were routine. The fact that an equally large picture of the former Party Secretary had just as much prominence showed that the Colonel had more than usual independence and character.

The office was spacious and well lighted by three large windows. The yellowish blinds and beige walls gave almost the impression of Grusev's grammar school room. Furniture filled the office. Twenty-five years before it had been elegant. The desk, bookcases, and table were of that light brown, somewhat oily looking veneer once common in railroad parlor cars. The chairs for visitors were of similar wood with heavy gray coverings. A group picture which included Stepan Yalinin, not the Colonel but the young Lieutenant of Stalingrad days, was the only other decoration.

Yalinin himself was a small, scholarly man. He was gray in appearance and manner. Chess master, bibliophile, and student of history looked out of his eyes without evidencing much interest in what they saw.

Major Grusev had little in common with his superior. The enthusiasm for everything, at least at first, that Alex brought to his duties caused his somewhat superficial manner to contrast all the more with the dour but thorough Colonel. Stepan Yalinin was a drudge. He was also an expert intelligence officer, which means he was doubtful of everything. His eyes scanned Grusev accusingly. He seemed critical of the Major's reaction to the report before he heard it.

"Well Grusev, our agent's report sounds interesting in a psychological way, but is ridiculously fantastic. Indeed, more like the work of a hysterical schoolboy. However, I suppose we must consider it."

"I agree in part, Comrade Colonel," replied Major Grusev. "However, we get very little information from U.S. G. Comp. Cen. (U.S. Government Computer Center), so we must study and use all we get. Our source has been quite reliable in the past."

"That may be, but now he is out of his head."

Grusev was disturbed. Both his natural enthusiasm for the work of one of his agents and an honest desire to do a good job, made him fear that Colonel Yalinin was being over cautious. After all, the Comrade Colonel was approaching fifty.

"It is true, Comrade, that the bulk of the report is most unusual and that the agent submits information in a flamboyant manner. Yet we cannot be choosy about our sources. It took a long time to train and plant him at Comp. Cen. We started him with a computer manufacturer ten years ago. This is his fourth job and the first one that is really useful for our purposes. And his retainer…"

"That sounds like a capitalistic line of reasoning. In other words since we paid for it, we should use it." Colonel Yalinin loved to worry his subordinates with that type of remark. It kept those younger fellows on their toes.

"The translator taped the report by reading from the original source material. I suggest we listen to it in its complete form. All you have is the brief and the agent's analysis."

Colonel Yalinin gave up. Actually, he was interested also. "All right, run it." He pressed a button under his table. Major Grusev stepped across the room. When he reached the wall a sliding panel had opened. A Baltic Model 2 repeating tape player was ready. He flipped a switch and adjusted the volume. The dry voice of a translator, amplified twice too much, blasted forth from concealed speakers.

Colonel Yalinin cursed Major Grusev in his (Yalinin's) native Ukrainian. However, Major Grusev had quickly corrected the amplification. The voice continued.

Report of Agent. Code-name 'Charles'. File 30745PCDP4. Appropriation 354 of 1965—1966. Origin: U.S. Government Computer Center, Arizona. USA Agent's report begins in the following section. End of identification.

I am presently working under cover as a computer programmer for the U.S. Government. It is very important to convey at once the immense size and power of the latest U.S. computers which are used at my location. They are unimaginably more powerful and are likely to allow some now un-thought-of programs and processes. Therefore I understand the vital importance of my task.

My present location is U.S. Government Computer Center—Secret, in western Arizona. We are located south of the Harcuvar Mountains, and north of the Southern Pacific Railroad. If you have satellite photos, you should look west of Aquila, Arizona. It is the most lonely, God-forsaken spot in the U.S., and that is saying something.

Colonel Yalinin broke in. "A fine Soviet agent you have developed. God is mentioned in the first thirty seconds of his report."

"Please, Comrade Colonel," Grusev replied, "remember he is nominally an American."

"I know that perfectly well. Did you suppose I thought…all right let it continue."

The translator's flat, accent-less voice went on.

And when you are alone at night with a giant electronic computer, in this isolated part of the United States, you are really alone. The machine just sits there, a great spinning, flashing beast. It has great virility, but no sex. We call it "it." The only sounds you hear are the whirring of the tape drives and the occasional movements of the computer operator. Outside there is an occasional wild, lonely whistle of a freight train answered in kind by the far and desolate cry of a coyote. It is a dreadful place.

It was on such a night, that I first identified the material with which my report is concerned. Only Earl, the night operator, and I were in the main computer room. The machines hummed quietly. The hours passed with a minimum of conversation. Since baseball season had not yet begun, Earl had little to say. I had reported to my superior that I would be working late to correct a defect in one of my computer programs. I had expected that this excuse would give me better access to the machine and so enable me to record some computer running times and possibly make an illegal copy of one or two tapes for delivery in the usual manner.

The main computer on which I was working is huge even by your standards. It has been deliberately designed with enormous over-capacity, so that it will accommodate all transactions and data for the next many years. There are capabilities and memory allocations for which they have no present requirements and cannot even imagine any in the future. As I indicated, I had made some purposeful errors in my computer program. That program, as corrected, ran for a long time. The night seemed to creep forward endlessly, without any completion of the computer processing.

The air in the large low room became increasingly stifling. The walls, a neutral color at best, seemed almost invisible. From time to time the night operator got up lazily to change tapes and then let the program continue.

Even the lights, the wild flickering console lights, seemed to slow their pace of agitation.

I think I was almost asleep. Then suddenly I sensed a disorder and almost a nervousness about the flashing of console lights and the whirring of the tape servos. The computer seemed to pick up speed and even Earl, the operator, stirred himself. Suddenly, from behind me, there was a mad clattering from the huge high-speed printer.

The operator turned, "This computer run doesn't call for printing. What's the matter with it?"

"I don't know," I said, "let me have a look." I had just started to walk over to the printer when a surprised exclamation for the operator stopped me. "Say," he said, "you are using a very high order of computer memory. I've never seen it in operation before." Earl had brought the processing to a controlled, temporary halt. Then he simply sat there, almost like part of the machine, waiting for my instructions.

I stepped over to the high-speed printer and began to read the material that follows in this report. At that point only one hundred or so lines had been printed. Even from this, I could see that I would need to act very carefully. I felt the hair on my neck rise.

Masking my nervousness, I turned to the night operator, "I've got an awful 'bug' in this program." Then I said tentatively, "I'm going to have to go all through the specifications, the flow charts, and the coding. Why don't you just knock off for the night? It looks like I'll be here until morning."

Computer operators obey orders. Especially government operators who are being offered unexpected time off. Even so, it seemed that it took Earl an hour to pick up his papers, get his jacket, and leave the room. It was no doubt, only minutes. Fortunately, his leaving did not involve closing down the machine. U.S. Government super-sized and maximum-readiness computers are never turned off.

I rushed back to the printer and reread the output. Then I hurried over to the control panel. A few tests confirmed my suspicions. An unintentional error in my computer program had catapulted me into very high order memory. Memory which was reserved for use well into the next decade. And yet, even in that memory, my program had executed further instructions which were spewing forth upon the high-speed printer, at the rate of almost 100 lines per minute, a most significant narrative. I pressed the 'start' button, and the clattering began again. On and on. Line after line. Page after page. Hour after hour. Carton of paper after carton of paper. The printing continued.

Colonel Yalinin broke in. "Grusev, stop the tape for a moment."

"Now Comrade Colonel, I know it doesn't sound like much so far," quickly interposed Major Grusev. He was concerned. Surely Colonel Yalinin had not already rejected the entire report. "This is only the discovery background and situation basis. You have that nearly complete in my brief. But the report itself. That's another story! Much too complex to brief at all, really. All sorts of peculiar circumstances and events. And several foreign intelligence organizations and personalities which are new to us."

"Grusev, what exactly is so—as you say—peculiar?" Colonel Yalinin sounded impatient.

"Well, for example, there is something about events in Poland. In 1945. Something of our 740th Guards Division being found wandering back from the front in a sort of daze. Some thought they were drunk, but they weren't." The words tumbled from Grusev's lips so rapidly that he missed the effect of his last statement.

Yalinin's machine gunners from the war would have known it. The expression on the Colonel's face said death and destruction, sorrow and sadness, and all that can be said of a ruined country and thirty million dead Russians. Yalinin was, however, a GRU officer and quickly mastered his feelings. Majors did not have to know everything known to Colonels. By the moment Grusev could have perceived Yalinin's changed expression, it was gone.

Major Grusev gave up. "I'll just discard the report, and put the source agent on an inactive status. We'll save several thousand rubles per year."

"Not at all," replied the Colonel, expressing a calm which he did not feel. "I want you to send out for some food. Perhaps some tea and some of those little sandwich cakes. And perhaps some apples."

Grusev, although not an apple lover, did as he was told. He also passed word to have his wife called and alerted her for his late return.

"Now then, Comrade Major," said Colonel Yalinin, "we will hear the rest of the report. Word for word. Tape for tape. Even if it takes until morning. Our source may be crazy, but even if so, it will be a good story. And if he isn't, well…"

Production

Chapter 2—Recruitment

Brahma

If this giant electronic computer is a good hiding place, I expect this story will be first, if at all, discovered and read sometime well into the next decade. This is my best estimate of the time it will take to advance memory utilization from the present date in the mid-1960's to the point at which this reserved, high-order memory will be required. It is possible that my plans will not work perfectly, but I will by then have had time to begin a new life, in a new place, and will not fear such discovery. Moreover, I am proud enough to wish to leave some record of my affairs. It is also my idea that I may need to use this narrative to call attention to certain of the proceedings of our government. While there is no black or white to these events, I think it may help me to make them known at some future time. But while proud, I am not unnecessarily foolish. So I do not want my story told unless I decide to do the telling.

Although I have had to use many names from time to time, I have first and longest answered to Humboldt Prior. I am for the moment a Senior Computer System Designer at United States Government Computer Center in Western Arizona. I helped design, system program, test, and install the government's newest computer, the gigantic Model 288-47. I now make use of my knowledge of the computer's innermost memory recesses to lodge in such places a somewhat remarkable tale.

Better than most men, I know exactly how I got here. I was tricked, deceived, and more or less enslaved by an intelligence agency of my government. At least that is what those involved tried to do. I understood most of it at the time and made a judgement that it was best for me to cooperate. While I usually did not like what I had to do, and have now successfully escaped it, I have to agree that most of what I did had to be done. This is the way of secret intelligence work. And always has been.

In the late 1950's and very early 1960's, the United States Central Intelligence Agency became well known and successful. These circumstances are sure, certain and rapid death for a secret intelligence organization. The CIA became in fact a massive bureaucracy. This has been the history of almost all intelligence agencies through history. Sooner or later they, like the CIA, become too well known to be effective in their work. Such work is necessarily secret, frequently illegal, and not infrequently unpalatable to the morals and sense of rightness of the general public. This holds equally true whether the organization is the U.S. CIA or NSA, the British MI6, or the Soviet KGB. In every case the head of the agency continues as a respected advisor to the government. The payrolls continue to increase. Operations are mounted in all parts of the world. Intelligence battles are lost and won. And the governing political body, be it the Communist Party, the British Parliament or the U.S. Congress, sleeps comfortably and soundly with the sure and certain knowledge that at last the evils of the 'national intelligence service' have been finally brought under civilian oversight and control. Little do they know.

In the case of the CIA, the nameless and faceless persons who constitute the U.S. intelligence establishment reacted to the CIA's notoriety by returning much of secret intelligence work to military control. An action like this brings a number of advantages. Financing becomes easy. A small but effective secret intelligence operation, even of the type in violent contact with enemy intelligence services around the world, can be financed for years for the cost of two or three jet fighter planes. Vast sums are not required to pay the salaries or bureaucrats or to construct conspicuous headquarters buildings. It is only necessary to provide a desk and a telephone in an obscure corner of the Pentagon. Place at this desk a not-too-bright, career noncommissioned officer. Then assign this purchasing agent the duties of paying certain charges invoiced by agencies of which he has never heard. Thereby you have financed your intelligence organization.

Other advantages to the military control lie in the areas of discipline and recruiting. Civilian intelligence operatives can walk off the job at a time of their own choosing. Soldiers cannot. Further, civilian intelligence personnel are seldom if ever severely disciplined. If a soldier, even an intelligence soldier, fails to obey orders he can be shot. And some have been! All operatives in this secret military intelligence organization were drafted soldiers. Draftees were selected because they have no choice as to the circumstances or locations at which they are first sent to serve. Only the best and most suitable men were put in position to be selected for the services required. Personnel records were laboriously screened. Certain needed qualifications were identified. Then the one individual who best met these was selected and taken. He was never really released.

All this I know now. I knew nothing of it that first night at Fort Ross overlooking San Francisco Bay. It was a beautiful night, even for guard duty. It was clear, without fog. San Francisco, Oakland, and their satellite towns were strung in lights around the black waters of the bay. Alcatraz Island lay in the center like a great, stationary ocean liner. The powerful searchlight on its masthead illuminated my sentry post at regular intervals. From motor pool to headquarters, from headquarters to motor pool, up and down, back and forth, I walked on that remembered evening. Walking guard duty on that night, I must have looked much as I do now. Over six feet tall, but not especially well built. Large head with eyes sometimes determined and sometimes evasive. Fair to sandy hair.

Up and down, back and forth. Long legs covering the ground easily. Weak eyes, needing glasses to detect anything not very large or very close that might menace the peaceful existence of the office buildings, supply sheds and repair shops of Fort Ross. There I was, a draftee soldier, with excellent intelligence, a German and Spanish linguist, and a sometimes devout coward, walking up and down with a loaded carbine on my shoulder, in what at the moment seemed the least important spot in the San Francisco Bay area.

"Cindy, oh Cindy, Cindy don't let me down…" Music, dimly heard from a nearby barracks.

At times like that I always think of the sad things. That's why I have an ulcer. Give me 15 minutes, much less four hours, of enforced mental idleness, and I'll do it every time. On this particular night I was thinking about a lady. When I had last seen her, over two years before, she was seated at a table in a cocktail lounge with a great shining diamond ring on her finger. That diamond, burning into my eyes, had not been mine. I still remember how, as I turned to leave, there was a laugh. A beautiful, silvery tinkling laugh. That night, I remembered well her eyes, her voice, how her hair looked, the shape of her body, and it had once felt against me. However, I remembered most that silvery laugh. I had since called her name to both oceans. Before another hour of guard duty would pass, most of the trees and buildings along my sentry post would likely know it too. I could feel creeping over my face that feeling of sadness which I get around my eyes instead of tears.

The arrival of Joel Martin, or rather Corporal Martin, a recent addition to our unit, was a moderately welcome diversion. He'd been stationed in Washington, D.C. and, as I now realize, had said very little about his duties there. While I did not know the man well, he had seemed friendly enough and more of my background than many of my fellow soldiers. When Joel's voice came from around the corner of a nearby building I was startled and probably jumped. Anyway, he laughed at me. That was nothing new at the time. People often seemed to do so. Then. Not anymore.

"Come on over here, Prior," Joel said, "I've got just the thing for this chilly night."

"It's not so chilly."

"I know," he laughed. "But what I have in this bottle is wet and it's got a little kick, and to you buddy, it's free."

"Well," I answered, "I've never been known to turn down an invitation like that." I stepped around to the side of the building. Sure enough, Joel had a jug of wine. It looked like the cheap, weak stuff we ordinarily bought. That was just as well because, even in my present state of mind, I knew I couldn't afford to be found drunk on guard duty. I dared not get into any trouble. I was too close to the end of my watch, and too close to the end of my two years in the army.

Joel Martin was acting particularly friendly that night. I thought at first he might want to borrow money, and was on my guard. However, it seemed that he was just in a good mood. He spoke again of how glad he was to be in the unit and how much he appreciated that fact that there were a few fellows like me that had common interests.

"We really run things around here," he said. "Those officers and noncoms don't do a thing. It's the draftees, the clerks, who hold this place together."

The only problem was that after the first small swig from his wine bottle, I found myself believing everything he said. Worse, I felt my head beginning to buzz.

Suddenly a car, which had evidently been parked further down the length of the building, drove up to us with its lights still out. Instantly, Joel's manner changed.

"All right Mr. Prior," he ordered, "please get into the car."

"Like hell I will," I said, staggering as I spoke. "What's going on? And what in the hell is in that wine? I feel half drunk already."

Nonetheless, as the car door opened, Joel steered me into it. There I was confronted by two more men whom I did not know then and do not know now. I never saw them again, nor did I ever again see Joel Martin, or whoever he really was.

"Mr. Humboldt Prior, we are about to present you with two alternatives," rasped out one of the unknowns. "We have given you drugged liquor. In one-half an hour you will be dead drunk. The first alternative is that you can spend the following hour in this car sleeping it off. The second alternative is that you can be found, within a few minutes, lying drunk at your guard post, with a bottle in your hand."

"Who the hell are you."

"You don't care about that until after you decide," replied the man who'd called himself Martin. The other two occupants of the car were silent. It was very dark and I couldn't see them clearly. The car was a Buick four-door sedan of indeterminate vintage. The two strangers were in front. I was in the back seat with Martin on my right. Slowly and carefully, as if to stretch my back and change position, I slipped the carbine off my shoulder. Then with one violent movement I slammed its stock into the side of Martin's head and lunged for the left-hand rear door. I heard a cry of pain and at the same time felt a stinging blow on the bridge of my nose. Red fires danced in my eyes. I heard Joel Martin cursing. I realized that the driver had been turned toward the back of the car and had clipped me very neatly as I hit the door.

"Mr. Prior, that was ineffective and in any event unnecessary," said the driver. "We are still prepared to be reasonable men."

For the first time the other man spoke. Although his voice was quieter, he appeared to be the senior officer. "I agree, Mr. Prior, and I can tell you, although we don't really care whether you believe us or not, that we all have the same employer. The United States Government. It is necessary for us to contact you in this unusual way. We want you to work for us. Whether you believe we are government officials or not is inoperative. If you believe us, you can join our organization believing that. If you don't believe us, you still have the choice of joining our organization or being court martialed and certainly imprisoned, if not shot, for being drunk on guard duty in a national emergency. You must decide quickly. The drug is beginning to have its effect."

Now Martin spoke again. "I'm not angry about that last trick of yours, Humboldt," he said. "We often meet that sort of thing from recruits who later prove to be our best people. In any event we are quite prepared for anything you can deliver."

The senior officer in the front passenger seat spoke again. "I'm going hand you five copies of a form. You do not have time to read it. It commits you to a five-year contractual extension of your government service and a transfer to a special military organization called ICAL. Your term of service will begin when you were due for your army discharge and will continue for five years or until the organization decides to release you."

Though already drugged, my mind raced as best it could. There was a chance that I could refuse and take my chances with the military justice system. Maybe my clean record would help? However, during almost two years of army service I'd seen much military 'injustice'. Like most soldiers, I felt a good deal of fear of the all-powerful government. Then there was a strange sense of curiosity and determination. There was nothing I liked waiting for me in civilian life. Maybe I was being shown my future?

With a trembling hand I signed the forms, but for many nights thereafter, I awakening crying out to be allowed to reverse that fateful decision.

Then I dropped off into a deep and dreamless sleep. It seemed to last about one hour, just as they said it would. As I was to soon learn they were usually right about such things. As I awakened, I felt them helping me out of the car. They started me walking on my guard post as if nothing had happened. Just as I left them, I felt a small plastic card being slipped into my pocket. Within a few minutes my relief guard appeared, and I was able to return to the barracks for the first of many sleepless nights.

The next morning I covertly examined the small plastic card. It read as follows 'ICAL Inc., Humboldt S. Prior, Representative'. They'd had a good deal of confidence in my so-called decision.

I felt instinctively that it would be most unwise to attempt to tell my commanding officer about the events of the previous night. I doubted that even the post chaplain would believe me. I therefore attempted to go about my duties as though nothing had happened and to await ICAL's next move.

Somehow I was not surprised to receive orders the next day but one. The orders transferred me to what was opaquely called the Army Supply Training Center at San Simon Creek, Arizona.

There began an intensive but unorthodox period of training, that was clearly timed to end on the date of my previously scheduled separation from army service. In effect, I had simply 're-upped'. The group of trainees consisted of several young men much like me, but we were under strict orders to avoid all but the most trivial conversation. Who we were and where we'd come from were totally forbidden topics. The training philosophy was not only to teach new things, but to intensify existing skills and characteristics. Among the interesting new skills we acquired were encoding and decoding, intelligence gathering, and endless practice with various weapons. As to existing capabilities, for my intelligence they had calculus reviews and advanced computer training. For foreign languages there were German and Spanish instructors. For developing my natural human fears, and the needed determination and sense of self-preservation, they had a number of interesting techniques. One especially.

On that day several of us were loaded into a station wagon and driven some distance away from the camp. While I was not sure that all my companions had been plucked out of army units, I knew I was not the only one to recognize our destination as a hand grenade practice range. The officer instructor spoke not a word even after we reached the throwing pits. Instead, he armed a grenade and hurled it down range. We naturally ducked behind the protective cement wall, and heard, many of us for the first time since basic training, the deafening roar of a fragmentation grenade exploding a close range. We stood up again. Another grenade was quickly thrown, this time into a small wooden enclosure somewhat closer to the barrier. Again we ducked. Again came the terrific explosion and the rain of fragmentation pellets even behind the barrier. This time the fragments were red and slippery looking. There had been something in the wooden enclosure. Something that had been alive, but wasn't any longer.

The remains of the thing were scattered over the range. At first you could see only shattered flesh and bone splinters. Then the debris of the enclosure were dragged aside. There had been a full-grown farm animal inside, now reduced to a bloody pulp. Two of my companions vomited.

Then the instructor spoke for the first time. "That is what a No. 3 fragmentation grenade does at close range. Now we are ready for your active participation in the training." He laughed. "Mr. Prior, appropriately, will be first."

One of the other range staff quickly brought forward a steel helmet. This was a reasonably welcome sight, at first! Then I saw this was no ordinary U.S. Army helmet. On the top had been welded a wide, heavy steel saucer.

"What's that thing?" one of the other students asked.

The instructor replied, "Just a little something we've borrowed from Nazi Waffen SS training. Mr. Prior will gladly demonstrate. Put the helmet on please."

Orders were orders. After almost two years in the army and especially after the type of training I been undergoing in the past months, I didn't hesitate. Then things only got worse.

"Next, Mr. Prior, please step around to the other side of the cement block barricade."

I stepped.

"Now, then Mr. Prior," said the instructor with almost casual unconcern, "I am going to place a live hand grenade on top of your steel helmet. Then I will pull the pin and I will jump back behind the wall. You will have two choices. If you stand at attention without moving, the explosion will be upwards and away from you. It will knock you unconscious, but you will not be killed or badly hurt. If on the other hand, you try to run or make any movement, the grenade will fall off and explode. What's left of you will join that cow out there."

My one advantage was that I had only two or three seconds in which to decide. Self-preservation did not desert me. I froze. I felt as though a sledgehammer blow had been delivered directly to the top of my brain. I awoke two hours later, bruised, but unhurt, back in our sleeping quarters. After that I knew more about fear and what to do about it.

Training continued for several more weeks. More of the tricks of espionage and more firearms practice. My foreign language skills were sharpened and I became more and more expert in computer systems.

Then I was released from the training school and nominally from the military service as well. I carried with me nothing but that little plastic card identifying me as an ICAL Representative. I also received a set of verbal instructions which were somewhat as follows: You will apply for a job as a computer programmer and systems designer at the U.S. Government Computer Center in the western part of the state of Arizona. You will be hired. You will subscribe to the southwest edition of the Wall Street Journal. Each day you will look at the personnel advertisement section. When your active services are required, ICAL will have a 'help wanted' advertisement for a computer programmer for service either in Germany or Spain. You will not apply. You will, however, immediately request and receive a leave of absence. You will fly to Washington, D.C., and report to the address on your ICAL card for further duty. That was that.

I did as instructed. By this time there seemed nothing else to do. I read the Wall Street Journal daily. Often I saw my advertisement. At first it seemed all too often. Later I became more proficient and did not care.

*   *   *

At this point Major Grusev took the liberty of stopping the tape. "Well Colonel," he said, "what do you think of the material thus far?"

"I begin to be interested," answered Colonel Yalinin. "But I do not understand their thinking in selecting and conscripting an agent who appears to me to be unsuitable because of his temperament."

"That is developed shortly in the report," Major Grusev replied.

"Well then, let us continue."

Chapter 3—First Conductor

"If the Red Slayer think he slays,"

It was a warm day in the early fall of 1964. John Kennedy was in his grave. Lyndon Johnson was president, but not yet President. Barry Goldwater had already lost the election although November was two months away. In spite of this, Arizona was smiling. The worst of summer in the desert was over. It had been a nice sunny day, with just enough breeze to make it pleasant. The distant mountains looked less forbidding, even to a midwesterner. My apartment seemed a little less like one of an enormous pile of shoeboxes. For once, things had even gone well at my nominal job at the U.S. Government Computer Center. We had recently hired a new programmer, luring him away from one of our computer suppliers. Because of salary differences, this was usually impossible for us to do. He was already making a big contribution and seemed unusually competent and particularly questioning and interested in our work. At little too much so in fact, but I lacked the time and opportunity to investigate him.

After work, the Wall Street Journal was waiting for me as usual. However, it had been over three months since my previous ICAL assignment. And since on that last ICAL mission I had been temporarily detained by the West German authorities, I was not expecting another call. Normally, ICAL cannot live with one of their 'Representatives' coming to the attention of the police or counter-intelligence services. When this happens it is a good sign that he will be retired and released from ICAL service. Then maybe, he can get on with his life.

Thus, even though I dutifully read the Journal's personnel advertisements, I had high hopes. I am sure that as my eyes passed over the help wanted ads, I was really looking more for another job than expecting an ICAL contact. I was half-reading an item pertaining to Intercontinental Computers Inc., a rising super-computer company, when the word 'programmer' dragged my eye to an adjacent column. I wished it hadn't, although that would have simply produced another notice in a future edition of the Journal. As I read the entire advertisement, it was all too clear. 'Programmer: Required for service in a multi-division corporation having offices in the U.S., West Germany, and Spain. Must speak and understand German and Spanish. Write ICAL Inc., Washington, D.C.

Innocent but deadly. Perfectly safe. Five applications or five hundred would all be rejected. The person they really wanted was already in their employ. Me.

The next day, my request for a month's special leave of absence was speedily granted. Obviously someone, as usual, told them I was needed elsewhere. Next came the bothersome chores of closing a bachelor's apartment for an extended period. Newspapers and mail had to be stopped. The landlady had to be told, plied with fictitious vacation plans, and worst of all paid in advance. Packing was easy. I had only to provide for the trip to Washington. A complete resupply of clothing that ICAL thought appropriate for my assignment would await me there. Only basic personal effects and personal weapons were required. Experienced representatives of ICAL are allowed to provide their own weapons. This provides some flexibility and is also less expensive.

My preference was a Mauser double-action military automatic pistol. 7.65 MM. Military pistols are generally bulkier, but this is the way the manufacturer provides strength and durability. They will take more abuse. The double action feature is handy. It means you can save seconds in firing it simply by pulling the trigger, without first cocking the hammer.

Those seconds can save a life, and have. I also carried with me a long, thin, battered looking attaché case into which I had fitted a heavily modified Kalashnikov AK-47 machine gun. There is no sense in not being prepared for opportunities.

As a favor to help with my 'vacation,' the duty driver at Comp Cen drove me to Phoenix, Arizona. From there I caught a plane for Washington, D.C. (Note: The reader will have noted that Prior is writing about a time in the 1960's before air travel security improvements would have made it impossible to bring his small arsenal aboard the airplane. Of course, ICAL if it still exists, may have ways around such regulations.)

My mood was not helped by the apprehensive feeling of anticipation and nervousness which always seems to pervade an airliner before departure. No amount of the bland, sexy-friendliness of the stewardesses could drive out the weary 'what now' from my mind. The flight was crowded. The usual number of returning tourists, businessmen, and government personnel seemed to be on board. The first free drinks appeared somewhere over Oklahoma. That's one good thing about working for ICAL, we do travel first class. By the second drink I had successfully disabused the gentleman across the aisle of the belief that he and I shared a common interest in the Goldwater election campaign. My seat companion, next to the window, was of somewhat more interest. From jealousy or for other reasons, the Federal Bureau of Investigation has been taking considerable interest in ICAL, and the man next to me had FBI written all over him. For the last 40 years J. Edgar Hoover has been doing a splendid job training FBI Agents. They now come off his production line like Cadillacs, and are about as easily recognized. This medium-height, athletically built, well-scrubbed and polished individual could just as well have been in uniform. Whether he was there to watch me or by coincidence, a few silly questions on my part confirmed his identity. He was most friendly and glad to talk about everything except his job.

I ordered us a third round of drinks as we began to approach the Appalachian Mountains. With their frequently rough flying conditions, this seemed as good a time as any. When we hit the first big air pocket my hand and my drink were out over the aisle. The FBI man's drink was right over the second button of his Brooks Brother's suit. Airplane, ICAL Representative, FBI Agent, and beverage glasses all dropped a good fifty feet. His slug of liquor remained for a second poised above his tummy. Then he had an unexpected bath! I was naturally quick to help with the toweling off. In the confusion, I was also able to remove his wallet for a quick inspection. Everything was in order, and I was sure he would be able to obtain another FBI identification card after not more than two or three weeks of explanation. Just another small battle in ICAL's struggle with the older security agencies. After all, a person has to sharpen his skills and have a little rough fun once in a while. Or any fun at all for that matter. And we might be able to use the card some time.

My wet friend and I crossed the Appalachians without further incident. We flew over a deserted Dulles Airport. It contained only a scattering of aircraft which lent further mockery to the Federal Government's belief that the American traveling public enjoys long taxicab rides. We pivoted on Mount Vernon and slid into a teaming National Airport. A quick cab ride would take me across the Potomac River into Washington.

All Washington cab drivers feel that they are expected to discuss politics and world affairs. This one's pro-Democrat, but anti-Social Security stance gave him something for everyone. I had just about convinced him that a fictitious criminal record had disenfranchised me when the cab hit the pavement of Washington, D.C.

I always think of Washington as part of another country. It seems like a little bit of Europe set down in the New World. Local people call it "the District" which adds to the air of separateness. Varied people they have got. All colors, shapes, and sizes. They have broad continental-type streets. The buildings too are quite European in appearance. It's the lack of skyscrapers that clinches it.

It didn't take long for the cab to reach ICAL's building on Vermont Avenue. I won't mention the exact address. It's a tall gray stone and brown brick building, narrow but otherwise not particularly unusual in appearance. I always think it must have been a medical professional building at one time, because the offices and conference rooms seem singularly small.

The first day or two was taken up by the customary debriefing. It is normal ICAL procedure to debrief their representatives not only after returning from an operation, but also when reporting for another assignment after a period of inactivity. They ask a lot of questions about what you have been doing, but the intent is clearly to detect changes in attitudes. This is very important to them. Personnel selection is their keynote and they want to be sure they know what they are working with. My strong points have always been intelligence, foreign languages, and a strong sense of self-preservation. I'm sure they once thought of the last as cowardice, but now they know better. I just always come back.

After several days of this and another day of medical checkups, inoculations and clothing resupply, I was ready to see my boss.

The next level up at ICAL is that of Associate. I am a Representative, but my boss is an Associate. His name is Walter Pearlman. He is an obnoxious, boorish, unpleasant, and egotistical boob. He is also a good intelligence officer, and not too bad to work for. ICAL Associates are full-time employees of ICAL, while Representatives like me have nominal jobs elsewhere with other government departments. The organization purports to be an international management-consulting firm. However, if you wanted to plan and construct a branch plant to manufacture cleated sprockets in Italy, I doubt that Walter Pearlman would be of much help. Anyway, he was unexpectedly away on vacation. That was okay with me, because it passed me on to Mrs. Lesky, his assistant.

I walked into her office at about 10:30 the next morning.

"Still an eager beaver aren't you, Humboldt S. Prior?" she said. I dislike having friends use my full name. She knows it. And I know she knows I know it.

"Yes, Mrs. Lesky."

"Have you been through the debrief?"

"Yes, Mrs. Lesky. Debriefed, tested, inoculated, new-suited, and moneyed. All wrapped up in tissue paper and tied with a blue ribbon, and I am ready for you."

"All right," she answered. Mrs. Lesky is not a bad person and I really didn't mind seeing her again. She is a refugee. A Polish Jew. But you don't tell her Polock jokes. Not to a Polish Jew who has had Nazi induced, but arrested, bone gangrene for 25 years. She is small and had no doubt once been attractive. Her original dark hair and complexion had both been grayed by time and agony. Her eyes were dull behind her thick glasses. Perhaps to compensate, she affected rather flowery print dresses. There weren't too many of each pattern of the print because she was lucky if she weighed 95 pounds. She was, in short, an older lady in years and in suffering and in disappointments. But her mind was bright and her voice was bright too.

Mrs. Lesky's office was small, but she obviously cared a good deal about it. Much of the furniture and fittings were hers not ICAL's. I doubt if her own apartment was as well fixed. Her small desk was dark wood and highly polished. Two or three Danish modern chairs, upholstered in gold fabric, matched the curtains, and contrasted nicely with the rich green carpeting. Three original oil paintings were the main decorations. The artists were unknown to me.

Mrs. Lesky began the briefing. "This is going to be a retrieval mission," she said.

I didn't like the sound of that. 'Retrieval' is what we call an assignment which involves the penetration of a foreign country and the removal to the U.S. of a person or an object too large to be easily concealed and carried by the ICAL Representative. This means the Representative has to get two things out of the country. Himself and whatever the retrieval target is. And it's usually much harder to get out than it was to get in.

Mrs. Lesky continued. "Mr. Pearlman will give you the operation orders. I am to background you. We are going to have to go back many years. Almost before you were born. I am sure that you have read that in the early 1930's, before Stalin realized Hitler's ambitions and ultimate purposes, there was a considerable de'tente between the Soviets and the Nazis. Foreign trade programs were in effect and military information was exchanged. German generals assisted in Soviet army training, while Soviet factories and testing grounds were used for the development of Nazi war machines. This situation was fruitful of risks for the military intelligence security of both countries. Even shortly after the First World War the Soviets had begun to plant a number of agents in Germany. This later led to the famous Rote Cappella or Red Orchestra resistance underground during the World War II."

I could see this was going to be a long session. "I'll buy a cup of coffee for you, Mrs. Lesky," I said. I knew what would come next.

"No," she answered, "we'll shake for it."

Out came the dice box. This was Mrs. Lesky's one vice. I've never understood the rules of her dice game. In spite of this, she usually loses. Sometimes I think she is just being nice because she makes more money than I do. This seemed to be one of those times. We helped ourselves to coffee (actually hot tea for me) from a machine down the hall. I also stuck Mrs. Lesky for a small package of cookies. They tasted as though they were left over from the Coolidge administration, but in front of Mrs. Lesky you don't waste food, so I finished them. The briefing proceeded.

"Our best information is," Mrs. Lesky continued, "that by approximately 1938, a key agent of the Soviet scientific espionage apparatus aimed at Germany had penetrated a highly technical bureau of the Schutzstaffel. You know that organization as the SS. All our information points to this. Reports from our own and from British agents indicate a marked increase in scientific intelligence information reaching the Soviets from Germany at about that time. The nature of the intelligence points to a source in the technical branch of the SS.

"The difficulty was, however, as far as the Soviets were concerned, that the Nazi Abwehr had made similar penetrations of the Soviet military high command. You will have read that this led to the notorious purges which Stalin carried out in 1938 and 1939. In addition to the Nazi sympathizers and Nazi intelligence agents, countless innocent Soviet officers and civilian officials were purged. Among these appear to have been the intelligence officers who made up the apparatus that controlled the Soviet agent with whom we are now concerned."

At this point Mrs. Lesky paused. I was more worried than ever about a retrieval operation that might involve an aging Soviet spy. Then, when I looked at Mrs. Lesky more carefully I could see she was under unusual tension. She wet her lips with her tongue, painfully and slowly adjusted her position in her huge chair, and continued.

"From all we know, it appears that the Soviet agent faced a crisis. He was marooned, so to speak. He was nominally a respected and trusted member of the SS. There was no hope of escape back to Russia, and probably as he saw it, little hope of avoiding detection by Nazi counterintelligence. His only chance must have been to be more Nazi than the Nazis. During the Second World War, his scientific abilities and training did not place him in frequent contact with Soviet prisoners, or the more unthinkable of the SS concentration camp activities." Here she paused and shuddered. "Even so Humboldt, we sense from captured documents a particularly vicious and sadistic treatment of captured Soviet scientific intelligence personnel. In fact none, so far as we know, survived their interrogation and captivity.

"By the hellish standards prevalent in the SS, these activities were grounds for the rapid promotion of the former Soviet agent. Thus in 1943 we have a new name as head of SS Scientific Warfare and Counter-Espionage. After this appointment the atrocities against Soviet and East European intelligence and scientific personnel seem to increase even more.

"Finally, after the July 20th attempt to kill Hitler, certain German scientific personnel were turned over to this man for questioning and subsequent elimination. It appears that Hitler suspected a third scientific arm of the military-intellectual conspiracy which almost led to his death. In any case, many scientists were ruthlessly interrogated and tortured. We have a description of at least one German chemical warfare specialist being hung over an iron railing. Every bone in his body was broken by expert beatings with a flexible steel rod. His vital organs were pulverized, but still he had sufficient life left in his body to moan out in pain-racked whispers the secret chemical warfare information required by the man we are discussing."

I could see Mrs. Lesky was exhausted by the lengthy briefing and her own recollections. "Let's break for lunch," I suggested. "I'll treat and then we can walk through that little gallery next to the restaurant. You can help me pick out a picture." That sort of suggestion had always worked with her before.

"Thank you, Humboldt," she answered, "but we're almost through. As I've said, Mr. Pearlman will give you the final operational orders. I have only the identification material left to give you. The ex-Soviet agent I've been telling you about is named Carl Petersen. At least that is the name he is presently using and has for many years. We believe him to be living somewhere in South America, and probably in Argentina. He is the man you are to bring back to us, voluntarily or not. And I want you to be especially careful this time."

It was typical of me that I didn't know exactly what to say. As with all new assignments, even after years of dangerous experience with ICAL work, I was already worried. I could feel my nerves tensing. Deep in thought, I hardly heard her next words.

"Say that again please, Mrs. Lesky."

"Humboldt, I said I'm not telling you this officially and if you quote me I'll deny saying it. But we are more than a little concerned with our own ICAL security in recent months and as to this case in particular. We will try not to mention this man's name again and please, you do the same. We have given him the code name '*Sunlight*'. Be careful to use that when you communicate with us. Now you'd better go back to the hotel and pack. Get to bed early too."

"What to you mean? Why do I need to do that? I was hoping for a little relaxation before Pearlman gets back to town."

"Sorry, but you are flying to Tel Aviv tomorrow!"

   *   *   *

Colonel Yalinin stopped the tape player by pressing the concealed button under his desk. His face was pale and grim. His desktop, normally so neat, was littered with torn papers and shattered pencils.

"Major Grusev," he said between clenched teeth, "we will have to take a short break. This matter is so serious that I want you to tell the staff to prepare to alert every one of our agents in South America."

Major Grusev replied, "With what you know so far I can agree with your concern, but you will not think it necessary when the report is completed."

Colonel Yalinin was adamant. "We can always cancel the preparations."

"Then I take it, Comrade Colonel, that you now find the report important." Major Grusev had to add that.

Colonel Yalinin merely glared at him and answered only by restarting the tape player.

Chapter 4—Shadows

"Or if the slain think he is slain,"

The night before I begin an ICAL assignment is a little bit like the night before running an important race. There seems to be little to do, but plenty of time to think. This is not good for me to do because it gets my ulcer going. Mrs. Lesky had simplified things by saying she'd pick me up the first thing in the morning and take me to the airport. When you travel light, packing is easy and so that can't be used to fill up the time. The starting process always seems to me as if I'm being launched down a chute. For the first few days, I seem to have little or no control over my speed and direction. Thus, when you've time on your hands and nothing routine to do, it is easy to think of all the bad things that can happen. In the first place, I wasn't partial to extracting desperate war criminals from the all too tender hands of the South American police authorities. I don't like to make people unhappy.

Also, my ulcer got busy about the peculiar addition of what seemed an unnecessary side trip to Tel Aviv. According to Mrs. Lesky, they were going to give me more background which I couldn't get in the U.S. This did not sound good or very believable. As I said, I was already known to police and intelligence authorities in Western Europe. I could easily spend two or three days walking around Tel Aviv with my face hanging out and then get it shot off. Many intelligence organizations, especially some of the newer ones, eliminate the opposition's agent first, and only then ask questions.

Lastly, I don't like to be followed. And if it wasn't so clumsy, I would have been sure I was. At first I thought it was some sort of agent's training exercise. Then I thought perhaps one of Hoover's boys was watching me with a view to squaring the episode of the spilled drink on the airplane. Also, I'd heard that the CIA were not above spraying hydrogen sulfide on ICAL representatives who had played the sort of trick I'd handed the FBI agent. Perhaps even J. Edgar was not above that sort of retaliation.

In any event, I checked out of the International Inn that afternoon, and after giving my unwanted follower a quick tour through the endless corridors of the Hilton Hotel Lobby, I jumped into a cab outside. Urging the driver to hurry, I ducked down, tossed a twenty-dollar bill onto the front seat, and was out the door and crouching behind a parked truck within a block or two. Then, seemingly alone, I strolled on and checked into the Carlton to which someone from ICAL had moved the rest of my gear.

Mrs. Lesky, with her ancient Morris Minor automobile in tow, met me at the hotel entrance early the next morning. Small owner and small car went well together. She had started me on operations before, so that I knew that in the right hand glove box would be a package of cookies, 'just for luck'. We worked our way to the airport through heavy traffic. Most of the motion was supplied by Mrs. Lesky rowing the shift lever through four or five gears at each intersection. Or so it seemed. I had a bag containing a newspaper, a New Yorker magazine, and three or four paperback books under one arm, as I walked with Mrs. Lesky through the terminal. With my soft hat, light raincoat, and small carry-on suitcase, I'm sure I looked like most of the other business travelers. Only I was sure that I had more than my share or doubts and worries, and only I had a Mauser automatic pistol inside my suit under the other arm. My briefcase with the machine gun was still at ICAL Headquarters. Even if Mrs. Lesky had been 100 percent lying about our security problem (and that was always possible) I couldn't see trying to carry a machinegun through U.S. and Israeli customs, no matter how well it was concealed.

Mrs. Lesky waited with me until my flight was called. This is usual procedure. She was acting as my case officer in Pearlman's absence. It's tough to be an agent about to be launched, as we say. But I guess it's tough to be pressing the launch button, too. Anyhow, Mrs. Lesky was most solicitous. She was full of talk of various Jewish relatives in Israel who might or might not have existed for all I knew. When they called the Eastern Airlines flight for New York she got down to business.

"Now Humboldt," she began, "your preliminary operation orders are in this envelope. You may not open them until you have left New York for Tel Aviv."

"What do I do for a start?"

"The substance is in the orders," she answered. "But briefly, we have to give you a little more field data on ImEx S.A. That stands for Import Export South America. It's an Israeli firm, or at least it is supposed to be. However, we think that it has a connection with the Israeli government's war-criminal search activities. The hard information we are getting is very new and as you'll see can't be taken out of the country. Therefore you are going to Israel. I wish I could go with you."

"In other words I have to hear something or see someone, and it is too important to rely on tapes or photographs." I was tired of not having the full story.

"Well, yes," she continued, not too happy at the interruption. "At ten AM on 25th of September you will meet our on-site representative at the corner of Rothschild Boulevard and Ben Yehuda Street in Tel Aviv. He will be wearing a felt hat, a tweed sport coat, and a white shirt with no necktie. He will have a briefcase in his left hand and a copy of the International Edition of Life Magazine under his right arm. You will be wearing the light brown suit which you have on now and a light cloth cap which you will find in your suitcase. You will have a brown paper parcel in your left hand, and you will be carrying a pipe, unlighted, in your right.

"You will say to him in English, 'can you tell me what the weather prediction is for tomorrow?' He will reply, 'Here and in Germany it is cold, but I hear it will be much warmer in South America.' If you fail to make contact on the 25th you will return two days later and repeat."

I said, "Thank you." It seemed the only reply.

Mrs. Lesky smiled. "You can see, Humboldt, that we are getting very professional."

"All that stuff is going to be awfully hard to remember."

"Well," she concluded, "you could just say 'Sam sent me'."

I'll never be sure whether she meant that or not.

El Al or Israel Airlines has a flight from Washington to Tel Aviv via New York and London. Air France also flies to Tel Aviv, but does so starting from New York. Therefore if most anyone interested in your travels to Tel Aviv knows you are flying Eastern Airlines to New York, they will assume that it's going to be Air France from there. Thus, joining the El Al flight in New York is thought to eliminate unwelcome traveling companions.

The flight to New York was as uneventful as any flight can be when you are in the midst of a crowd of businessmen, all of whom, between drinks, are trying to sell each other something. Happily, we reached Kennedy Airport according to our fast schedule, so I was able to get my bag and spend an hour waiting for the El Al jet which I could have caught in Washington. Waiting in an airline terminal is okay for about the first five minutes, but after that, for me it's a drag. I sometimes think that when some of these nuts are through sitting on flagpoles or being buried alive, there will be a competition to see who can remain in an airline terminal building for the longest time. The record number of days will not be large. Anyway that's my bet.

El Al, in the form of a 707 jet, left Kennedy on time with typical Israeli, I almost said "German," efficiency. There was no one in the seat next to me which was fine with me. I don't particularly like company and anyway maybe one of the stewardesses will sit down there, or Sophia Loren will get on at the next stop, or something.

As it turned out, I didn't even get to see too much of the stewardesses. We didn't seem to be crowded, but perhaps they found better company elsewhere. One did come along and asked me the time. It's hard to build a romance on that type of a beginning but as I did have one of those new electric watches, we had a little talk about that. I was getting up my nerve to progress the conversation to something leading to more permanence than the time of day, but then she had to serve dinner, and so I lost her. That's one of the stories of my life. Because we were flying east, into the time zones, its was night when we reached London. The plane didn't wait long there and I didn't get off.

We picked up a good many more passengers. A cloud of students and a scattering of commercial and diplomatic types. There were one or two beautiful young ladies to whom I was as usual, too slow or too shy to offer the vacant seat next to me. No one in fact, seemed very interested in me. But if you are intelligence agent that's the way you are supposed to like it.

Finally, I did get a traveling companion. He was a little, brown, dusty looking chap, who turned out to be a Professor of Archeology. This was swell because I've always liked to read about that subject. The flight to Tel Aviv was overnight, and I should have taken a good night's rest. However, I spent most of it pumping my archeologist companion about his work. He seemed to have a lot of new findings about the Dead Sea Scrolls. He had also just made some new finds at a dig of in Iraq and was trying to correlate the two. By one or two o'clock in the morning I was ready to trade jobs with him and was thinking of asking if he needed an assistant. Maybe I will some day.

We hit the concrete in Tel Aviv at about 10:00 AM local time. As the weather was clear and our approach was from the northwest, I could see the ancient city of Caesaria and the clock tower in old Jaffa, the city from which Tel Aviv has grown. It was just a short ride to the Dan Hotel which was where ICAL travel office had booked me. Since the meeting with our local representative was not until the next day, I had plenty of time to kill. I didn't mind that at all since the archeology class on the plane had cost me a night's rest. Consequently I turned in at mid-day after just a shower and one trip out of the hotel to change some dollars into local currency. I awoke again at about 4:00 PM in the warm afternoon.

The minute I was fully awake I realized I had completely forgotten to open Pearlman's preliminary operation orders. While I was fumbling with the envelope, I was hoping that I hadn't been supposed to leave the aircraft in London and do something or other. That sort of thing had happened to me before. Sometimes ICAL gives you a nice complicated courier job enroute just to save on expenses. Luckily the orders were nothing more than a repeat of what Mrs. Lesky had told me, plus the fact that Pearlman thought that since I had been, as we say 'blown' in Western Europe that I should move around very conspicuously. His hope was that anyone who was interested would either fix me operationally in the Eastern Hemisphere or would think that I was no longer with the organization. It occurred to me that they might also think that it would be a good idea to give me a nice shot with a cyanide dart just to simplify their paper work. I called Pearlman a few choice names as I always do under such circumstances. Then I had a shower, dressed and went out to move around conspicuously, obeying orders which I also always do under such circumstances.

I had dinner at the Ramot Aviv and then took in a little of the entertainment at the Accadia Grand Hotel. Because of the Orthodox influence on entertainment in some Israeli settings, I wished afterwards that I had reversed the procedure. But I guess that's another story of my life.

The next day was even hotter. You could see the blue hills of Moab only through a heat haze. I was wearing a reasonably lightweight tropical suit, and still was pretty sticky so I didn't envy my contact in his tweed jacket. Anyway, there he was at Rothschild and Ben Yehuda, the only person there with hat, jacket, and Life Magazine. Probably the only one in Tel Aviv with such an outfit for that matter. I didn't remember the greeting and apparently he didn't either. We each started to say 'Hello' at the same moment. Then we both smiled and got down to business.

His name turned out to be Samuel, so Mrs. Lesky's joke about 'Sam sent me' might have been okay, although backwards.

By agreement, we quickly parted. While he went to collect his Renault automobile, I walked back in the direction of the Dan Hotel. Then I suddenly caught a taxi, rode to the French Embassy, got out, walked in, stood around for five minutes and came out. Samuel was there to pick me up. Hopefully these ICAL-prescribed antics provided added interest for anyone who might be watching.

Samuel took me on to his office in an implement dealership on the outskirts of the city. This didn't seem too helpful until I noticed as we drove up that his business shared a common rear wall with a larger new building conspicuously marked as the headquarters of ImEx S.A. No one can say that ICAL's representatives don't have prime office space!

Samuel's office was cluttered with the usual array of papers and catalogs. Other than this, it was quite austere. Austerity and simplicity did not extend to the short wave radio transmitter which was hidden in the rear of a large filing cabinet, and to the Series 309 high-sensitivity listening device which he had inserted in the rear wall of his office. Even as we stepped into the room he motioned me to silence.

"Be still," he whispered, "they are in the office next to us. I can tell from the audiometer which I've connected to the listening bug under their conference table. Please listen carefully and remember the names and voices."

He handed me one of two sets of earphones, donned the other himself, and we sat down to hear the entertainment. After the first minutes I didn't think it was so darn entertaining after all. It got even less so as our eavesdropping continued. The voices were clear and spoke in English or occasionally in German. In either case the speakers had little accent. Samuel had one of those erasable slates on which he quickly wrote 'An ImEX person called Goldson, speaking to his associate, a woman whose name I have not learned.'

The next words we heard were, "There are two complications in the Argentine matter."

"Indeed?" the woman answered. It was a voice that I was soon to know well.

"Yes," the man's voice continued. "First, I was just getting a good feel for the lead we had on the war-criminal we have been discussing. Now however, my source wants more money, much more money."

"That will be very difficult."

"Maybe so," Goldson retorted," but if they want the object of this search they are going to have to pay for it. And pay me too. Those fools think that we are supposed to be working simply from a sense of loyalty to the cause. Maybe they are. Not me. They can take the 'causes', but I'll take the 'effects'. The personal 'effects'." He laughed at his pun.

"Hiam please, you know I don't like to hear you say things like that." She added more calmly, "For now, let's just see how we can find a way to get our job done."

"All right. In a nutshell, the second complication is that those Germans, the group from Bonn, seem to be taking an interest in our war-criminal."

"The Kreisau Gruppe?" she asked.

"That's right, my dear."

"You mean that old Cornitz and that wild von Hausenberg."

"Exactly," Goldson answered. "Also a younger person. Somebody's daughter, I think it's von Hausenberg's, who seems now to be working with them." Goldson's voice sounded particularly irritated. Perhaps he didn't care for lady spies.

He continued, "We have a recording of a small portion of this morning's radio transmission between Cornitz and one of his local people here in Tel Aviv. Will you please put the tape on the player? I want to hear it again and also learn what you think of it."

A harsh old man's voice crackled in our headphones. "Do the Israelis at ImEx have any idea about Petersen?"

Goldson's voice broke in. "That's Cornitz talking."

"No," replied the local man, "not insofar as any hard information we have indicates. However, there is a new development. Do you have a file on that American operative named 'Herman Prior'?" Damn him, he might at least have gotten my name right.

"Yes, I think we do, I'll have Kathi check it."

"Well, he's here in Tel Aviv, staying at the Dan."

Nice going Pearlman, I thought. Here I am in the city less than 48 hours and both of the apparent competitors on the project have me identified.

Cornitz replied, "How does he relate to the picture?"

The other voice went on, "I don't know for certain, he may not. For one thing I don't think he is tough enough to tackle Petersen."

Cornitz' voice rasped with disdain, "Then I know some of us who are, plenty strong enough. Now I want you to…"

Goldson's voice interrupted. "That's all that we could get on tape. I'm going to have a 24-hour watch put on the Dan Hotel. We'll soon see what the American, Herr Prior, is up to. And deal with him."

This was all nice to know, but I knew that an organization as arrogant as ICAL wouldn't let such interference go unchallenged. Samuel and I talked over the situation and I waited while he communicated with someone by coded short wave radio transmission. Then he indicated, after giving me such additional information, as he possessed, that the preliminary field-data phase of the operation was about to end. He had orders to send me back to Washington. And to give me certain special instructions for my departure.

When I left the Dan Hotel that evening, I didn't want a taxi driver for company on the way to the airport. Therefore I discretely hired a car. I couldn't go in Samuel's car because he was going to need it elsewhere. It didn't take me long to see that I had someone tailing me. A small car, with two occupants, pulled in behind me and stayed there. It looked like a Volkswagen, but in the dark I couldn't be sure. No amount of slowing down or turning off changed the situation. The airport isn't far from Tel Aviv by the direct route, but you can also reach it by a roundabout way leaving from the other side of the city and circling back through less traveled roads.

After about fifteen minutes of driving, the road passed through a narrow cut between two low hills. The sort of place preferred by the ICAL training manuals. As my car approached this point, I could feel tension building and the sadness coming around my eyes. I could just see Samuel's car parked in the brush beside the road, and I blinked my headlights as I went by. In the cut I slowed and ducked far forward in the seat, pressing against the steering wheel. Then I hit the accelerator as hard as I could and got out of the way.

Samuel's Sten gun carefully put one cover shot through the rear window of my car and then hosed and rehosed bullets into the following Volkswagen. It veered sharply to the right, out of control, and with the front mounted gas tank and front seat a sheet of flame. A burning 'thing' half-crawled from the car just before it exploded.

One thing about me, I'm a little scared only before, never after. There had just been two more casualties in a war that has no beginning and no end. The Israeli newspapers would simply say that two motorists had been ambushed by Arab terrorists. One car escaped, one did not. Samuel may have intended only to disable the tail, not to cancel it. But in our line of work precise calculations are not always possible. Still some of us grieve. It doesn't do any good, but we do.

It took several drinks and most of the flight back to New York to clear from my mind the picture of that 'thing' trying to crawl out of the burning Volkswagen.

*   *   *

Here the first deck on the tape player was exhausted. Major Alex Grusev stood up, stretched, and stepped over to restart the machine.

Colonel Yalinin turned to him; "Do reports from Tel Aviv confirm any of this material?"

"Yes, Comrade Colonel," replied Major Grusev. "The two dead ImEx men were found the next day. The man Samuel was killed in a mysterious light plane crash a few months ago."

The Colonel repeated a proverb. "In a nest of snakes, all are bitten," and signaled Major Grusev to restart the recording.

Chapter 5—Pearlman's Office

"They know not well the subtle ways,"

The sight of its pagoda-like control tower reminded me that we were landing at Dulles Airport. Since I had slept for most of the flight from New York, the long cab ride would be useful in a way. I could review my situation and the information I had collected in Tel Aviv. I wanted to be ready to talk to Pearlman.

First, however, there was the little matter of clearing U.S. Customs. Normally my U.S. Government Officer I.D. card made this a formality. Not so that day. By the time two or three very unfriendly customs officials had turned my luggage inside out, felt the lining of the suitcases, and messed up my remaining clean shirts, I was sure I recognized FBI retaliation. It is easy to leak some vague information about a narcotics smuggler fitting my general description. Luckily they did not search me personally. While ICAL representatives carry a presidential authorization to be armed at all times, we are not supposed to show it except in dire emergency. Short of doing so, I didn't want to discuss my double-action Mauser pistol with the customs people. Especially not in front of the sizable crowd that had collected in line behind me. Anyway, the FBI was now even, or perhaps one up, for the spilled drink and stolen credentials episode on the plane from Arizona.

The lengthy taxicab ride to central Washington D.C. did not pass quickly. However, I had a good deal with which to occupy me. In the first place there had already been two deaths in an operation that had scarcely begun. I couldn't get the burning car outside Tel Aviv completely out of my mind. In fact, once in a while I can still see it. Then in the second place, there were evidently 'other armies in the field'. The Germans, making up the Kreisau Gruppe, were an unknown quantity. I would have to check them out immediately. We knew a good deal more about ImEx, the Israeli organization tasked to search for war criminals. They had a reputation for playing very rough. It was clear that both groups knew something about my operation. Further, the Israelis had evidently penetrated the Kreisau Gruppe's communications. At least in part.

The more I thought about it the less I liked it, and the less I liked it the more worried I became. And from worried it's just a short step to 'ulcer symptoms'. That was the way I was beginning to feel when we reached the outskirts of the 'District'. From my standpoint, it looked like I was going to be landing in the middle of a stinging hornets' nest of Israelis and Germans of various descriptions. Added the list of serious 'stingers' would be South American National Police organizations who do not take kindly to recovery or retrieval operations conducted in their countries, especially when on behalf of their much disliked, giant neighbor to the north.

I felt a stab of pain below the left side of my chest. That was my ulcer telling me that I was worrying too much. I tried an antacid and a little sightseeing as we drove through government Washington, but it didn't seem to help very much. I kept thinking of the operation at hand. Then, trying to find the 'silver lining', my mind kept coming back to the voice of the Israeli woman whom we overheard talking to Hiam Goldson in Tel Aviv. She at least sounded okay. Perhaps this could add a little interest to the next few weeks.

By the time we reached the familiar building on Vermont Avenue my mind had put together a pretty complete set of impressions of the environment in which I was to be working. Indeed, I had already turned to various possibilities for action. Most of them involved unpleasant amounts of danger and violence. That's the trouble with having an active imagination. However, we are taught that it is better to be acting against the enemy than reacting to him.

I checked in with Mrs. Lesky, who seemed unusually glad to see me.

"Good afternoon, Mr. Humboldt Prior," she said. "You've been having some exciting days we understand."

"Yes."

"Things have moved ahead since you left us. We have some more solid information about Carl Petersen, your potential traveling companion on your return from South America. If I were you, I wouldn't make any plans for a long stay in Washington."

As nice as she was, I found myself resenting her oversimplifying words. "Thanks, but no thanks," I retorted. "And Pearlman is damn well going to have to buy me some clean shirts. Or I'll have to start using the identity of a penniless immigrant."

"We've booked you at the Hilton. There's a complete new clothing supply in your room. So is that gangster weapon." That was what Mrs. Lesky called my machine gun.

"All right," I said. "What do I do first?"

"Mr. Pearlman wants to see you right away. He said to send you up the minute you came in."

"Well, so you've sent me." It was not the first time.

As I've said before, according to our masquerade as an international management-consulting firm, I have the job title of ICAL Representative. The next level up is 'Associate'. That is the title they give my boss Walter Pearlman, and the other ICAL case officers. Associates get to have private offices on the upper floors of the building. Those who are particularly able, or particularly demanding, have larger offices or corner locations. It was typical of Pearlman that he had both a large office and a corner location.

When I appeared, Stella, Pearlman's very attractive private secretary was bent over filing papers in the outer office. I've always suspected Stella has some special personal qualifications that appeal uniquely to Walter Pearlman. She doesn't like ICAL field representatives in general or me in particular. And I don't suppose I looked very presentable after a 24-hour airplane ride. Anyway, she seemed to resent it when I gave her a friendly pat from behind, on the most "patable" surface available.

"Damn," she yelled, "it's the wonder boy of the Arizona desert. I'd like to tell you to get the hell out of here, but he wants to see you. So, the word is get the hell in there."

"Yes, ma'am," I said. I'm really very courteous.

Pearlman was studying a file. His office was symphony of artificial lighting, artificial plants, artificial mahogany, artificial fibers, and decidedly artificial paintings. All of this was stacked up on carpeting with a pile so thick that footsteps were completely silenced. Anyway, I waited standing in front of Pearlman's desk for a minute or two before he looked up and saw me.

His greeting was characteristic "Unless you're here to resign, ha ha, sit down because we're going to be a while."

"Good afternoon, sir."

"Good afternoon, Prior. I see you are still shaking." This could either have been a reference to the ruckus outside Tel Aviv or to the airplane trip. Or it could have been a general purpose Pearlman insult referring to nothing in particular.

Walter Pearlman is a big man. Over six foot two inches tall with a pale face and heavy black hair cut short and held in place with an excessive amount of rather oily hair tonic. Even 50 extra pounds did not fully obscure the form of the one-time star football player. Pearlman was loud and generally unpleasant. He was also, in my judgement, a highly competent intelligence officer, and one who had a single sterling virtue. His operations usually worked.

"I understand Lesky has briefed you on the '*Sunlight*' operation?"

"Yes, sir." The use of 'Lesky' instead of 'Mrs. Lesky' was typical.

"And you've obtained the field information in Tel Aviv?"

"Yes, sir."

"And now you're back?"

"No." I could only put up with so much.

Pearlman regarded me harshly, and then turned to look out the window for a good minute. Then he swung back to face me. By the time he did so I was bent over tying a shoelace. When I rose to face him again, Pearlman glared at me and then removed his glasses and began to clean them on his trousers. I recognized this as another deliberate irritant. The trousers must not have been very clean, for the results didn't satisfy. Next he pulled out his front shirttail to finish the job. I couldn't top that. Score one for Walter Pearlman.

"Tomorrow you are starting for Buenos Aires."

"All right."

"Once there," Pearlman continued, "you will proceed as your judgement, such as it is, indicates. We will also give you documentation for Paraguay and Brazil, as those are the other likely operational areas. It is amazing how well your capabilities fit this assignment. Your knowledge of both German and Spanish will be helpful. I also think that with all your education you ought to know enough chemistry to do that part of the job."

The chemistry part was a new wrinkle. "What do I have to do, dissolve the man?"

Pearlman ignored the question. "And your well known sense of self-preservation, which by the way we used to think was just plain cowardice, should keep you on your toes. Hopefully that will be enough so to counteract the adverse effects of your bad manners."

I could see we were just about getting down to the substance of our meeting. Pearlman wanted to seem rough and crude, but wasn't really too bad to work for. He could really 'chew ass' when necessary and he had high standards. However, he would do a good deal to protect his field representatives and was by no means stingy insofar as salary, expenses and accommodations.

"How do I get to South America?" I didn't mean this question in terms of transportation and Pearlman knew this. I was asking for an explanation of the plausible grounds that I would have for suddenly appearing in

South America, and then, no doubt, meandering all over the countryside while attempting to establish contact with my target.

Pearlman's plan surprised me both for its cleverness and for its added danger. He began "You're first going to New Orleans. There, just after you have arrived, curiously enough, there will be a serious civil rights incident. Someone is going to take a shot at the local president of the NAACP. No harm will be done, but the attempt on his life will receive a great deal of publicity. Especially in newspapers which circulate in South America.

"The day after the shooting in New Orleans, you will continue to Buenos Aires, Argentina. By the time you arrive one or two of the newspapers will have made reference to a possible suspect fitting your description. A few days later still another local paper will mention you by name, saying you had been picked up for questioning, but quickly released for lack of evidence.

Just to see what Pearlman would say, I asked, "What if someone In New Orleans takes the law into their own hands before I can get away?"

He answered, "They won't, and anyway if they do, you have a certain reputation for being able to run pretty fast."

"I guess you're right. Otherwise it sounds okay." It really did. Pearlman was good at fixing up covers of this kind. His philosophy was that it was much better to make up a cover story about a real person than to require, on short notice, that a field representative assume a complete false identity. The latter left too many opportunities for mistakes. And I guess if any North American would be sure of a favorable welcome in Latin American Neo-Nazi circles it would be a white-racist, action-man type.

"Now then Prior," Pearlman continued, "about this man Carl Petersen, whom we've named '*Sunlight*'. Lesky's briefing has told you that he was originally a Soviet scientific intelligence agent who fell in with SS operations as a matter of pure self-preservation. However, he is not, absolutely not, our target as a war criminal. If he was, this would not be a retrieval mission. Here is the nub of what we are doing. While functioning as a part of the SS scientific apparatus, he either developed or acquired some extraordinarily deadly poison gas and neurological warfare materials. When he escaped from Nazi Germany, he seems to have had the formulas, the manufacturing processes, and amazingly, actual possession of the compounds themselves. We have to have them!

"Our last real contact with him, an actual positive contact, occurs when the German armies were retreating through western Poland early in 1945. At first we had the impression that the Soviets had rounded up '*Sunlight*' and the rest of his technical group as a result of the Russian winter offensive. We have assumed for years that his information has been the basis for the Soviet chemical and bacteriological warfare development since the Second World War. We have also supposed that after all useful information had been extracted from him, what was left of him was simply turned over to the KGB executioners for elimination. After all, the Soviets have long memories and he had been inhumanely thorough in his efforts to destroy all Soviet scientific personnel with whom he came in contact during the war." Pearlman yawned. "Are you with me so far."

"Yes."

"Well then," he continued, "more recently some additional information began to appear. At first there were just vague stories. Then we bought a portion of the diary of a Polish refugee. This man had spent a good deal of time in concentration camps and was pretty shaky by the time he escaped. What we got from him is a disjointed story about having walked right through the Russian lines while making his escape to the West. This wouldn't mean too much except that he also says that the Russian soldiers seemed afraid of him. This story came to us several years ago. We, not ICAL actually, but the CIA, just circulated the information and filed it away.

We were reminded of it later, when we, meaning 'we' ICAL this time, were debriefing one of our agents who had returned from West Germany. In the course of his assignment he had a certain amount of interaction with East German veterans' organizations, and mentioned a discussion with one of their historians.

It seems that one of the last remaining German armored spearheads was probing eastward in an effort to reestablish contact with other German army formations cut off in western Poland. Their progress was so easy that they began to be suspicious. It seems that everywhere the Russians turned and fled, or were simply found wandering between the lines in a state of extreme nervous shock. I gathered that the Germans simply machine-gunned most of them, but those that they captured were little better than vegetables. They also had an animal-like fear of other human beings.

"In short," Pearlman concluded, "it looks very much as though the Russian army unit had been subjected to some form of neurological warfare attack, presumably a nerve gas."

I probed for the connection. "I gather you assume that Petersen or those under his command, doused the Russian soldiers with nerve gas and used the opportunity to escape to the West. Is that it?"

"Yes, that's what we think. And we, and doubtless the Soviets also, have been searching for him ever since." He turned to the intercom, pressed a button and spoke, "Hi Stella, tell Mr. Zavaleta to come in." He turned back to me and said quickly, "You do not know Mr. Zavaleta and, except in dire emergencies, you will not know him if you ever meet again. That's an order."

I knew what he meant. Evidently there wasn't time to transcribe Zavaleta's material or else, for some reason, they wanted me to hear it first hand. An order never to know a person again is not uncommon in our business. It simply means that never in the future are you to indicate that you recognize him, unless he initiates the contact.

A middle aged, rather swarthy-complexioned individual stepped into Pearlman's office.

"Mr. Zavaleta," Pearlman ordered, "this is Mr. Prior. I want you to tell him very briefly about the circumstances you discussed with me yesterday."

"Well," Zavaleta answered, "it has to do with the contaminants in the Parana River. The Argentine Government, although they haven't said anything officially, were most seriously concerned. They seem to have found very dilute neurological compounds, although no one is doing much talking about them. At first pesticides were suspected, but these new compounds were slightly different from anything that was known. And anyway there was no evidence of a pesticide application or any manufacturing to account for the contamination. It was more as though some neurological materials were being disposed of, periodically, by dumping them in the river."

I asked quietly, "Only in Argentina or coming from up river?" The Parana touches Paraguay and Brazil also.

Walter Pearlman glared, but then nodded, following my thinking. Zavaleta paused and thought a moment. Then he continued.

"I've only heard of it in Argentina, and nothing about any international implications. I've developed all this information in Argentina at Mr. Pearlman's request. You'll please recall however," here Zavaleta was speaking to Pearlman, "that the particulars about which I first communicated to you related to the art objects."

"What art objects?" I was getting tired of Mr. Zavaleta and wanted to bring the briefing to a close.

He answered, "Five or six small paintings from the old Royal Museum of Warsaw. They disappeared during the Second World War and have remained unaccounted for since that time. They were very nice and very valuable paintings. One, a..."

Pearlman cut him short. "That will be enough Mr. Zavaleta. Mr. Prior is not an art fancier."

I don't tell Pearlman everything.

"Suffice it to say," Pearlman continued carefully, "that someone in South America, apparently in Argentina but possibly in Paraguay, is dumping neurological contaminants into the Parana River. And somebody, possibly the same somebody, is maintaining his standard of living by selling art objects stolen in Poland by the SS during World War II."

I finished the discussion for him. "And you think that it's *Sunlight*."

Pearlman shooed Mr. Zavaleta out of his office and then continued. "Yes I do, or as a matter of fact, we all do, meaning that you have been assigned to an ICAL top-approval operation. I mean from the very top! Your mission is to locate Carl Petersen, code named '*Sunlight*'. After that there are two options. If you can persuade or force him to return to the United States with you, you are to do so. If not, then he is to be dead, with absolute certainty, when you leave South America."

I didn't like missions of that kind and probably showed it. "What do I have to do, bring back an arm for proof?"

"No. We will know one way or another, whether or not you have carried out your mission. As you will remember, we always know."

Pearlman concluded his instructions. "Starting with 0800 hours tomorrow you are to remain in constant readiness to proceed to New Orleans to commence the operation. From this moment max-security precautions are in effect. You will require a code name for this operation. Of those we have ready for use, I have selected 'Ralph'."

"Any particular reason?" I asked.

"No, but if you really don't like it, that next one on the list is 'Susan'."

"Oh."

* * *

By this time it was early evening in Kuybyshev. Major Grusev yawned and stretched.

Colonel Yalinin turned to him and said, "Their methods seem to be a little dated, but it will be interesting to see how they developed the operation."

Major Grusev nodded. He agreed.

Chapter 6—Enroute

"I keep and pass and turn again."

I was glad to get away from Pearlman's office. As always at the start of an operation there is a feeling of holding on to the organization and your case officer. After all, if you fail you may not get back alive. However, even if you are as worried as I always am, the actual commencement of an operation relieves a good deal of tension. Often you are too busy to think.

Consequently, I didn't care a thing about waiting at the Hilton for a day or two, until they were ready to launch me. Undoubtedly certain arrangements had to be made and they probably wanted Mr. Zavaleta back on station in South America before I departed. Then too, they had to arrange transportation, finances, and anything else that I might need. I had a passport that was good enough for Argentina, but Paraguay was quite another matter. There you have to have a visa, a health certificate, and a certificate of good conduct from your local police department. Paraguay is about the only country that requires the latter. I doubt that any police department that knew anything about me would have certified to my good conduct. Fortunately the Paraguayans are not very skillful at detecting forgeries.

Other than the opportunity for general purpose worrying, the enforced wait at the hotel gave me time for two things. First, reading. Mrs. Lesky and Stella both assured me that the thin file I was given contained all that ICAL knew about the Kreisau Gruppe. Perhaps they were telling the truth. There were several pages, but the substance was that nothing was known. I also quickly read several booklets on chemical warfare that I'd surreptitiously drawn from the ICAL library. Chemistry knowledge indeed!

Second, I could give some thought to the individual who followed me from ICAL headquarters back to the Hilton. It's just a few blocks and normally even someone with my unusual apprehensions would not have identified a 'tail' in such a short distance. However, he was easy to spot. A medium height, nondescript person, dressed in an out-of-style suit and wearing a straw hat. He had a rather bland look about him, as though he was a junior level clerk, which nominally he very possibly was.

I didn't really mind a tail from New Orleans once the business there was done. It might even help my cover. Before that I could do without it. Contacting ICAL headquarters was out of the question. Once an ICAL representative is in a readiness state, they refuse to accept contact except in emergency. Being followed was not such an emergency, especially for someone with my experience. I was supposed to know how to take care of that type of difficulty.

I could tell that preparations were progressing because, when I returned from dinner that evening, I found a large envelope containing all the necessary papers and money. There were plenty of Argentine pesos and Paraguayan guaranis. There was also a folder of railroad tickets which took me to New Orleans via Chicago. Mrs. Lesky and I had worked that one out. Intelligence operatives normally travel by the fastest and most direct means available, so we thought that perhaps a railroad trip would confuse any observers.

The tickets indicated that I was booked out of Washington the next afternoon, but I had known of changes even at this stage on an operation launch, so I stayed by the telephone. At noon the next day I got a call. It wasn't Mrs. Lesky or Pearlman, but a voice that I was sure I'd never heard before. With just the trace of a foreign accent, the caller said, "Good day, Mr. Prior. This is Rail Traveler Information Service. We just want to confirm your reservation on this afternoon's B & O train to Chicago."

Without thinking, I said, "Thank you." Then I kicked myself around the room several times. Somebody had me pegged as a train buff. The Washington Union Station does not provide that kind of service. This lapse was particularly bothersome because it looked like there might be a leak in our internal security arrangements. However, it was too late to do anything about it.

Anyway, the telephone rang again. This time a voice that sounded a good deal like Stella's said only two words. "Ralph, go."

And so I went.

The overnight portion of the trip to Chicago was pretty uneventful. Fortunately I had a good-sized compartment to myself. I was carrying a large suitcase, a battered briefcase, and the equally worn attaché case containing the machinegun. None of these, especially the latter would have stood any degree of scrutiny from inquisitive baggage men.

The next morning in the dining car, things got more lively. I was seated at a four-place table next to the window, which meant there was a vacant seat on my right. Dining car stewards and waiters are usually friendly and fun to talk to. These were no exception. There weren't very many people in the car so I got a good deal of attention. After I finished a large and excellent breakfast, and paid for it including a big tip courtesy of ICAL, I was ready to return to my compartment.

The steward was standing by my table and just as I started to slide out to the aisle, he removed the unoccupied outer chair. This no doubt seemed the courteous thing to do. But as I was relying on it for support, I landed on the floor of the dining car, and slid part way under the table. As I was rolling to my feet and apologizing to the steward for all the commotion, I felt another hand helping me up, one hand only. The other hand was starting to work its way into my back pocket to extract my wallet.

We are supposed to know how to react in these situations. I came to my feet very fast and pushed an elbow firmly in the direction of the would-be pickpocket. All very easy and casual. I didn't want to make any trouble. At that time.

"Excuse me," I said, "thanks for the lift."
"No trouble at all." This from the pickpocket.
"I am very terribly sorry, sir." This from the steward.

My injured dignity, my wallet, and I hustled back to my compartment to wait for our arrival in Chicago and to engage in some good serious thinking. The helpful gentleman who was interested in the contents of my wallet had turned out to be the same small nondescript clerk-like person who had followed me from ICAL headquarters. And his voice sounded a good deal like the very courteous representative of the nonexistent Washington Railroad Traveler Service.

I didn't have too much time between trains in Chicago. Only enough to make the burdensome transfer to the Illinois Central Station and board the train.

The ride to New Orleans is not particularly interesting, so I thought perhaps I could do something to liven things up. Both for me and for my unwelcome traveling companion. The trip was going to be an all-day affair and would get us to destination late in the evening. Since this was just a day train, I was limited as to the accommodations that I could select. And with the 'tail' on board, I didn't dare get very far away from my luggage. Luckily however, I hiked the length of the train before getting on and discovered that the last car was an old-fashioned observation lounge car. Or rather one-half such a car, with the front half containing a few Pullman rooms. I was able to talk the conductor out of one of these for an additional charge and made my headquarters there. This gave me a considerable sense of security. With my treasured master key it was possible to lock the compartment when going to lunch and dinner. Thus, with my housekeeping arrangements well in hand, I was able to sit and watch the Southern Illinois countryside slide by. Sit back and think of a way of providing some excitement for my unwanted traveling companion.

It was tough to figure the 'clerk', as I'd mentally named him. For all I knew he might be working for some agency of the U.S. Government. He might even be working for ICAL, simply sent along either to watch me or as a chaperon on the first leg of my journey. In a foreign country and under different circumstances there would have been a good many ways of eliminating him, either temporarily or permanently. A good strong laxative put into his food for instance. Somehow, he didn't look quite experienced enough to be one of our own people, so I thought I'd take a chance.

Fortunately, the train was nearly empty. I'd already observed that he was sitting in one of the shabby armchairs of the lounge car, watching my compartment. He was ready to follow should I go elsewhere. Or, more likely go through my luggage. He was going to be hard to get at, and for all I knew he might be as well armed as I was.

I stepped out of my room into the passageway and turning, addressed some words to a nonexistent porter. While doing this, I shielded the door with my body and managed to lock it. This was already step two of the program. Step one, completed in the privacy of the compartment, had been to pull the double-action Mauser pistol from its armpit holster and operate the slide in order to load. Then I carefully let the hammer down and replaced the gun in its holster.

There were only one or two other people in the lounge car, so I merely sat down next to my friend and began to read a newspaper. He acted ill at ease which was another indication that he was sort of a second stringer.

Time and miles passed. The plains along the Mississippi took on a certain worn-ness. A well-used look in common with the aging interior of the railroad car. After what seemed like an hour, and may well have been, the last of our fellow travelers got up and moved away to the forward cars of the train. I had a copy of the Illinois Central timetable and a quick look out the window at a milepost sign told me we were shortly coming to a brief stop at a small town. This seemed as good a place as any for what I had in mind.

"Are you enjoying the trip?" I asked the 'clerk'.

"Why, uh, yes I am," he replied.

"Are you traveling far?"

"Why, um, yes I believe I am."

"Are you traveling alone?" I certainly hoped so, but I didn't expect a straight answer.

The clerk hesitated and then said, "Yes."

I slipped the pistol out of my holster and pointed it at him behind the newspaper I was holding.

"I have a small friend with me. His name is Mr. Mauser. You can see him if you will look behind my newspaper."

"What do you and your friend have in mind?" He didn't even bother to look and was apparently quite ready to believe me. He was trying to put on a good front, but I could see he had already caved in.

"Well," I said, "there's a small town at which we will stop in about five minutes. I think that is about as far as you're going."

"Why yes, I guess it is," he sighed. "I suppose I was pretty clumsy in the dining car this morning."

"You were pretty clumsy when you started following me on Vermont Avenue in Washington. I don't know who you are or who you work for. And you can be pretty thankful for that. Because if I knew you might be getting off the train right now. Head first."

He looked badly frightened, but said nothing. Already we were slowing to a stop.

"Now," I continued, "I'm in a bit of a difficulty. I find I don't have enough money for the rest of my trip. You'll be lending me yours. I want you to take your wallet out and your belt off and put them in your jacket pocket. And no sudden movements."

He looked surprised, but did as he was told.

"Next, please take off your jacket and hand it slowly to me." I took it from him and dropped it behind one of the easy chairs. Now get up and let's walk slowly to the door of the car. Then you'll get off the train."

The last I saw of him, he was standing on the platform of the little station, looking rather bewildered. He was not a large man and his clothes were a little too big for him. With no belt, one hand was occupied in holding up his trousers. This was not really the reason for taking his belt.

Second raters, as he apparently was, would often think to use a money belt. If he was a little smarter he might have something sewn into the lining of his suit coat. In any event, without wallet, jacket, and belt, I doubted he would be able to do very much or get very far very quickly.

The rest of the trip to New Orleans was uneventful. This gave me time for more thinking. First, as a minor oddity, I'd examined the personal effects of my departed fellow traveler and found absolutely nothing interesting except some money. Worse, here I was on a tough operation traveling thousands of miles away from friends and safety and it looked more and more like our security had already been penetrated. We arrived at New Orleans late in the evening, so I was glad it was only a short cab ride to the Jung Hotel. I checked in there.

I had not been in New Orleans for some time. So, the next morning I wandered around showing myself in the city, while waiting for Pearlman to arrange the incident he had in mind. To make it work, I needed to have been seen. I guess New Orleans is a pleasant city, but I've never really enjoyed it. A former lady friend and I once planned a trip to Mardi Gras. We had talked about it all winter. Several arrangements had been made and I already, unfortunately, had spent a good deal of money on tickets and reservations. Then as always seems to happen, things started to change. More and more often, when I called her she was busy, or she didn't feel well, or she was going home for the weekend. Finally, she ran out of excuses. 'I just can't go with you' was the last one. That took some forgetting.

I was sitting at the hotel lunch counter, two mornings later, finishing a second piece of toast. And feeling guilty about it because of my waistline. Actually there was a pretty nice looking waitress working behind the counter, so perhaps even a third piece of toast was in the offing. One thing about wearing glasses is that it somewhat disguises one's eye movements. I was doing a little staring. I let my eyes play over the graceful curve of her body, up, down, and back. I made the trip a couple of times as my eyes strayed over the smooth surface of her waitress uniform. She raised her arm to take one of those little individual cereal boxes off the top shelf. My eyes caught a small, metal ventilation eyelet on her uniform under her arm. Sic transit illusion.

The telephone in my room rang later that morning.

"Good morning Ralph, meet me in St. Louie." It sounded like Mrs. Lesky and I hoped it was. Not only would I enjoy a visit with her, but I imagined she was getting considerable pleasure out of a trip to New Orleans. I was also glad to think that Pearlman thought enough of her to let her make the final arrangements for my cover story.

The cemetery of St. Louis, a common ICAL meeting place to which the call referred, is just a few blocks from the Jung Hotel. The old cemeteries of New Orleans consist entirely of aboveground tombs. These are like tall, deep sets of stone shelves, closed in front, on which the remains were laid. At the back of the shelves is an open well, a final resting-place, into which the bones are pushed after time has done its work. It's not a pleasant thought. However, I like the old cemetery. It is now a sort of tourist attraction, with guides, anecdotes about famous residents, and such things. Apparently, some of the old families have died out, for some of the tombs have fallen into great disrepair. One in particular was in considerable decay with moss and grasses growing out of cracks in the stones and even a small bush which had taken root in some cranny in the roof of the tomb. It looked a lot like a Canaletto painting and I wished I had a camera with me. It was a pleasant place to sit and think. This was where Mrs. Lesky found me.

"Good afternoon Humboldt," she greeted me. As usual she was very businesslike although I did detect a slight holiday air. Probably she was glad to get away from ICAL headquarters for a while.

"How are you today ma'am," I replied.

"Fine, thank you. Did you have a successful trip?"

"Yes I did. I even found some company on the train. Unfortunately he had to get off a little sooner than he expected."

"I know," she said. "We understand that he's been turned over to the St. Louis FBI. They don't know too much about him yet, but he seems to be an employee of a multinational South American trade organization. His passport is Bolivian, according to the records, but he seems to have lost it."

I had it in my pocket and since I thought that perhaps ICAL would want it, I handed it over. "Maybe this will help him return to a more congenial climate."

"I should think it will," Mrs. Lesky smiled. "Anyway, Humboldt, you are on your way. Buy a ticket for Buenos Aires, on Varig Airlines, for this evening. I know that actually you already have your plane ticket, but the purchase is part of the cover plan. And now I thought you might like to see the lead story of the early edition of the afternoon's paper."

The headlines were big, black, and bold. 'LOCAL CIVIL RIGHTS LEADER HAS NARROW ESCAPE. TWO SHOTS FIRED FROM AMBUSH. POLICE HAVE A LEAD.'

I said goodbye to Mrs. Lesky and was on my way. With all the publicity I didn't want to wait around.

It's a long ride out to the New Orleans airport. In fact it was one of those cab trips that seem almost as long as the following airplane trip. Of course, this wasn't really the case because Argentina is a long way away. However, once I was on board, the flight to Buenos Aires seemed to pass rather quickly. The plane was crowded with a number of people who were at least interesting to look at. I'm a stewardess watcher from way back.

The couple across the aisle from me seemed to spend most of their time discussing whether or not their children would voluntarily go to church when their parents were not there to take them. After about 45 minutes of eavesdropping on this subject, I concluded that the children would attend, and turned to see what my seat companion was up to. It wasn't hard to get him talking. He turned out to be the editor of a dog-food industry trade magazine. I did not know that we had such a formally organized dog-food industry or much less that it had a trade magazine, but I was willing to learn. By the time we were over Buenos Aires, I was almost ready to become a subscriber to his magazine, if not a consumer of his product.

As we taxied to a halt at the beautiful modern airport of Buenos Aires, my new editor friend stretched, turned to me, and said quietly, "This has certainly been a pleasant trip Mr. Prior, much better and more peaceful than train travel don't you think?"

I hadn't told him my name and if he knew that, I was pretty sure I also knew the meaning of the reference to train travel.

*   *   *

Colonel Yalinin spoke, "I certainly hope that wasn't one of our agents that Prior dumped off the train in such an embarrassing fashion."

Major Grusev replied, "No, although similar things have happened. It's a pretty old trick."

"Yes," Colonel Yalinin continued. "I think we'll have to try it on one of those ICAL people sometime. Anyway, this man Prior seems to have been a little more effective than I had first thought. And I presume he had to be, to cope with those persons in Buenos Aires."

Chapter 7—Porte'nos All

"Far or forgot to me is near,"

At Buenos Aires International Airport you meet your luggage at the entrance to the main terminal building and then carry it down a long corridor. This corridor is made to seem even longer because unlike those in the United States, there is no advertising material to read as you walk. At the end you find yourself at the Customs office and counter.

When you are carrying unusual luggage as I was, you are always concerned with customs inspectors. I very much hoped that my large attaché case, with the small machinegun hidden behind a false side panel, would pass unnoticed in a large crowd of incoming visitors. However, there didn't seem to be very many people walking down the corridor. Just as I was starting to get very worried, I had an idea. That's the way it usually is.

A Catholic priest was waiting just ahead of me. Not one of those elderly, dimpled types from the movies, but a big, tall swarthy young fellow. I thought he might need some exercise. Anyway, I stopped and mopped my forehead. Then I took a step or two and stumbled. The good father was quick to oblige.

"May I help you with one of those three bags?" he asked.

"I would surely appreciate it, Father."

"I'll be most pleased to. I didn't think you were going to able to carry them all the way to Customs."

I said hopefully, "Perhaps you'd be kind enough to carry the sample case. The longer one. But it's pretty heavy."

"With much pleasure."

The Argentine Customs officers were brisk and efficient. Although they gave my suitcase and briefcase a pretty thorough going over, they found nothing incriminating or contraband. My clerical helper, complete with machinegun, sailed right through without a single question. A friend in need is a friend indeed.

I bade him farewell by the bus stop. "Thank you again, Father. Wish me luck." I'm going to need it, I thought.

"You're most welcome. Go with God." Then he was on his way. And so, shortly, was I.

Buenos Aires was new to me, and so I even enjoyed the microbus ride from the airport. I had only seen the city in films, but had thought it seemed to be a heck of a nice place. My first actual impressions were equally favorable. It was a beautiful day in what was, since I was now in the Southern Hemisphere, late spring. Everything was green in the outskirts of the city, and even in the more built-up area flowers, green plants and some trees were to be seen. I hadn't seen anything of my traveling friend, the dog-food man, since I'd cleared customs. But just in case he was still interested in my affairs, I directed the microbus to the Plaza Hotel, and got out very quickly. I was fumbling for a tip as the doorman carried my bags up the steps into the hotel. Inside the hotel, I took all three bags from him quickly, and dropped several coins at his feet so that he wouldn't see the direction of my departure. Then I stepped quickly out of a side door and into one of the limousines which ICAL told me are usually parked outside Argentine hotels. Then I told the driver to take me to the City Hotel and checked in there.

The organization's suggested arrival stunt had worked fine. ICAL is usually pretty good at that sort of thing. Once in a while they'll tell you that there's a side door when there isn't, but not often. And for all I knew the priest who carried my hidden machinegun through Customs was one of our local ICAL people!

I spent the rest of the day getting cleaned up and resting. I also took care of a few housekeeping details like street maps and so forth, and looked around for a car to rent. Even with the unpleasant memories of events in Tel Aviv, I selected a nondescript Volkswagen. I had dinner in the hotel and, since I was able to get a reasonably North American type of meal, was able to get a good night's sleep. In my few forays south of the Rio Grande I've learned that Latin American cooking and my ulcer don't mix. The next morning I had a light and again northern breakfast, and then took a walk in the town. All of this by way of preparing and learning.

Buenos Aires looked like a nice place in which to do my kind of work. There were large bench-filled plazas, and sidewalk cafes which they call confiterias. The Porte'nos have got it made in many ways. The main street in the central area is the Avenida de Mayo, with the Plaza de Mayo at one end and the Plaza Del Congresso at the other. Nearby is the Avenida 9 Julio. A huge underground garage beneath all this keeps parked cars off the streets and so creates a nice impression of the city. Several other streets opening off the main ones also looked inviting.

It was a fine day and the walk was most enjoyable. It was even a pleasure just to sit and relax on a bench on the Plaza de Mayo. I did so, resting and rubbernecking for five or ten minutes. Then I began to 'fiddle', as a person sometimes idly does, running my hands over the smooth wood, occasionally drumming my fingers, and so forth. At one point I just happened to move a small, white thumbtack which was sticking in the lower board of the bench backrest. I moved it to the upper board. Perhaps someone else sitting on the bench would be pleased to find it there.

Then I took a trolley bus back to the hotel. Taxis are hard to find in Buenos Aires, but since they have subways, streetcars, buses and microbuses, as well as trolleys, it is not too hard to get around. Taking a rather roundabout way back to the hotel, I was able to see more of the sights of Buenos Aires. The Plaza San Martin with its large statue was particularly impressive.

General San Martin was Argentina's liberator and is respected in much the same way as George Washington is in the U.S.

I was a little tired after my long morning's walk, so I stayed around the hotel. I just thought I might receive a telephone call. Surprisingly enough I did too, that very afternoon.

"Good afternoon, Ralph," said a rather thick, husky voice. "A little bird is telling you that you want to meet me. There is a little café called Florida on the Calle Corrientes. Be there."

"Thank you, little bird," I said.

It seemed like a rather odd message, but then we work with some pretty odd people. The caller had not mentioned a time but didn't need to do so. Some desk-bound genius at ICAL headquarters had worked up a new wrinkle. The meeting was to take place six hours after the telephone contact. The call had been at 3:30 in the afternoon, so the system required me to meet the caller at 9:30 in the evening. I was glad that my contact person had seen the white thumbtack early in the day. This permitted an afternoon phone call. I would not have wanted him to wait until after 6:00 PM. I don't fancy seeing new places and meeting new friends at midnight.

You can't get dinner in Buenos Aires soon enough after luncheon to keep an ulcer happy. So I tried to put on my best British manner and had tea and cakes served to me in my room at about 5:00. Then I went downstairs for some lobby sitting. That is a good way to pass the time in a strange city. There wasn't too much traffic, but what there was looked interesting. Airline stewardesses are usually the best, but even without them, there was a pretty good selection for some mental speculation. That seemed to be all I'd had time for in the last many weeks.

For some reason I didn't care too much for the gentleman sitting across the aisle from me. They say that cops look the same the world over. At least this one did. I tried him with a few quick trips out the side door, around the block and back into the hotel lobby. He always seemed to want to take the air just when I did. I found the same wonderful coincidence of interest in the magazines displayed at the cigar stand and even in the frequency with which it seemed necessary to visit the men's lounge.

I kept him busy with these activities until about nine in the evening. Then I got up in what I hoped was a casual manner, and left the hotel through the revolving doors leading to the side street. I was exiting the revolving door just as he reached it. Without turning back I gave it as hard a push as I possibly could. I felt the jarring halt and heard a yell of pain as the door pinned him against its frame. I didn't look around but instead jumped into a waiting hotel limousine. I had it drive me about half way around the block and then hopped out and into a bus which took me down to the Calle Corrientes.

The Florida was a small place and was not crowded. It didn't seem very secure, but I had to suppose that my contact knew his business. ICAL's local friends usually do.

I failed to see anyone who looked especially like a bird, so I took a chance. The man opposite whom I seated myself weighed easily 250 pounds. He was short, with great rolls of fat from the neck down. His eyes were bright and intelligent looking, even though the rest of him suggested otherwise. He'd obviously been drinking, for his uniform coat hung open and his necktie had been loosened. On his shoulder straps reposed the small silver eagles which indicate a colonel in the Argentine air force, just as they do in ours.

"Good evening, Colonel," I began. "May I join you for a drink? Birds of a feather should flock together." 'Birds' was the key word. In his condition I hoped he'd caught it. At first his heavy, rather North African features gave no indication. Then he heaved himself partway up out of his chair and surveyed the neighboring booths.

The Colonel spoke, "I am Colonel Manzano. I am required to believe that you are Mr. Ralph. I don't, but am pleased to make your acquaintance none the less. Now," he suggested, "let's have that drink. At your expense of course."

"All right," I said, "but then I'd like to get started with what I came here to do. I don't have much time."

"In your country you get things done by hurrying. Here we make haste more slowly. And we drink."

There was no answer to that. So we had one. And another with dinner. Then he took me with him to a military reception. Such affairs are characteristic of a society in which the military caste plays a prominent part.

On the way Colonel Manzano told me that he was merely serving as a courier and contact man. He said he knew nothing about my assignment, but had instructions to provide me with an invitation to a certain military reception, which was taking place that evening. It was being held by the Army and Navy Officers Society at a very large private home in Belgrano. Belgrano is the Anglo-American suburb north of Buenos Aires proper. It is where Americans pretend they are living in Silver Springs, Maryland, British pretend they are living in 1900, and Germans pretend they aren't living at all. Even in the dark it looked like a pretty ritzy area.

On the way out to Belgrano I told the Colonel about the incident with the policeman in the hotel.

He smiled. "That was entirely my doing. I told the police you were an eccentric American millionaire. I suggested that they provide constant police protection because, with your great wealth and unpredictable ways, you are a likely target for a robbery or abduction. The people in Washington said you would probably react the way you did. This means our local police will by now have washed their hands of you."

I wondered whether to believe him. "In other words," I said, "that means there will never be a cop around when I want one."

"That's exactly it," he replied as we arrived at the reception. I'd been joking, but somehow I thought that was exactly the way things would be.

Experience told me otherwise, but I still wasn't exactly sure why the organization wanted me at an affair like this. In my rather rumpled lightweight suit, I didn't cut much of a figure among all the dress uniforms, gold and silver braid, multitudinous medals, and highly polished boots of the senior military officers who were in attendance. Even the Argentine civilians were considerably more presentable than I.

However, here I was. I thought I might start by seeing if I could pick up anything about the stolen paintings we believed Carl Petersen was selling. Consequently, I paused before one of the many paintings which adorned the walls of the large ballroom, and waited for someone else to come along so that I could try to strike up a conversation. This produced no results. Maybe there weren't any art lovers in attendance. So, I wandered about the room.

Large-scale receptions seem pretty much the same all over the world. A small orchestra, which you can hardly hear over the chatter. Crowds of people lined up two deep at the hors d'oeuvre's table, and three deep at the bar. Although writers of television commercials would not believe it, there were absolutely no little groups of folks standing around having spirited discussions about cigarettes or reasons to stop smoking them. (Note: Again, Prior is writing about events in the 1960s, before cigarette advertising was banned in the U.S.)

Other than remarks about the weather and a few words about forthcoming soccer matches, I didn't do too well in the conversation department. My Spanish was good enough, but most of the people present seemed to know one another. I was pretty obviously tabbed as a stranger, possibly there either on sufferance or by mistake. Anyway, I hoped they were getting used to me, and that I was becoming accustomed to them.

Without really meaning to, I found myself standing again in front of one of the oil paintings. This was a big one, a fair reproduction of Gerard's painting of 'The Emperor at Austerlitz'. I've always enjoyed that picture and I guess I was quite absorbed in it. Anyway I was surprised to hear a voice at my elbow.

"Are you interested in the art of the Imperial period?" The voice was soft and regular. The words were uttered courteously, but without a great deal of interest in whatever answer I might have. I turned to the speaker. He was a middle-sized, middle-aged, stern looking fellow. His rather large head sat on a wiry body. His long, graying sandy hair, still richly thick, was brushed straight back from a heavily tanned face. It was an approachable face except that the eyes were very hard. They were more nearly yellow than any other color that can be named. He smiled thinly as he continued, "I've always enjoyed these battle scenes." His English was precise and distinctly European.

"I do also," I said.

He continued, "In fact any type of scene involving combat appeals to me. I believe you are not frequently in this society. Most of the men here know me as a fighter. In fact at times they call me the jaguar killer." He laughed, "It is a recreation of mine." Up to this time he'd had his hands in his pockets. Later I was to learn that this was a characteristic pose. And for sufficient reason. When he removed his right hand to point to the artist's representation of Napoleon's General Rapp, I was in succession, very pleased and a bit frightened. In angling terms, I thought I might have a nibble. The tips of the man's fingers had been almost entirely cut away, leaving peculiar chisel shaped surfaces of scar tissue below the nails. Taking the fingerprints of this particular art enthusiast would have been a waste of time. He had none.

I thought I'd take a chance. "I am really very fond of paintings," I said, "but I seldom have enough money to buy what I like."

The thrust went home. "Perhaps I can help you," he replied. "I have some good sources for old European paintings at remarkably low prices. You know the situation. Old families in financial difficulty, who are forced to liquidate. That sort of thing. And I know of imports, without duty, for sale at several small shops down in the Boca."

The Boca is the waterfront district of Buenos Aires. "That sounds very interesting," I said. "Perhaps I'll call on you in the next few days. May I have your business card?" He handed it over. I just glanced at it and continued with scarcely a pause. "It is nice to have met you, Señor Petersen. I'll be calling on you in a day or so. Sorry I don't have a card with me. And now if you'll excuse me, I see a friend beckoning to me from across the room."

"Until then," he answered, his yellow eyes glaring.

I really did see someone waving from the other side of the room. Colonel Manzano was trying to attract my attention. With him was a small, dark, vivacious looking young woman. Her clothing looked well, especially on her, but was simple and probably inexpensive. I met the Colonel and his companion halfway across the ballroom.

Colonel Manzano spoke quickly. "Here is Miss Sharen, a young friend of mine. Please make yourself acquainted and entertain her. I must rush off and see the General for a few minutes."

That sounded fine to me. "Good evening," I said. My name is Humboldt Prior. I am a North American. Shall we dance while we can still hear the music? I mean before the crowd at the bar completely overcomes it."

"I am pleased to make your acquaintance, Mr. Prior." Her voice was deeper than I expected, speaking English that was fluent but not natural to her. She continued, "And I will greatly enjoy a dance. Colonel Manzano is interesting to speak to, but not much fun. My name, by the way, is Sharon. Now I think the music is beginning, shall we…"

I expect that I stumbled around the dance floor even more awkwardly than I normally do. In my line of work, establishing contact with Carl Petersen so quickly and easily was an almost unheard of piece of good fortune. Indeed, even then it seemed a little too easy. However, that was still, after all, the reason I was at the reception. Beggars can't be choosers.

Meeting Sharon was another matter. She was a most charming young lady. Even in a very few minutes, as sometimes happens, I was strongly attracted to her. By this I mean I would have been most interested in her, even if hers had not been a voice I had heard not long before. It had been coming from the bugged Shin Bet office next to the back room of an implement dealer, next to ImEx headquarters in Tel Aviv.

*   *   *

"Do we have anything on this Manzano?" inquired Colonel Yalinin.

"Yes, Comrade Colonel, but until now we only knew that he was not just what he pretends to be. We rather thought he was working for the Brazilians."

"Well," continued Colonel Yalinin, "as the Americans say, you learn something new every day. Or," and he yawned, "every night in our case."

Major Grusev was still a little afraid that Colonel Yalinin would lose interest. So, the Major added with his characteristic enthusiasm, "But you will agree that the manner in which they so quickly made contact with the criminal Petersen is most interesting?"

Colonel Yalinin however, would not give the enthusiastic Grusev the satisfaction of his agreement. He said nothing and the tape continued.

Chapter 8—Sharon

"Shadow and sunlight are the same,"

It was after 1:00 o'clock in the morning when I finally said goodbye to Sharon and left the reception. So when I turned in, back at the hotel, I was definitely looking forward to sleeping late. This was not to be.

It must have been well before 9:00 AM when I became, at first vaguely and then more positively, conscious of movement next door in the sitting room of my hotel suite. I raised my head from the pillow and listened. Yes. Certainly someone was fumbling around in the next room. And not very skillfully from the sound of it. There were muttered curses in Spanish and occasionally a louder noise as a chair was bumped or a drawer opened.

I had been brought up not to welcome unannounced visitors at that time in the morning, but I thought I had better prepare some sort of reception. One of the first things you learn with ICAL is how and where to conceal your personal weapon. In all types of circumstances. For example, when sleeping, hiding your gun under your bed pillow is not one of the recommended places. They look there first and if you start to slide your hand under your pillow someone just might blow it off. Further, it's damn hard to sleep with your head on a gun, especially if you've the beginnings of a hangover. I prefer to leave an open book on the floor next to the bed, on the side away from the door. Then I slide the pistol under it. When, as silently as possible, I rolled out of the bed, it was easy to retrieve the gun, load and cock it. I waited. Nothing. Then I stepped quietly across the room and pushed the door open, crouching in the approved ICAL shooting position just to the side of the opening.

Yes, I had company. Colonel Manzano was bent over the sideboard helping himself to what was probably not his first drink of the morning. I leaned back into the bedroom to place the pistol, now uncocked, on a nearby dresser. Then, resplendent in my not-too-new pajamas, I walked into the living room to greet my guest.

"Good morning Colonel," I began. "I hope you've found whatever you were looking for."

His big dark oval face beaming, he was not the least embarrassed. "Good morning to you, Señor Prior. Will you join me in a drink of your bourbon?" His uniform, if possible, was even more disheveled.

"I'm too old to drink this early in the day," I replied. "And to what do I owe the unexpected pleasure of an early morning visit from you? And, while we're on the subject, next time, knock. You might catch me in a less friendly mood."

"Come now Prior, you're never unfriendly. At least you certainly appeared friendly enough late last evening." This was true. Once Sharon and I got together, it had been a swell night.

"I'm only friendly after working hours. At this time in the morning I'm only curious."

Colonel Manzano turned, walked over to the sofa, and lowered his huge haunches into it. He beamed more good spirits. "I just wanted to see how you were getting along. That is one of my many duties. How are you getting along?"

"Well," I answered, "last night you introduced me to a very nice lady and also I ran into an interesting gentleman who wants to sell me some pictures. What more could I ask for?"

"So you made some valuable contacts?"

"I think so and I surely plan on contacting one of the contacts again."

Colonel Manzano laughed. "I guessed that. Otherwise I don't suppose you really plan to tell me anything?"

"No, I really don't," I answered.

He sighed. "That may do for now. I'll toddle along then."

"So toddle."

He heaved himself up and headed for the door.

"Why not tuck that other bottle of bourbon in your briefcase?" After all, he seemed like a pretty nice fellow.

"Thank you so much, Mr. Prior." He grinned and left.

Just as I was turning to go into the bedroom to dress, there was a frantic pounding on the door. 'What next' I thought as I opened it. Here was the good Colonel again.

"I knew I wanted to see you for something else," he said hurriedly. "Our surveillance at the airport reports some additional visitors. ICAL tells me you may be interested in them. A von Hausenberg and another man traveling as his servant. Also a daughter, or wife or mistress or something. Anyway, a woman traveling with them." The Argentine culture, or the Colonel's high rank, precluded any real interest in the names of servants and women.

Now I was very glad I'd been nice to him. "Okay, Colonel, thanks for the word. If I need to see you again, I'll put another tack on that bench on the Plaza de Mayo. Well, so long and thanks again."

I dressed quickly and went downstairs for a late, light breakfast. Then I thought I'd spend a little more time sitting in the hotel lobby. I wanted to see who, if anyone, had the duty of watching Mr. Prior that morning. It's always nice to be the center of attention. If you know it!

There didn't seem to be anyone at first. Just the usual crowd. You can normally tell if someone is trying to make it look as if he isn't watching you. And there didn't seem to be anyone loitering in the alcoves either. All the same I had the feeling I was being watched. Because of the work we do, we are taught to always respect such feelings until we prove the situation to the contrary. I did so. I had selected a comfortable, overstuffed plush chair with a good view of most of the City Hotel's ornate lobby. At right angles to my chair was a small, equally plushy davenport, with a low table between us in the angle. There was someone seated at the far end of the davenport. All that I could tell at first was that my neighbor was a youngish woman, because her face and upper body were buried behind a newspaper. As I turned to take one more long look toward the cigar stand, my eyes caught a well-placed mirror on the opposite wall. From the mirror, it was easy to see that the young woman's face was behind the newspaper only when I was looking her way.

She looked to be about my age. Face just a little too full. Otherwise pleasant regular features and a particularly pretty mouth. Her countenance was serious and she was obviously very intent on her business. And that seemed to involve me. But her eyes really stopped me. She had the brightest, happiest pair of eyes I have ever seen. You could almost hear the laughter in them. Otherwise I couldn't see too much. This was another interesting development I mused, wondering where she might fit into the picture I was mentally painting. Perhaps not naturally suited to her present assignment, but doing her level best.

But, with some regret, I decided I didn't have time to strike up an acquaintance just then. I had an idea to take a little drive and more fully familiarize myself with Buenos Aires and its environs. And too, I thought I should spend a little time checking further on my new acquaintance, Carl Petersen. Anyway, after a moment's thought I stood up and as if by accident used my knee to overturn the small table between us. This sent two ashtrays, both of them unfortunately rather full, cascading over and almost onto the lap of my watchful companion. Then I scooted for the nearest exit. As I went out the door I was feeling more guilty about the trick I'd just played, than anything I had yet done on the operation. For I had caught her eyes directly, not in the mirror. They looked hurt and startled, almost as though I had injured a friend. But they still laughed too.

I quickly retrieved the Volkswagen from its parking garage and started to drive over to the other side of the city. That was where Petersen lived, as nearly as I could tell from the Buenos Aires road map and the address on his business card. Or at least it was where he had an office. I didn't drive there directly. First I took steps to eliminate any other company that I might have accumulated. You don't do this by driving 60 miles an hour and going around corners on two wheels. This just gets you traffic citations. Even in Buenos Aires. I simply drove leisurely and quite aimlessly through the city. I made a good deal of use of lightly traveled side streets, which will usually show you if anyone is following. I didn't seem to have another watcher, so after five more minutes of evasive tactics and 15 minutes more of blundering about trying to find my bearings, I got back on course and shortly thereafter arrived at the Plaza Britannica.

This was where Petersen seemed to be located. His address was that of a fairly new building. There were small and expensive looking shops on the ground floor with apartments and offices on the first and second floors above. This looked good for me and the job I had to do. New buildings are, generally speaking, more straightforward as far as an intelligence operative is concerned. The walls are thinner so eavesdropping is easier. They are laid out in a simple symmetrical manner so you don't have trouble finding your way around. And, usually the individual apartments have but one exit. I parked the car and wandered around on the Plaza. I was careful not to either concentrate on Petersen's building or avoid it. That's one secret of successful intelligence work. It isn't a case of being casual, but rather of acting normally. And that takes a lot of concentration.

After I had the lay of the land pretty well tied down, I stepped into the nearer shops, one after another, asking what I hoped were some oblique questions about Petersen. Unfortunately nobody seemed to know anything useful.

There were two or three booksellers fronting on the Plaza and so, having concluded that either Petersen didn't move about very much or, as is often true, wasn't well known by name, I walked into one of the bookstores. I always enjoy browsing. And once in a while I find something I like. Military history is one of my favorite subjects, and I thought I might run across a good volume of war memoirs. I found one, written in

German, that looked pretty good and was leafing through it to see what it had in the way of photographs and maps.

Then a voice at my elbow said, "May I help you?"

I reacted without enough thought, which can be very dangerous. "Yes, thanks, I was just looking for Petersen."

"Yes I think we still have it."

What the heck did that mean? Anyway, the clerk had hurried over to his card index and was thumbing through it.

"Yes indeed," he continued triumphantly, "right over this way please."

By the time I had joined him at the other end of the small store, he had picked up a book. He held it out to me as I reached his side. The title of the book was, literally translated, 'Tiger Killer'. It was one of those soft cover books which have become so popular in the last few years. The picture, or rather the photograph, on the cover was that of a snarling jaguar. I turned the book over. Sure enough, there on the back cover, was Mr. Petersen. He looked a good deal younger with his jungle dress and jaguar spear. His foot was aggressively forward, resting on the spotted body of a slain jungle cat. The clerk had made a sale!

I had several things to think about on the way back to the hotel. For one thing, Petersen was obviously either pretty vain or feeling pretty secure. Probably both, for people in hiding seldom publish books in their own names. And, again obviously, he wasn't the type of individual who was going to fold up the first time I told him it was time to come and work for ICAL in the United States. Not when he liked fooling around with jaguars armed only with a spear. That set me to worrying. It also got me a bit angry. I've always liked cats of any kind and I don't like to see or hear of them being killed. Even a poor little dead alley cat, lying crushed in the street, is a hurt to me.

When I got through with that first subject, I spent more time pondering the risks of Colonel Manzano's blundering efforts to be helpful. Next came the problems of the arrival of the German contingent, possibly members of the Kreisau Gruppe; of the unknown woman at the hotel (who was probably now my enemy for life); and lastly, of Sharon. She at least was a pleasant subject and I let her occupy my mind the rest of the way back to the hotel. And indeed for sometime after while I was resting in my room.

As sometimes happens I spent quite a while deciding whether or not to call her. On the one hand I needed to know more about her and ImEx, the Israeli organization for which she appeared to work. On the other hand I doubted that ImEx would intend to be of any assistance to my operation. On the contrary. But on the 'third' hand I just wanted to see her again. Even though she had given me her full name, Sharon Sharen, her address, and her local telephone number, I felt a little shy about calling her. I've never liked doing that. After all, sometimes you get turned down. Finally I talked myself into moving over to the telephone and working the dial. For once I was lucky or so I thought at the time.

"Hello."

"Hello, Sharon, this is Humboldt Prior, the dancer with the two left feet."

There was a pause, just a little bit too long, and then she replied. "Oh hello, Humboldt, I'm glad to hear from you."

"I hope so."

"Yes, Humboldt Prior, I really am." She certainly sounded enthusiastic, although I was later to learn this was her normal mode. "I mean I really am. I was hoping you'd call. After we met last night, I had a very fine time with you, and I was hoping that could continue. I was thinking maybe you'd take me to dinner tonight."

I don't pass up such invitations. "I'll see you shortly," I answered. "And this time we won't have Manzano along as a chaperone." I laughed. So did she, with just the slightest trace of a suggestion in her laugh.

I hustled through a shave and a shower and quickly dressed for what I hoped would be a most enjoyable late afternoon and evening. Then I collected the Volkswagen and tooled it out to Belgrano, where Sharon's apartment was located.

Her apartment was in one of those large new developments. These always have, at least to me, a rather antiseptic almost hospital like quality to them. All surfaces are metal, glass, polished stone, or plastic, as if prepared for sterilization. But I didn't have much chance to reflect on the lobby and hallways. Sharon's door opened at the first knock. I was just starting to say "Hello" when she pecked a light kiss on my check and dragged me into the living room. Never a dull moment.

"Come in, Humboldt dear, there's a person here who wants to meet you."

A somewhat older man was seated in the living room. He was dark, slender, and athletic looking. Casually well dressed, I judged he had a good deal of money to spend. He had one of those long aristocratic heads that I, at least, always associate with the British upper classes. He rose and came forward to shake hands.

Sharon introduced us. "Humboldt, this is my cousin Hiam Goldson. Hiam, this is Humboldt Prior. We met at last night's party."

We exchanged pleasantries. I got the impression that Hiam had not planned on going anywhere, but Sharon quickly shooed him out. "Hiam is just leaving. He has a number of business interests here in Buenos Aires and they keep him pretty busy...don't they?" This last to him.

He evidently took orders from her, at least for the moment. He walked to the door, turned, and said, "Nice to have met you, Mr. Prior. Cousin Sharon seems to think that 'two is company' and so forth. I do also, and anyway I've got to go make some money."

I'll always remember the adventure of that afternoon and evening with Sharon Sharen. To her, everything was interesting and agreeable and fun and exciting. It was always 'Oh look at that' or 'Isn't that wonderful' or 'You are so right'. We prowled in and out of the stores and shops in the area, but mostly we just wandered. This was somewhat pleasant and relaxing, although I had to keep on my toes. I wasn't supposed to know who she was and what she was and who she worked for. And I didn't dare let the knowledge color my words and attitudes. Carefully, I had to try to find out what the ImEx people were up to, and how that was going to affect my task with Petersen.

Sharon was really quite a picture. Small and dark with sharp features. Altogether a nice little package. And wearing one of those simple, lightweight silk, summer dresses, which was just enough too small for her to make it interesting. Darned interesting in places.

Along about 8:00 o'clock, she dragged me into an Italian restaurant. For me, this is normally a mistake because my ulcer is pretty sure to resent any type of Italian food. However, by that time I was feeling so relaxed and companionable that even my ulcer didn't seem to mind. It was one of those restaurants where they really make a production out of serving a meal. Six or seven courses. And, so it seemed six or seven different wines with each course.

Sharon talked almost constantly, mostly in the form of questions about me and in various forms, 'What I was doing in Argentina?' I had to be more and more careful with my answers, which was difficult because I was getting into a rather affectionate frame of mind. With each glass of wine this mood became even more so. As a matter of fact while trying to keep my wits about me, I even tried to remember some of the ICAL training for this sort of situation. However, it didn't really equip you to cope with matters when you are sitting next to a lovely young woman in a dark restaurant, and she starts tickling the palm of your hand, and at the same time leans over and kisses you ever so lightly. That sort of behavior is pretty sure to lead to more of the same, and then on to neck rubs, community showers and all the rest of it. At least at that point, I hoped so.

It didn't take us long to get out of the restaurant and into one the scarce taxicabs. On the way back to Sharon's apartment, I was very fervently hoping that Hiam's business had kept him away for the evening also. I rather suspected that it might have been planned that way.

The street in front of Sharon's building was empty, save for one car parked across the street. I gave little thought to that at the time. I paid off the cab driver, giving him in my haste, as I later discovered, about five times too much money. Sharon was waiting for me at the doorway. Nothing would do but that I should carry her over the threshold. I had an idea of making a nonstop trip right through another doorway to her bedroom. Fortunately however, something told me we ought to have another drink first. She made us a couple of large ready mixed Manhattans and then poured a little whiskey in for something extra.

Sharon and I, and the two Manhattans, were getting along very well, there on the davenport with the room completely dark, when something or somebody started trying to tear down the front door. I definitely did not need an interruption, and my suit coat, with my gun in its built-in shoulder holster, was on a chair across the room. I dumped Sharon on the floor and reached the chair with one long sliding step. I pulled the Mauser out, worked the slide, opened the door, and then quickly jammed the loaded pistol into my trouser band. For there, with his usual helpful smile, was Colonel Manzano, big as life.

"What the flying hell do you want?"

"It's an emergency," the Colonel replied urgently, "right here in the building. It's on fire. Everyone must get out."

Sharon had, by this time, also scrambled to the doorway. She looked genuinely surprised. I grabbed my suit coat and we all scuttled down the stairs and out into the dark street. Sure enough, firemen were everywhere and black smoke was billowing from the window of an adjacent apartment. Just to complete things, Hiam Goldson had arrived almost simultaneously with the fire department.

Under these new and unwelcome circumstances, Sharon and I said our good-byes there on the street. As Hiam had said earlier, 'three is a crowd'. And with Colonel Manzano we had four. I found the rented Volkswagen and drove the Colonel back to the center of the city. For a while neither of us spoke. I, for one, was seething.

Finally, I was cooled off enough for some conversation. "That certainly was nice timing my dear Colonel," I said sarcastically. "I was just wishing for a smoke grenade nearby! I don't know how I can ever thank you."

"You recognized the effect?" he asked with disappointment.

"Yes."

"It seemed to only way to rescue you," he said innocently. "I hope the firemen aren't too annoyed. Fortunately, there is a small vacant apartment next to that rented by your friends Sharon Sharen and Señor Goldson. Even so it is going to take quite a time to clear the smoke. It was necessary for me to place three smoke grenades there. Two are going now and one has a delayed fuse."

"Necessary?"

"Well yes," he answered. "We received this telephone call. From a woman. Said she was an acquaintance of yours. She further informed us that you were going to get in a lot of trouble if we didn't get you out of that apartment right away."

Whoever she was, she was right. Damn it.

* * *

"A typical Yankee intelligence operation going full blast," Colonel Yalinin said sarcastically. "That's the big difference between their operations and those of ours. A Soviet operative would never indulge in such frivolous side activities."

Major Grusev said nothing. But as he remembered it, frivolity wasn't so bad.

Chapter 9—July 20th

"The vanished gods to me appear,"

Colonel Manzano had learned at least one thing from the episodes of the previous day and evening. Instead of just entering unannounced, he actually knocked on the door of my hotel suite. This time it didn't make too much difference, because I had been up and around for some time. In fact, after all the excitement, I'd had a good deal of trouble sleeping. I woke up early and pitched and tossed for hours. At such times I know it's fatal to let my mind start working, but it did so and that eliminated all prospect of sleep.

There had been a good deal to reflect upon. In the first place, I thought over all that I already knew about Carl Petersen or '*Sunlight*' as ICAL wanted me to call him. This is included his residence, his activities as an art dealer and the jaguar hunting avocation. I didn't yet know quite what to make of the last or whether I could use it to my advantage in any way. Next, I gave myself some credit for getting to know the Israeli operatives. My evening of davenport wrestling with Sharon made me feel a little bit like one of the family. The other ImEx agent Goldson looked as if he might be difficult. There were still plenty of uncertainties. These included the woman who'd watched me in the hotel lobby, Colonel Manzano's unidentified caller of last evening, and the assorted Germans who were now on the scene. Indeed, the place seemed to be getting a bit crowded.

It was already hot and the Colonel's uniform jacket was damp with perspiration. We exchanged greetings and remarks about our uncaring ICAL bosses' insistence on having work done in such weather. Colonel Manzano was, as usual, in positive spirits. Both from his manner and because he didn't even ask me for a drink, it was clear that he'd made a stop or two on his way to my hotel. In spite of this, he got right down to ICAL business.

"Now then Señor Prior. I trust you slept well. Ha ha. And I think you are at least somewhat acquainted with the ImEx people my country is currently entertaining. Now there is more. I have tapped Goldson's telephone. There have been several hurried overseas calls. They think Señorita Sharen has gone too far with you and has possibly become involved. She has been put under Goldson's orders for the balance of the operation."

I didn't especially care about being reminded of the events of the previous evening. I knew I'd been less than totally professional, and I certainly wasn't happy to hear that my new lady friend was in difficulties. I'm afraid I didn't sound very appreciative of the Colonel's news.

"So what else is new? I'd just like to complete my job and get the hell out of here. The place is starting to get on my nerves. So are some of the people." This last was apparently a bit too subtle for the Colonel. Anyway, he went on.

"My sources have also learned a little more about this so-called Kreisau Gruppe. I understand from our bosses at the ICAL home office that you've already had some exposure to them. From what I'm told, there appear to three of them. Von Hausenberg seems to be in command. He's a doctor from the old East Prussia. Apparently, he had a rough time during the second war. He has his daughter with him too. She is Katherin or is sometimes referred to in the messages as Kathi. I don't think she could have much of a role in whatever they are attempting. Probably she is a beginner and just along for the trip. Then there is a sort of elder statesman. A Hasso Cornitz. He's said to be a peculiar old fellow. Unpredictable and crotchety. Bill von Hausenberg on the other hand is a fanatic." Manzano spat out the word 'fanatic' describing a mind set totally outside his comprehension. I wondered about the Colonel. Was he really working loyally for ICAL, or only so far as it served Argentina's interests?

He summed up the situation. "All in all, they are one of the vengeance groups. Germans squaring their consciences or trying to undo the past. However, we are told that von Hausenberg goes pretty far in his efforts."

Manzano was carrying a different briefcase. He placed it on the low table in front of us and opened it. He said, "I've got a recorder in my case containing a conversation from one of Hausenberg's telephone lines. They are staying over at the Claridge Hotel. It's what you would call an old-world type of place. Very upper class. He took out a small, Japanese-made wire recorder. He pressed one button, then another and the machine began to speak.

"…and so Kathi lost him."

Colonel Manzano interrupted. "That's von Hausenberg. He's speaking from his hotel room to Cornitz who has rented a house out in Belgrano. It's a small place and not too far from where your Israeli friends are staying. Then the tape continued.

"So." That was evidently Cornitz talking.

"We've had difficulty in getting information on that devil Petersen through our local German people," continued Hausenberg. "Nobody seems to want to say anything. It isn't like our previous cases. People don't seem to like him, but feel they'd better cover for him. Or, they're very afraid of him."

"But we will get him." Cornitz's old voice had iron in it, and he said the words with great emphasis.

Bill von Hausenberg agreed. "Yes, I haven't forgotten what he did to Klaus after the 20th July attack on Hitler. I can still hear the screams and my cell was 20 meters away. I have Kathi watching his apartment now."

Cornitz sounded concerned. "Isn't that rather dangerous?"

"No, she's learning to take care of herself. And if it is, well, that's the way things must go. Anyway, let's get on with it. Have you started with your approach?"

Cornitz replied, "Yes. I've passed the word around that I represent the Berlin Museum of Art, and that I'm in Argentina looking for German paintings to buy back for the Museum. With no questions about origins or ownership. Perhaps that will help us get somewhere. You know the story goes that Petersen had dozens of paintings with him when he left on that U-boat twenty years ago."

Von Hausenberg sounded encouraged. "Fine, you pursue that. And I'll...." The wire recording ended and Colonel Manzano switched off the machine.

"Well, that's all we have. What will you do now, Señor Prior?"

I couldn't really think of anything that would lead directly to Petersen's agreeing to come to the United States. In spite of what I'd said to Manzano about my impatience, it seemed I'd have to let things continue to happen gradually. That's sometimes the way it is in an operation. Often the agent, who tries direct action right from the start, doesn't get as far as the one who lets things come to him. Anyway, I didn't want the Colonel in my hair anymore and thought he didn't have to know all of my plans. I had a more indirect idea stirring in my brain.

"I think I'll just sit tight for a day or two," I said. "I don't like the way things are developing. Perhaps someone will do something that will help me sort things out. There are too many interacting and conflicting forces in the field. I think we'll have to be more patient." I was trying to sound worried and cautious.

I don't know that Colonel Manzano believed me, but in any event he closed his case, and after one or two pleasantries and a less pleasant remark about the previous evening, he left my hotel suite.

Actually I had no intention of doing nothing for days. Indeed, I thought I might provoke something by paying a call on Hasso Cornitz. Manzano had given me the address of Cornitz' rented house. As I said, I had just the germ of an approach twisting around in my mind. I couldn't have described it fully at that point, but I felt that it might be good for Petersen's soul, assuming he had one, to have a little contact with some of my competitors. Later, this might just make him more receptive to what I had to offer. Anyway, I left the hotel and again "Volkswagened" out to Belgrano. I was beginning to feel like a native as far as that part of Buenos Aires was concerned.

Hasso Cornitz answered the door himself. He was quite a sight. A man of at least 70 years. A great mountain of sagging flesh, topped by a huge red face and close-cut white hair. Walking with difficulty and with a noticeable limp. His clothing had probably been expensive when it was purchased 20 or 30 years before. Now it was shiny and threadbare with age and wear. It was also disheveled and not too clean. Obviously there was no woman around to keep him spruced up. I told him that I understood he was in the market for paintings with indefinite backgrounds. He invited me in. After we were seated in his sparsely furnished living room, I introduced myself more fully.

"Good morning, Herr Cornitz. Thank you for seeing me without an appointment. I trust you are enjoying your visit to Buenos Aires."

He was unresponsive except to say, "Yes, and so?" His old eyes simply regarded me with a vacant, tired expression.

I continued, "I am Humboldt Prior, a North American. I too am interested in paintings."

Again, no response other than a shift of position in the huge chair. It was none too large for him.

"And," I said, "I have a potential client who has fallen on hard times. He tells me he will have to part with everything in his collection. I may be able to get you some good prices. Perhaps I..."

Cornitz interrupted me, although not directly. It was almost as though he was speaking with someone else or perhaps to himself alone.

"When you crossed the border from Poland into Ost Elbia (literally 'east of the River Elbe', a German expression for Prussia) it was like going from night into day. It took us 500 years do you hear, 500 years! But we a country built. Five hundred years of building, draining fields, planting, making roads and later railroads. And all the time holding back the Slav hordes! We were the bulwark of Europe. And the Nazis," he snarled, "ruined it. They destroyed it and they gave it away. They caused most of our best people to be killed, and, in 1945, let the rest be driven across the ice of the Baltic. With Soviet planes machine-gunning our people and dropping bombs to break the ice.

"Now you come here, you young swine." He paused for breath. In a way I felt that for Cornitz this was a somewhat friendly expression. "You come to me and tell me you have sources for pictures. Once I had plenty of pictures. They were all stolen from me. And my associate Hausenberg heard his brother scream out his life in a prison cell. And he lost his wife to the Soviet rapists and he now has only his daughter. And he is lucky to have her because after what they did to him, he'll never have any more children." Again Cornitz stopped to regain his strength. He changed position in his chair and then continued, his forehead heavy with perspiration.

"I know perfectly well why you are here in Argentina. You are interested in the same thing we are. A man. I don't know what you want with him, but you won't get him, because we will!"

After that outburst, I didn't know exactly what to say. "It seems to me," I said carefully, "that someone once said that vengeance is sweet only in anticipation. When you get it, it is like dust between the lips."

"Vengeance was never in the vocabulary of the Prussian officer," retorted Cornitz, "only duty."

I thanked him again for seeing me, and said, clumsily, that I respected his views. He seemed to have nothing more to say. I could think of nothing more either. So I left.

It began to look as if Carl Petersen would not be a good life insurance risk. And the Kreisau people obviously weren't going to want my assistance in making contact with him. There didn't seem to be much that I could do for the rest of the morning, so I motored back to the central city and had lunch. Then I went upstairs to my hotel suite. There I spent a couple of hours trying to figure out how to use the latest code system that the staff people at ICAL Headquarters had designed. It seemed to me that it was about time I put someone else in the picture. After about five or six unsuccessful attempts, I found an error in the instructions. It made the code unusable. Therefore, I sent Pearlman a postcard. It simply said 'Having fine time. Wish you were here. Business activity very brisk and city crowded. Living costs at an all time high.' The last sentence was intended as a reminder to Mrs. Lesky, so that she would be sure to send the operating funds due me at each first of the week. Perhaps the Argentine counter-intelligence mail-watchers would overlook postcards.

I spent another hour or so turning things over in my mind, but couldn't come up with anything very constructive. I wondered if Petersen was as worried as I was. On the whole I doubted it, although he had to have concerns about me and all the other attention he was attracting. I thought perhaps I could profitably add to those concerns, so finally I decided I couldn't put off a call on him any longer.

After making sure that my Mauser pistol was loaded, and had a round in the firing chamber, I went out. This time I took a bus over to Petersen's location in the Plaza Britannica. Sometimes an automobile is more of an encumbrance than a help. I got off the bus two or three blocks away from the Plaza and hiked the rest of the distance, looking about very carefully as I went. I thought perhaps some of the competition might have a watch on Petersen's arrivals and departures and wanted to arrive as inconspicuously as possible.

When I got within half a block of the Plaza I was glad I had taken precautions. Apparently the Argentine authorities did not want Petersen disturbed. An elderly Chevrolet was parked in one of the side streets. In it were two uniformed policemen. They presented a problem.

I certainly did not want to appear on the report of those who had called on Mr. Petersen. I couldn't think at the moment how best to get rid of them, so I took another walk around the block. When I came back they were, unfortunately, still there. And I didn't want to do anything violent, at least not right near where Carl Petersen was living. I wanted him worried, but I also wanted him to stay put. Finally, I had an idea. I stepped into a nearby shop and found a telephone and a directory. The number for Police Headquarters was prominently printed. I dialed the number. Using my most enraged Spanish, I almost shouted into the phone. "This is a concerned citizen calling," I said. "I must report I saw a police car in the Plaza Britannica. Both of the lazy bums inside were asleep. What kind of a government have we got now anyway?"

I thought that possibly would stir things up a bit. Sure enough, by the time I was back peering around the corner at the police car, things were happening. One officer was angrily looking around the Plaza. The other was talking excitedly on his car's radiophone. Apparently the explanations weren't satisfactory. In Argentina, as elsewhere, everyone is all too ready to believe that a policeman is loafing. Anyway they started the car and drove away.

That gave me a chance to enter the Plaza itself, and take a seat on a bench. I had a pretty good view of the whole place. The afternoon sun was hot and I just sat lazily for a while. Watching and waiting can be pretty boring. I thought I was unobserved, but I wanted to be sure. When I got up and walked to another bench I had a surprise. From a corner of the Plaza that I couldn't see well from my first vantage-point, another person was watching Petersen's apartment.

The square was becoming more crowded. People were enjoying a stroll, or just a rest in the late afternoon sun, before completing their homeward journeys to supper. Although I couldn't be completely sure, I was pretty confident that the young woman on the bench at the far corner was my friend from the hotel lobby. The same light-haired lady with the laughing eyes. From the recording Colonel Manzano played for me, I thought I also knew her name. Occasionally she would rise and walk over to a water fountain. She had a pleasingly light step. Then she would return to her book and bag of popcorn. It must have been salty, as the trips to the fountain were frequent.

I was pretty sure she didn't see me, which was fine because I was enjoying watching her. I have pretty good vision even at a distance, so when there weren't crowds of people between us, I could see her clearly. Her attention was divided between her book, the popcorn, and Petersen's building. Her face had a look of serious concentration and also some anxiety. But her eyes still laughed.

Then I saw something that I didn't like. There was a small delivery van parked down the street from where she was sitting. It was one of those Volkswagen vans with the sliding side doors. One of the doors was open just a crack. I thought I saw movement through the crack, behind the door. Somebody was watching the watcher. Either backup or opposition. Under the circumstances I doubted it was the former, and as I had disposed of the police watch, and as Petersen could do his observing perfectly well from his apartment, this left the Israeli Hiam Goldson as the logical candidate.

I joined the crowd of walkers and followed along as inconspicuously as possible. The flow of people seemed to move round and round the Plaza Britannica as skaters on an ice rink. As I came up even with her, the young woman on the bench got up and started across the street. Either she had seen me watching her, or she was through observing for the day.

At about that same moment whoever it was in the panel truck had regained the driver's seat, and I could tell things were going to get ugly. Just as she crossed into the street, the van accelerated forward with a screech of tires. I could see what was intended, so I slid between two people in front of me, and as fast as I could, tripped against her from behind. Both of us stumbled clear of the speeding van, although I felt a stinging blow as its bumper caught my trailing leg. No permanent damage was done, except to Goldson's intentions.

The woman ran to the far curb and paused, turning toward me. There was the same look in her eyes, hurt but still with laughter. Then she saw the speeding Volkswagen van disappearing down the street, and another look came into her eyes.

I thought I'd better speak to her. "I beg you pardon, sincerely I do. I always seem to be upsetting you. First, in the hotel the other day, and now I stumble into you in the street. I'm very sorry for being so clumsy."

Her eyes read me carefully. The she smiled and answered. "Yesterday I knew that you did what you had to do. Also, I know what you did just now, and will remember how you helped me. But in some ways I wish you hadn't been here to do it. There are enough difficulties as it is."

I wasn't sure what to say next, so I temporized. "I hope I didn't hurt you. I'm afraid I had to push rather roughly."

"No," she said with another little smile, "but I must go now. You should go too. Please." She turned and quickly disappeared into the crowd. The look of her eyes remained with me.

Apparently everybody else interested in Petersen's apartment had cleared out, including the driver of the van who had indeed looked very like Goldson. It seemed that this might be the time for me to call on Carl Petersen. I was into his building very quickly, checked his apartment number on the lobby directory, and ran up two flights of stairs. I knocked, but there was no answer, so I pushed hard on the door. It was open and the apartment was empty.

Everything pointed to a hurried departure. Odds and ends were scattered about the room. In the wastebasket lay a hastily torn note, audaciously typed on Police Department stationery. Quoting from something or other, it simply said 'Shake the dust from thy feet.' Evidently Petersen didn't need a visit from me to worry him.

Without time to search thoroughly, there wasn't too much else to see among his papers. Just the usual array of bills and unimportant letters. Then I found something more interesting, a small but unusual photograph album half hidden behind some books. I scanned it hurriedly. It contained a selection of passport photographs or rather copies of them, obviously made by someone working in Argentine Customs at the Buenos Aires airport. Several recent arrivals were pictured. The one of Humboldt

Prior was unflattering, but recognizable. It even had the letters "I, C, A, and L" written across the lower margin.

The pictures of Sharon Sharen and Hasso Cornitz were not much better. The scholarly face of Bill von Hausenberg looked out of the album next to the picture of his daughter. With some help from a friend at the airport, Carl Petersen had a complete rogue's gallery. Even to von Hausenberg's daughter Kathi, whose laughing eyes looked out of the picture at me just as they had on the street a few minutes before. For some reason, I kept that one.

*   *   *

Major Grusev spoke, "I imagine Prior easily fell for all that Fascist propaganda that old Cornitz was spouting."

Colonel Yalinin didn't answer. He remembered.

Chapter 10—Driven

"And one to me are shame and fame."

I woke up the next morning with my leg and ankle hurting like the devil. At first I couldn't figure out why, but then the events of the previous day began to come back to me. At least now I knew a little more about the Kreisau Gruppe. It looked as if they were going to cause difficulty. Old Cornitz was definitely a fanatic, if a somewhat immobile one. Fanatics of any kind always cause complications in my business. The other man, Bill von Hausenberg was still unknown, but sounded dangerous. And impulsive, which was worse. There seemed to be much more to the girl, Kathi, but I wasn't sure how she would affect what I was assigned to do. Anyway I was glad I'd been able to save her from Goldson's attempted hit and run.

That meant the ImEx people were starting to play rough. Mr. Hiam Goldson was obviously a tough customer. And while I was much attracted to Sharon, she struck me as being a little dangerous also.

There were still more loose ends, but I didn't see how I could be expected to have everything tied together in such a short time. The worst problem was that it looked like my target, Carl Petersen, had left for parts unknown. Obviously someone had warned him. I and others were supposed to think that someone was with the police, but that wasn't clear. What the warning was about was clear. Who the warning had been about was not clear.

It was still pretty early, but I got up anyway. After breakfast I took a short walk. Not with any particular purpose in mind but just to see if things would sort themselves out. I didn't realize it at first, but it was Sunday. Not too many people were on the streets. This made it easy to be sure no one was tailing me. Either everyone had lost interest or, which was more likely; they felt they already had an understanding of my intentions and capabilities. I hoped to surprise them later.

It was a warm day and the walking was pleasant. The streets in that part of town were lined with attractive looking newer buildings, two or three-story blocks of flats, many decorated with small balconies on the upper floors. Little patches of green grass fronted the buildings, usually surrounded by cast iron railings. Some of the buildings had automobile storage on the ground floor, sometimes with one of those small turntables which help the garage attendants maneuver the cars around tight corners. I wondered momentarily if I should try to talk Pearlman into authorizing me to rent one as a base of operations. Slowly I found myself relaxing after the hurly-burly of the previous day, but that didn't help get my mind going. I still needed a clever tactic for finding Petersen.

I was also a bit surprised that there had been no sign of Manzano. I'd been worried that his morning visits would become his routine way of keeping an eye on me. I could do without that, but might now require his help. I wondered for a while if he had been the one who warned Petersen that things were getting dangerous. Finally, I dismissed that idea. Air Force Colonel Manzano could have done it and would have been clever enough to use police stationery as a blind. But he certainly would not have thought of the almost lyrical one-line, Biblical warning. It was too affected for my friend the colonel. That was worrisome because it meant that there was another force in the field. One that I had not yet identified.

The only thing that occurred to me was to have another look at Petersen's apartment. But I couldn't exactly see how to do it. Not with local police, Germans and heaven knows who else watching the entrance. Also, I had to assume that it now was locked tight. Finally I had an idea, but I didn't like it very well. However, I don't like a lot of the things I have to do. So I went back to the hotel and composed a report to Pearlman. Hopefully he would remember the obsolete code I had to use. Damn those staff people. Then I rested until evening.

    I had noticed several things during my last visit to Petersen's flat. In the first place, the building appeared to have a central courtyard, opening on the next street. The less expensive apartments probably looked out onto it. Secondly, the street outside, while well lighted as to pavement and the ground floors, was pretty dark above. I left my hotel at about 8:30 in the evening. Since things had been getting a little rough, I carried my machinegun, still hidden in it's attaché case. I thought it might be well to have some extra protection. After a considerable wait, and a good deal of whistling and waving, which didn't seem to be the standard methods in Buenos Aires, I finally found a taxi. I had it leave me two or three blocks from Petersen's flat, on the street behind the block of buildings looking out on the Plaza Britannica. It was a warm, dark, summery night, with just a hint of a storm brewing.

    I walked slowly and very quietly toward the rear of Petersen's building, trying to stay in the shadows. The streets were deserted. To do this sort of work you've got to act quickly. So I picked out one door, which looked like it led to a central hallway, walked rapidly across the street, and opened the door. I found myself in a car-storage garage at the rear of the ground floor. Fortunately, there was no one about. As I had come through the door running, I was across the storage area, between two cars and had opened and climbed through a window before I had much time to think about what I was doing. I'd made a certain amount of racket, so for a few minutes I crouched in a dark corner of the courtyard. Nobody seemed to be stirring. The wait gave me some time to think about whether or not I still had the nerve for the next part of my plan. From the insubstantial look of the small decorative balconies which projected from each of the first and second floor apartments, I rather doubted it. They didn't appear very solid and were certainly not designed to carry any great amount of weight. Just for show, as a matter of fact. On the plus side, apartments opened on the courtyard only on one side. On the other three, blank walls rose, offering no view of my planned activities.

After about fifteen minutes I got up the nerve to open the attaché case and remove from it the lightweight machinegun and a small ICAL designed scaling ladder. This had looked easy to use in the training film, but now I wondered. I slung the machinegun over my shoulder, adjusting the carrying strap so that it hung down behind me. That is the approved method and at least I knew that worked. You don't want the barrel pointing upwards for it may catch on something or become fouled. I selected successive apartments, one above the other, that were totally dark and hopefully unoccupied. This moved me down toward the corner of the large building, about 200 feet from Petersen's flat. Then I spent about five minutes trying to throw the scaling ladder quietly up onto the first balcony. Finally the grapple caught and I climbed up. The second time it was easier and soon I found myself, still apparently unobserved, on the second floor balcony.

The edge of the roof wasn't too far above my head at that point. I threw the grapple over the top and tugged it tentatively. At first it moved and I could hear it grating over the roof toward the edge. I got ready to catch it above my head, as I didn't want it to go crashing down the side of the building. Finally, it stopped and held. After waiting and listening for any sign of discovery, I started to climb up. So far I had resisted the sometimes-fatal temptation to look down. Just as I got to the edge of the roof, I did take a look and promptly froze. My stomach turned. Although the drop couldn't have been more 35 or 40 feet it looked like 500. I shivered and felt the palms of my hands growing damp. Then I half shut my eyes and completed the climb, rolling over the edge of the roof to avoid a silhouette for any watchers to see. The things we have to do!

A light mist had started to fall. The roof was not completely flat and the rain made it slippery. I moved cautiously along the roof, being very careful not to make extra noise. Although it would be more dangerous on the front of the building, I had an idea of resetting the ladder and, taking advantage of the dark front of the building, dropping down onto Petersen's balcony. There I could hopefully force an entrance through the window. That I had done before.

However, I had better luck. There was a skylight which apparently lighted the hallway outside his apartment. Sometimes these aren't much good because they don't open, but this one did. I opened it a little and after looking carefully up and down the hall, used the scaling ladder to let myself down. It wasn't hard to use a thin bladed knife on the latch of Petersen's door. I had done that before too.

A more thorough and unobserved search of his flat was now possible. However, it didn't look like it was going to do me much good. The rooms, which on the previous day had only shown signs of a hurried departure, now looked as though a cyclone had roared through them. Chair cushions carried great knife slashes, where someone had probed their interiors. Drawers had been pulled out of cabinets and overturned. Petersen had not had a great deal of personal gear in the apartment, but what there was had been thoroughly trashed. Obviously someone else was extremely interested in him and his possessions. Just on a hunch I took another look at the kitchen wastebasket. Often times searchers omit these, forgetting or not wanting to paw through garbage. There I hit the jackpot. An Argentine airline schedule with checkmarks next to two or three different flights to Asunción, Paraguay. This looked promising, especially since the neurological compound traces in the Parana River suggested a source somewhere in that direction.

Just as I was ready to leave I saw a flicker of light pass across the ceiling of the living room. An automobile had driven up and stopped outside. Keeping well away from the front window, I moved across to the wall next to it and took a quick look outside. Two or three cars. From their model and markings they had to be police. This seemed like a good time to leave quietly. But when I opened the apartment door, I thought I heard them in the lower hallway. Evidently the lighted car was not the first. They weren't coming up very fast, and I could hear arguing in Spanish. None wanted to be first.

Working as quietly as possible, I was able to get the scaling ladder back in the skylight before they were even up to the second floor. They seemed very cautious, as though they were expecting trouble. I prefer not to fulfill such expectations, but I thought I had a certain obligation not send them away empty-handed.

I slipped the sub-machinegun around to a more businesslike position, flicked the selector to the semiautomatic setting, and carefully put one round through the large light globe which illuminated both upper hallway and stairway landing. Then I shifted to full automatic and fired a short burst down the stairs. Bullets ricocheted and sparked off the metal stair railings. There were yells and a mad scramble to get down stairs and out of the building. I stepped back to the door of Petersen's flat and fired another few rounds right through the apartment, smashing the front window. Then I slammed the door and was up the scaling ladder and onto the roof as fast as I could go.

By this time, all hell had broken loose on the street outside. Certain that they had an armed and barricaded enemy to deal with, the police were taking extra and unusual precautions. Though for all I knew, Petersen often had visitors of my demeanor. There were shouts and random revolver shots and spotlights played on the front of the building. Sirens wailed and motors roared as reinforcements arrived. I pulled up the scaling ladder, was across the roof in a flash and, probably a bit carelessly, fixed the ladder to the back edge of the roof and released it to drop its full length. I was about halfway down when it let go. I fell probably ten feet onto my bad leg. It hurt badly and I again felt sick to my stomach. But I did what we do best in such circumstances. I ran. Pausing only to find the attaché case and stuff the gun and ladder into it, I was across the courtyard, through the window of the garage, and out the door to the back street in little more than a minute. Luckily for me there were as yet no police in the back street. I ran, heart pounding and leg aching, to the end of the block, crossed the street and then walked away in what I hoped was an innocent looking manner. Just a peaceful businessman returning from a late evening at the office. And taking a lot of work home.

From what I could glimpse of the square, things there were pretty exciting. Police were running every which way, although endeavoring always to keep something solid between them and Petersen's building. It was the burst of fire through the window that had done it. It would not occur to most people, or to most police, that an unseen opponent would attract attention with all that shooting and then immediately disappear.

I was pretty proud of myself when I got back safely to the hotel. Although there was someone who looked very much like Bill von Hausenberg watching from across the street, I walked boldly up to the entrance and into the lobby. There, I paid two weeks' suite rental in advance and then bought a ticket to Asunción, Paraguay on Argentine Airlines. The first flight was at 5:00 AM the next morning. I don't like getting up that early, but at the same time I thought it might be well to have a change of scenery. There had been a little too much attention paid to Humboldt Prior in Buenos Aires.

The flight to Asunción was pretty routine. We North Americans like to think that we have pioneered commercial aviation. Maybe so. But it's more important, relatively speaking, in other parts of the world. Countries such as Argentina, Paraguay, Brazil and other South American countries lack the high-capacity railway networks and superhighway systems which are found north of the Rio Grande. Flying is by far the best and cheapest way of getting around. Everybody does it.

The two young girls across from me were typical. Both in their early teens and from ordinary families. In a few years, one would be most attractive. The other would never be. They kept up a continuing chatter, the pretty one describing her social life, probably on a much-exaggerated scale. The not so pretty one asked question after question, apparently getting as much vicarious enjoyment from the stories as there had been in the original affairs.

We flew northwest from Buenos Aires, following the Parana River, and thereby avoiding Uruguayan air space. This was northern Argentina, which is much more heavily settled than the southern Pampas. Ahead was the Chaco, the great plain of Argentina, interspersed by many rivers. I was surprised by the number of villages and towns. Since there wasn't anyone sitting where they could observe me closely, I slipped a Minox miniature camera out of my pocket, palmed it, and took pictures of two small railway yards. This is routine for ICAL agents when we have the chance to do it. The right people can make reliable estimates of a country's economic and military potential just by knowing the capacity of its railway terminals. Just about the time I had the Minox put away, I had company.

The pretty, dark-skinned stewardess asked, "Could I get you anything, sir."

I said, "A weak Manhattan would be nice if you have one."

"I am sorry Señor, I do not know that one."

"What do you know?"

"I know Martini."

That's one thing the ulcer doesn't tolerate, so the flight had to be dry. I was rather sorry about that, because sober, and with nothing to do, I had more time for thinking. Several years of ICAL work have given me a good-sized store of things that are not pleasant to think about. But think I did. I remembered my first assignment. Organizing spontaneous, but carefully controlled, anti-nuclear bomb demonstrations outside a submarine base in Scotland. This is not too unusual in intelligence work. Very frequently, instead of letting them spring up spontaneously, such demonstrations are organized so that they can be controlled by the proper people. I'll always remember that the whole thing worked pretty well, and that we fooled the young student protesters into thinking they really had something going. One young woman, a humanities teacher and pacifist, but pretty loveable all the same, had not been so much fun to fool.

Next in my mind, rose an undercover study of communist activity in West German universities. That was an interesting operation and went well, until the opposition arranged for me to be invited to join an old fashioned dueling fraternity. Characteristically, I maneuvered my hapless first opponent into challenging me not with sabers but with pistols. On firm ground with those, I winged him and left town quickly, sans dueling scar. Pearlman had been pretty mad about that.

And then there had been one terrible short trip to India to observe the cancellation of a defecting ICAL representative. I had known this man quite well. They gave the actual killing assignment to one of ICAL's local people, but they wanted someone from Washington along to verify. It was pretty rough. They did the deed with a shotgun in broad daylight. The charge caught him full in the face and I still remember the red spray of flesh and blood that erupted as he was bowled over backwards onto the pavement. It took the Indian police two days to identify him. I was glad when we were coming into Asunción, because I didn't want to think about that type of thing anymore.

It has been popular in the 1960s to talk down about Paraguay. Really, it is not such a bad place. You just have to remember that it's a small country, with limited resources and a small, mostly uneducated, population. Paraguay is a farming country. And even the capitol city is just a small town. It lies on a low plain by the Paraguay River. They've got a water system, but it's not hard to tell they have no real sewers.

The layout and architecture are Spanish, with the usual parks and squares. Just as in Argentina, the few people who are at all wealthy want to live in Colonial haciendas or newly built replicas of them. I checked into the Grand Hotel de Paraguay in the late afternoon. I had a small room. The furniture wasn't new, but things seemed reasonably clean. There was an enclosed stool, a washbasin on one wall, and one of the original two closets had been made into a very small shower. There was even a rickety television in one corner, although I could never make it work during my stay.

Asunción does have some disadvantages, however. The police, and the military guards that are to be found on many street corners, are apt to be quick tempered and arbitrary. Normally I've a pretty good level of respect for law and order, but I couldn't afford to be too cooperative with these particular authority figures. So I took the Mauser pistol along thinking that if worst came to worst I could defend myself.

You can 'do' Asunción on foot in an hour or so. Although you must be careful where you step. I hiked past their version of the Roman Pantheon, which is where the dead dictators are buried, and then on to the government palace. There I asked one of the guards if there was an art gallery nearby. He didn't reply, but merely pointed his carbine down the street. I wondered what he would have done had I pointed back with what was in my shoulder holster.

The art gallery really didn't amount to much. Just a couple of rooms in what they call the opera house. Except for one very old, very beautiful painting of a religious theme, there were no pictures of much value. A few by local artists, and several large, poorly done murals depicting the glories of past and present regimes. I asked one or two questions of the attendant, thinking I might get a lead back to Carl Petersen through his art dealings. It seemed that the attendant was going to tell me something but then thought better of it. That's an unpleasant feeling, meaning briefly that 'the word is out'. Anyway my tactic didn't work, so I walked back to the hotel. I didn't particularly want to be on the streets after nightfall. I'd been told that sometimes one of the palace guards will take a shot at a passerby just for the fun of it.

After a look at the local newspaper I got cleaned up and went down to dinner in the grand dining room. I was not too surprised to see some people I knew.

"Good evening Sharon, good evening Mr. Goldson." If they were not expecting to see me, they didn't show it. Evidently ImEx trains well.

"Why Humboldt dear, what a nice surprise. We were just speaking of you."

Hiam Goldson continued, "Yes, we were saying how dull it would be for Sharon up here in the hinterlands."

"Yes," Sharon said, "Hiam has his business interests to see to, but I was afraid I would just be desolate here with nothing to do."

"I'm sure we can find something to amuse you," I said archly, but somehow not liking my tone or choice of words. Briefly, I wondered why.

"When did you arrive?'" Goldson asked.

"Just today." I didn't see any advantage in lying.

"I've been up here for several days." Evidently Hiam did.

"And I came up yesterday," Sharon added.

"Yes," Hiam continued, "while I'm busy Sharon is going to look for old paintings. She is a collector and has heard that some may be purchased even in this out-of-the-way place. And then, when I'm free, we thought we might have a go at jaguar hunting. Sharon is anxious to try it."

"Do you know any jaguar hunters," I asked politely. Neither of them had an answer to that.

*   *   *

Colonel Yalinin turned to Major Grusev. "Do we have verification of any of these episodes? Personally, I think they are beginning to sound a little fantastic."

"Yes, Comrade Colonel," the Major replied. "We have a contact with the Buenos Aires riot police who was actually present in the Plaza Britannica when Prior fired the shots through the window. It was such a strange action, under the circumstances, that the police didn't know what to make of it."

"And does our contact say anything about this warning that Petersen allegedly received from the police department?" Colonel Yalinin was mildly curious.

"That is developed in detail later in the report," replied Major Alex Grusev, "however I do recall from the summary that the note wasn't from the police."

"Well," answered the Colonel, "let's get on with it."

Chapter 11-Staff Major Anadon

"They reckon ill who leave me out,"

I started the next day with breakfast in the hotel restaurant. They didn't have many items on the menu, and even fewer that were things I could safely eat. I stayed with tea and toast. Someone had told me that in Paraguay you could drink the water, but not the milk. Anyway I hoped the tea involved boiling water.

I was still somewhat at a loss as to how to start putting the pieces of my assignment back together. ICAL had no usable contacts in Paraguay, so I was on my own. In some ways this wasn't too bad, but in others it was going to cause problems. I thought to myself that before I was through I'd even be missing Colonel Manzano.

It didn't look like I was going to have much success in finding Petersen in my capacity as a buyer of old paintings. Not unless he wanted to be found. So I spent an hour or so after breakfast just sitting in my room lost in deep thought. Often this is quite helpful. Experience and testing have shown that I am usually somewhat smarter than the average person, and training has made me much more resourceful. And more deceitful also. Most of the time, if I think long enough and hard enough I find the answer. However this didn't seem to be one of those times. Perhaps, my deep thought works only in the Northern Hemisphere.

Asunción did seem a lazy place. I was getting to feel that way too. Probably as an after effect from the strenuous days in Buenos Aires. Or maybe I was getting too old for what I was doing. The small hotel room seemed not conducive to good thinking. It was hot and a small fan served only to stir up the dust. The only idea that I could come up with was to try to reestablish contact through persons or businesses engaged in outfitting hunting parties. If there were any such in the city, perhaps they would know Petersen and where to find him. This didn't sound very promising, but I thought I'd better try it for want of something better. With that intention, I was just getting ready to leave when the telephone buzzed.

Sharon's voice bubbled over the wire. "I'm in room 300A and I wish you were too."

That was a distinct improvement on what I'd been planning to do. I said, "That sounds a little like 'Come up and see me sometime'."

She laughed. "That's just because you have a naughty mind."

I laughed in turn. "I'll be there in five minutes, ready or not."

Although she had sounded her usual enthusiastic self over the phone, Sharon seemed somewhat restrained when I got to her room.

"How are you today Sharon," I began.

"Relative to what," she quipped quoting, perhaps unintentionally, an American comedian. "Really, Humboldt, I'm fine. But more than a little concerned."

"You look swell," I said, "and I don't think you have much to be concerned about. After all, you're supposed to be on holiday."

"I'm concerned for you, Humboldt Prior. I think you are going to get into difficulties. And I think I am too."

"We almost did that in your apartment a few nights ago. It didn't seem so bad then."

"No you dear dope, that's not what I mean. That was fun. This is business and I think we're in for trouble. And I think you are also."

"Who is 'we'?" I asked.

Sharon had been seated on the couch as we were talking. She paused to glance at a letter or memorandum which was lying on the cushion next to her. I didn't have anything else ready to say, so I had time to do a little looking. She looked great. Dressed in a pale yellow, lightweight summer sheath dress and barefoot. Her dark hair, with just a slight wave, was hanging down to her shoulders. All in all, an enticing little picture. Between us was a modern looking coffee table of the kind that consists only of a circle of plate glass with a central wooden support. She placed the letter face down on the table and carelessly slid an ashtray on top of it, as though to hold it in place against the slight breeze created by the ventilating fan.

"I'll fix us a couple of drinks, Humboldt," she said, "and then you'll come and sit next to me, really close, and we'll talk about things."

She disappeared into what was presumably the kitchenette alcove of her hotel room. I didn't have anything like that in mine, but she couldn't see me from where she was standing. She had obviously been well trained. There wouldn't be time for me to mark the position of the ashtray carefully enough to keep her from knowing if I had examined the letter. But there was, unfortunately for her, nothing to stop me from taking the Minox camera out of my pocket, holding it in my hand under the table and shooting a picture up through the glass tabletop. That is what I did. I'd probably never know what was shown on the photograph, but it might interest someone at ICAL.

I had just finished this activity when she came back with the drinks. On a hot morning, the gin and tonic tasted great, although I knew my ulcer would be unhappy about it later on. In fact, I thought I felt a little burning as the first cool gulp slipped down my throat. Remembering her request, I moved over to the couch and sat down next to her. I follow orders.

Sharon began seriously. "Humboldt, we're good friends aren't we?"

"Good and close, I hope."

"Well then let's stop fooling each other. Or rather let's stop trying to. I don't know exactly who you work for, but I do know you are after Carl Petersen. So am I and I have the right to get him. You don't!"

"What do you mean?" Sometimes it doesn't hurt to seem a little dense. She answered sharply. "I can see I'm going to have to tell you a few things. Although I can't believe you don't know most of it. And if you do, you should be ashamed of yourself for not telling me."

"I'll listen," I said.

"Anyway," she continued, "I work for a small office of my government. Our job is to locate war criminals and return them for trial in Israel. These are terrible men, Humboldt. You can't have any idea of them. Awful Nazis. Murderers and monsters." The words tumbled passionately from her lips.

"I've read of such organizations," I said with vague interest. "Do you think there could be war criminals even in this remote corner of the world?"

Sharon continued with just the slightest touch of exasperation in her voice. "Of course there are, Humboldt, what are you thinking of. That man Petersen is such a criminal. One of the very worst. And a thief. My government will have him. No matter what or who," she added meaningfully, "stands in our way."

I let her continue talking to give me time for some quick thinking. Then I had an idea. "This sounds really serious," I said cautiously. "We had no information of this nature. I represent a very specialized recruiting firm. We heard this Carl Petersen had some specialized scientific ability. We thought he might do as a sales engineer for one of our clients. Do you mean to tell me he's a Nazi?"

"Nazi," she literally spat out the word. "Yes, of course he's a Nazi, a murdering, Jew killing Nazi. Now do you know? Now do you understand why we have to have him? And why we will stop at nothing to get him?"

"I believe I do," I said.

"And Humboldt," she continued, "you could help us a little if you would. We've got to work quickly. Things are starting to go wrong. We're beginning to think that our organization has been compromised."

"What do you mean by 'compromised'?" I asked. I thought I might learn something more, and it didn't hurt to have her go on thinking I didn't know much about her business.

"I don't like to tell you," she answered, "but I guess I must. We think we've been penetrated by Nazi sympathizers. Yes, there are still such people. You wouldn't understand how we know that this has happened, but we do. Things have stopped working the way they used to work. Worst of all, the leaks seem to becoming from someone in the organization who is close to me. We have some evidence that points to that and there are banking transactions that aren't otherwise explainable."

"That doesn't sound good for you." I felt concerned for her and wanted to show it.

"No," Sharon sighed, "and even though my organization has assured me that I've been cleared of any suspicion, I'm having a lot of difficulty getting my job done. And beyond all the internal trouble, we have competition. Not just from whatever you were doing, but real competition."

I was glad to hear that she thought I didn't amount to much of a threat. That could help me later on. I wanted her to tell me more, so I asked, "Who on earth would want to find a Nazi criminal except for your group?"

"More than you would think," she answered. "In this case there are some Germans, strangers, recently arrived in Buenos Aires. We've just heard about them. Hiam tried, but tells me he was unable even to find out where they are staying.

"Anyway," Sharon concluded, "don't you dare breathe a word of any of this. And will you please help me now that you know."

"I think I can," I said cautiously. "I'll have to be sure I don't cause too much trouble for my employer and I can't do anything right now. I have to go out, but I should be back here late this afternoon. I'll call you then. In the meantime, take care of yourself." Then I left.

I liked Sharon and she was very persuasive. So I thought I'd better get away before she had me completely roped into her operation. And I had a few more things to worry about. For example, her friend Hiam Goldson obviously wasn't telling her everything. I remembered that he had spent a good 45 minutes spying on Kathi von Hausenberg.

The block on which the hotel was located narrowed sharply at one end. Just before that point there was a short, narrow alleyway which led to the other street, and from there to the main shopping area. As a shortcut, I'd walked through this alley two or three times already, saving a few steps under the hot sun.

Today things didn't work out that way. As I walked into the alley I heard an automobile turn into it right behind me. The car was moving slowly and I stood to one side to let it pass. But it didn't pass. Instead it suddenly nosed in just in front of me, pinning me against the alley wall. There were two or three occupants of the car. All were wearing the uniform of the National Military Police. There was only one machinegun visible, but that was enough for me. It was pointed right at my stomach. When the rear door opened, I didn't need to be told what to do.

The ride to Military Police Headquarters was not long. I was glad of that because the Military Policemen reeked of perspiration, tobacco smoke and, worst of all, garlic. If that was their way of softening me up for interrogation, they did a good job. As we walked into the long, low headquarters building I could see my escorts square their shoulders. We entered an office not far from the entrance. As we did, my companions snapped to attention.

The man behind the desk scarcely looked up, but hissed out a command. "Leave us," were his only words.

The guards turned about and nearly collided with one another in their haste to be out of the room. I'm afraid I laughed, but just a little. All in all, the situation didn't seem that amusing.

The man at the desk was clearly of African descent. Rather full faced with small, cloudy but very intelligent eyes. Very greasy hair. His uniform was rumpled and none too clean. His desk was covered with cigarette ash.

But he spoke with authority. His voice was calm and intelligent sounding, even with just the trace of a lisp.

"Kindly sit down Señor Prior. Or should I say…Field Representative Prior."

That was a shocker. I didn't expect to be addressed by my ICAL title in the United States, let alone in this out-of-the-way corner of South America. I tried to cover my surprise with a courteous greeting and what I hoped was a polite comment about his office.

"Good morning, Major," for that was his rank if I remembered my review of Paraguayan military insignia. "You have a nice room here." He did too. The office was clean and neat. The first air conditioner I had seen in Paraguay hummed in the window. New metal furniture, light carpeting, and even an abstract print on the wall, all contributed to an impression of the office which was not fully consistent with that given by the questionable appearance of its occupant.

"Thank you very much, Señor Prior, I'm pleased that you approve. We try to be civilized and up to date. We have so many visitors now a days. What a lot of interesting visitors, Señor Prior. Do you know why?"

"I don't know Major, and while we're at it, may I respectfully ask who is asking these questions? Your friends with the machinegun didn't introduce us."

"I beg your pardon," he answered with some sarcasm, "I am Staff Major Anadon. I am forgetful. And most people here know me. But you are a stranger. And that is interesting to me. Why is it that you, a representative of the ICAL of the great United States, have selected our modest, rural capitol city as a place to visit? Surely there was more color and excitement in Buenos Aires."

"You seem remarkably well informed even for a senior police official in a modest capitol," I replied, wondering how Pearlman would react to this penetration of our security.

"Thank you again," he said with just a slight smile, "but let us return to the question at hand. I am still wondering why you chose to visit us? And all the other visitors, why have they arrived? You were seen dining with some of them last evening. And now these others. The ones that flew here this morning on a private aircraft. I understand that, before you left Buenos Aires, you had a discussion on subjects of a historical nature with one of these latest arrivals."

That sounded suspiciously as though he was talking about the old man Cornitz and the Hausenbergs. I suppose that I knew it was inevitable that they would soon come on the scene. Nonetheless I had not expected them so quickly. And somehow, for some reason about which I wasn't very clear, I didn't like the idea of the girl, Kathi, being further involved with the operation. Here in Paraguay, everything seemed to be more complicated and more dangerous, and I would have enough to do just to look out for myself. That thought in itself surprised me. Why was I worrying about her? I'd evidently been silent too long to suit Major Anadon, for he pressed me.

"I'm waiting Señor Prior," he said with exaggerated patience. I thought maybe the cover story that ICAL had dreamed up might still work, so I tried it.

"Well Major," I answered, "I got into a little trouble in New Orleans. I made a mistake or two. Things got to looking pretty hot for me in the States."

"Come now, Señor Prior. You and I both know there is absolutely no connection between you and that racial shooting incident. And furthermore, please don't try to sound like a criminal of some kind. It doesn't suit you." I agreed with that. Staff Major Anadon seemed to have all the answers to all the questions. Just for a change I thought I might try a question on him.

"Actually I'm really trying to locate a potential business partner. A man I met briefly in Buenos Aires. We were going to do some transactions together, but then it seems that he was called out of town. Knowing he has interests here, I thought I'd just follow along and see if I could meet him again here in Paraguay. His name is Carl Petersen. Perhaps you know him?"

The Major smiled thinly. "Now you are being more sensible, Señor Prior. We are not at all adverse to business contacts between foreigners. Herr Petersen has a house not far from here. It is an interesting place. You will enjoy seeing it. It has most unique surroundings. A high wall, with barbed wire and search lights. Also electrification and angry, suspicious guards who dislike strangers. All devoted to the peace of mind and security of your friend. You'll be pleased to find him so well taken care of."

I wasn't so sure about that, but said nothing for a moment. Staff Major Anadon's office was not overly quiet, even when he wasn't talking, and the air conditioner added some noise of its own. Still, we both heard a muffled explosion. Followed by another, and then by the unmistakable buzzing rattle of a light machinegun.

Major Anadon kept his cool beautifully. He simply flicked an intercom switch and without waiting for a response said, "Find out about that" and flicked off the switch.

Then he spoke to me. "Probably nothing very consequential. Sometimes our soldiers don't fully understand things and react foolishly. Unfortunately, people get hurt."

I wondered what was coming next, but apparently we were just going to wait. We did so for about five minutes. Then suddenly the Major said, with a puzzled look on his dark face, "Why not with two 'L's?"

"What do you mean?"

"I know ICAL supposedly means 'I see all'. What became of the second 'L'?"

I didn't know the answer, but then an interruption arrived in the form of a young, junior officer who knocked sharply and then rushed into the room before Major Anadon could respond. He started to speak rapidly in Spanish. The Major interrupted him.

"This person understands our language, but you may be reasonably complete in your report."

"It looks like another bungled assassination attempt. But unusual. Two men were in a car. They actually bombed the gate of the big house. One was killed. And a guard also."

Major Anadon was quickly on his feet and on his way out of the door. He yelled back to the Lieutenant, "Bring this person along with you."

I could tell it was Petersen's house from the Major's description of it. I could also tell that the assassination had been unsuccessful. The guards were still protecting the shattered entrance gateway. Apparently the would-be assassins had tried to blast their way in.

The air was full of dust and still reeked from the sharp odor of explosives. What was left of one of the private guards was lying in the street. He must have caught a hand grenade full on. Blood and shreds of flesh were everywhere, but that didn't seem to disturb or even interest Major Anadon. He was talking quietly to the remaining guards, speaking in Spanish and Guarani, the native Indian language. Military police soldiers had arrived and were driving away the throng of onlookers. The young Lieutenant stuck to me like a shadow.

Probably because of this, the guards let me pass through the wreckage of the gateway and into the courtyard which fronted the main building. There had been dying there too. What was left of Hasso Cornitz was sprawled in a heap next to the wall. The machinegun burst had killed him instantly. There was a lot more blood. To the extent that I could see the expression on his face, it was resigned but not unhappy. He had done his duty. Old Germany started dying in 1914. Bit by bit. Now another bit was dead.

I somehow wasn't surprised to hear Carl Petersen's voice at my elbow. For a man that had seen and done as much killing as he had, he looked a little jumpy and scared, too. Perhaps he was getting old.

"There were two of them, Prior," he said excitedly. "One is dead, but so is one of my men. The other got away. He will no doubt return and then there will be more killing."

"I thought killing was a specialty of yours."

He answered quickly. "What do you mean? I only kill the big cats. The jaguars. I don't like killing people."

I didn't know whether or not he knew what I really meant. Maybe he was a little too shaken to reason clearly.

Thinking I had an opening, I said softly, "I might be able to help you arrange some new business opportunities and a permanent change of scenery. Especially if you can do me a favor or two in return."

He looked startled. "I could be interested," he said, "but your friend the Staff Major may not cooperate. I expect that even now he is ordering that the airport be sealed off."

"Have you an automobile?" I asked. "Perhaps tomorrow we could go for a long drive in the country. We could speak about business as we go."

He paused to think. "Yes, why not," he answered resignedly.

Staff Major Anadon didn't seem to have me in mind at the moment, so I asked the young Lieutenant if he and the Major would each like 5,000 guaranis to spend. He took the money and turned his back. I left quickly, wondering whether the Major would get his share. I hoped so.

I was not sorry to have met Major Anadon. He seemed to know all about my assignment, but that hadn't kept him from helping put it back on track. Or maybe he had to do so. Before I finally fell asleep that night, two ideas kept bothering my mind. First, it was very obvious that the ICAL security for my operation had been blown to smithereens. In spite of this, it looked like just maybe I could pull it off anyway and get out in one piece. And second, although I had Carl Petersen on the stringer at last, I found myself somewhat sorry to be leaving Asunción. I kept seeing those laughing eyes through which Kathi von Hausenberg looked out over the world. From the manner in which her father operated, it was easy to think she would need more protecting. I would have liked to do that, but it seemed I wasn't going to be able to do so.

*   *   *

Major Grusev spoke first. "So you see Comrade Colonel, the old German didn't last long."

"No," answered Colonel Yalinin, "he did not. This report grows more amazing. The Americans, the Israelis, and the Germans bungle things at every turn. And who would have imagined that a Paraguayan police official would prove to be the only competent person on the scene."

Chapter 12—Onward

"When me they fly, I am the wings,"

I had arranged with Petersen that we would meet at noon the next day. We would then drive in the direction of Concepción, a smaller city somewhat to the north of the capitol. That meant I was going to have a busy morning. My first task was to create more interest for those engaged in keeping me under surveillance. I dialed the hotel switchboard and asked to be put through to the airport. When I had the connection, I asked for a reservation and ticket for the next day's flight back to Buenos Aires. The clerk with whom I was put in contact left the telephone for several minutes. Unnecessarily long, I thought, unless the delay was required in order that anyone watching my doings could be advised. However, when the clerk returned, the reservation was confirmed.

Then I went to the lobby to let them know I would be checking out early the next day. On the grounds of the need to make a hurried departure in the morning, I paid my bill in advance. I don't cheat hotels, or rather ICAL doesn't.

My planned driving trip was going to require certain preparations. Under the circumstances, I wanted to travel light. So I made a quick trip to an outfitter's store and obtained a large backpack made of strong canvas. This meant that even with the battered attaché case with its concealed machinegun, I could walk with one hand free. Or if necessary the whole business could be stuffed into the pack. Then I sent the rest of my luggage and belongings to the airport for checking on the next day's flight back to Argentina.

I also thought I had better try to get in touch with the home folks at ICAL. Our arrangements had been that when and if I had Petersen in the bag, I was to contact headquarters and have someone of higher authority, i.e. Walter Pearlman, come out to take charge of him. I don't know exactly why they wanted this done, for I could have brought him to Washington, D.C. myself. I suppose that they thought it would allow them to de-brief Carl Petersen and me more quickly. And perhaps too, Pearlman wanted some of the credit for himself.

Making the required contact meant another bout with the codebook. This time I was more successful. I found what had to be the typographical error that caused all my previous difficulty. I didn't like the idea of sending the complete coded message to ICAL by way of Buenos Aires, for I was still just a bit doubtful about Colonel Manzano. Instead I sent it to Abel Zavaleta in Rio de Janeiro. The message was short and to the point. It read as follows: 'Shipment nearly ready for delivery. Final arrangements and routing still pending. Suggest you take first steps to have facilities open for processing. Ralph.' I hoped that was clear enough and at the same time oblique enough to be secure even if the code was broken. Then I took the message to the telegraph office and sent it off.

I had not seen Sharon Sharen or Hiam Goldson since the previous day. I did call Sharon's room once or twice, but no one was there or at least no one chose to answer. I had things pretty well set for my trip by about 10:30 in the morning, so I thought I would take one last stroll through Asunción. I had the Minox camera with me with the intention of taking a few pictures for ICAL files. We always try to do this, especially in more remote places, for you can never tell when a photograph will assist in verification of information or in the briefing of an incoming agent.

There was not much traffic on the streets, but there seldom is in Asunción. There was however, one little red Volkswagen which was rolling slowly down the street behind me. It didn't seem to be going anywhere in a great hurry. In fact, curiously enough, the driver was moving at just the same pace at which I was walking. I wasn't in any mood to be followed out of town, so I thought I'd better attend to the tail quickly.

Just then I was passing a large general store. This had several entrances on the street, each leading to one or more of its component departments. I walked down to the last door and then turned and darted into the building. Out of the corner of my eye I saw the Volkswagen pause and then pull over to the curb. I walked quickly back through the store, paralleling the front, and blundering as always seems the case, right through departments intended exclusively for women. I'm not an expert, but the women to whom the store catered, seemed to like styles right out of the 1930's and 1940's.

I paused just short of the first door of the store and took a look outside. The Volkswagen was still parked at the curb. It had only one occupant. If anyone was going to follow me, I was very glad that it was Kathi Hausenberg. I was also glad to see that she was all right and had not been harmed in the Germans' escapade of the previous day.

Then I did something I hadn't expected to do. Sometimes this is healthy and also surprises the opposition. Anyway, I walked quickly out of the store, reached the curb before she saw me, opened the passenger side door, and got into her car.

"Is this cab for hire?" I asked politely. "And how are you today. I'm glad to see you again."

She was quite flustered and showed it. Rather prettily I thought. "Why…I'm…well." And then as an afterthought, "What are you doing in my car?"

"I thought that as long as I had your company on my morning wander, we might as well do it together. After all, we seem to have a common interest in what I'm doing."

Then she laughed. It was a strangely musical laughter that sounded wonderful, especially as I hadn't heard much real laughter lately. She turned her beautiful eyes on me, and said, "Yes, I suppose I've been rather clumsy about it. There are only two of us now, and there were things my father had to do this morning. So he told me to watch the hotel and follow whoever came out. And how is it with you? I hear you were out there yesterday."

I knew she meant Petersen's residence and I enjoyed hearing her talk. There was a certain freshness and truthfulness in her voice. I was unaccustomed to that and therefore heard it with all the more pleasure. Her voice had a silvery ring to it, almost as a little bell.

"Yes I was there," I told her. "It was pretty bad and, I regret to say, badly executed also. I don't think they ever had a chance of success. I'm very sorry about your old friend Hasso Cornitz. I guess, according to his views, he had good cause for what he was trying to do."

She sighed. "Yes, he had lost everything. Mostly to the Nazis. Then all the rest to the Russians. He spent the rest of his life brooding and seeking to get even. Now it's over for him."

"Is your father all right?"

"He is. They didn't know about the guards inside. They thought that all they had to do was blow up the gate and go in and get him. Hasso threw the grenades and then ran through the wreckage of the gate, yelling their slogan, '20th July.' Father was right behind him in the car. He saw Hasso go down and drove away as quickly as he could. There are bullet holes in the back of his car. I don't know how he'll explain that to the owner."

I tried to reassure her on that minor point. "Perhaps that won't be so hard to do in this city."

She smiled a little. "But what about you," she continued. "We think you're involved in this too. I don't even know your name, although I think my father does. Are you working for the Jews? Or the Russians?"

"No Kathi," I answered. "In the first place, I guess I'm sorry to say that I'm not. They've got better reasons for wanting Petersen than I have. And second, I'm sorry I didn't introduce myself. I felt I knew you already. My name is Humboldt Prior."

She answered, "It's nice to know you Humboldt, although as I said once before there are too many involvements as it is." With that she started the car. We drove slowly down the street. I was thinking how nice it was to hear her say my name. Then she spoke again. "Why do you think you're sorry in the first place." She was very quick, catching meaning that I'd revealed unintentionally.

I should have made up something to tell her, but I was getting tired of lies and secrets. And somehow I didn't want to make things any more complicated for her. "Kathi, I'm employed by the United States Government, technically by a front organization. They want Petersen back in the States because he can help us offset the Soviets' advantages in neurological warfare. I'm sorry to be working against your father. For me, this is just a job I have to do."

Kathi von Hausenberg half turned and answered with irony, "Oh. Just a job. For me it's supposed to be a holy cause, or at least that's what I've always been told. But I remember almost none of it. You see it all happened when I was only a child. And children are fortunate, they forget." About this time she had turned the car and we were heading back down the street toward my hotel. Then Kathi went on. "But now my father has no one else. So I must help him, you see."

"Yes, Kathi, I see. And I understand." Saying that I also wondered who would help her if I didn't. But I didn't say so. Instead, I found myself saying sadly, "It looks as if we'll be on a difficult road together, until one or the other of us is successful, or dead or we both are."

She stopped the car by the hotel entrance, but said nothing.

After waiting for her to speak, I continued. "We should both be extra careful. That man Petersen is hard as steel and has killed many times."

Then she surprised me. "At least," she said, "let it be that we ourselves are friends. Maybe that will help." Then she smiled at me. It was a beautiful, luminous, shining smile. Eyes, lips, everything smiling.

I couldn't think of anything to say in reply, so I reached over and squeezed her hand. Then I got out of the car. I looked back just before I went into the hotel. By that time the red Volkswagen was speeding up the street.

At noon I picked up my gear, left the hotel and took a wretched, dirty taxicab to the prearranged meeting place on the outskirts of the city. I hoped Petersen hadn't changed his mind. Noon is a pretty good time to begin a trip of this kind. Starting a long drive at that time doesn't occur to a lot of people, which sometimes helps. And in Asunción, most of the citizens were on siesta at that time. They might well be, for it was hot as Hades. By the time Petersen's dusty old car rolled up, sweat was pouring from my forehead and many other locations as well.

Carl Petersen was again calm and determined, having recovered from the beginnings of panic which he had exhibited the previous day. His automobile was an elderly Mercedes 220. The old body style from the 1950s. I imagine that it had originally been black, but now it was a kind of mottled gray, with spots of rust showing through. I threw my stuff into the backseat and then slid in beside him. I kept my Mauser pistol with me.

At first Petersen drove in a leisurely manner, as if we were going nowhere in particular. No one seemed to be following. He evidently decided this just about at the same time I did. The car suddenly picked up speed and we started flying down country roads leading to the main road to Concepción and the north.

We only saw one car. It was parked in the shade of a grove of trees, just at the place at which we turned onto the main highway. I couldn't see too clearly, but a man in the parked car waved as we went by. He looked a lot like Major Anadon.

The Mercedes Benz 220 is a good car in which to travel long distances in poor conditions. For its size, it rides well and is quite fast. It also holds up well, so you don't have unwelcome mechanical failures. This is true even with an older model, out in the middle of nowhere. That was a good thing because that was where we were going. Urban Paraguay, such as it is, is limited mainly to Asunción. The rest of the country is mostly farms, country people and Guarani Indians, together with dust, dirt, and heat.

Qualified automobile repairmen are few and far between. So are automobiles for that matter.

Neither Petersen nor I spoke much for the first half-hour or so. Each of us was lost in thought. When his words came, they came with sudden violence.

"All right now, Mr. Prior," he began with an angry tone, "let us get a few matters cleared up. I know perfectly well you are no art fancier. Nor a sports enthusiast. Nor a hunter. I am confident that you are working for someone. And whoever that is wants to make contact with me. I have no objection to that on principle, but I dislike to have people think that they can trick me. Now then, who are you and what do you want? And who are you working for and what do they want?" He had me there. His sudden verbal offensive didn't leave me much time to make up a good answer, but I thought quickly. Most of the truth might do it.

I began, "You already know my name. I'm employed by a consulting firm in the United States. One that specializes in doing confidential work for government agencies and government contractors. One of our clients is a gigantic chemical company. They foresee an upsurge of interest in neurological warfare materials. And somehow or other they have a lead to the effect that you are an expert on that subject. I'm authorized to make you an offer of employment; a firm offer of $80,000 a year for the next 30 years payable in advance, if you will come and work for my client in the U.S."

"Discounted by what rate?" He was sharp!

"Undiscounted. In other words $2,400,000." I thought he might laugh in my face, but he did not do so.

"That doesn't sound out of the question. Obviously," he said grimly, "I'll have to have many particulars later. However, as you learned yesterday, if you didn't know it before, unpleasant things seem to happen near me. Down here they understand such problems and allow one to take appropriate precautions. What type of guarantee of my safety can be offered in the U.S.?"

That hadn't been mentioned in my instructions, so I thought quickly. The answer had to be plausible but not too pat. "We only talked about that in general terms, wanting to know your views. The client sees one of two solutions. They can give you a maximum-security residence and laboratory, but with limited opportunity for free movement. Or, they can locate you in a section of our country that should be reasonably safe. Smaller cities and towns either in the Deep South or the Southwest are good in that way. The local police are active and there are fewer foreign nationals."

Petersen laughed unpleasantly. "Yes, I imagine there are people in those areas who would understand my situation. They might know how it is when a man spends some of the best years of his life doing a very unpopular job. A job that has to be done. Then because unexpected winners change the rules, the man is turned into a criminal."

I replied, "It's hard to do a good job sometimes, even if they don't change the rules later."

Then he continued, his words coming in rapid bursts, like gunfire. "I was a government officer, a scientific security official. We had certain problems. Solutions to these problems were requested at a higher level and properly approved. It was for men like me to design and execute those solutions." I caught the double meaning and wondered if it was intentional. He was telling his lies as a German, his deeper identity as a Russian agent buried under his long taken cover story.

Petersen continued. "Germany was surrounded by enemies. With other dangerous enemies working from within. They used all available means to destroy us. So we had to fight back. You Americans have learned more about Communist brainwashing during the Korean War. Undergoing that is a pleasure compared to some of the things they put our people through. So we retaliated. That's all it was, retaliation and the execution of orders."

Although it sickened me, especially coming from a Soviet turncoat, I had an answer for this line of talk. "Our client understands that. Their executives know there have been certain difficult associations. However, they believe that since these occurred many years ago, and under different circumstances, such matters need not be a bar to the type of employment the client has in mind."

"Ah." Petersen said else nothing in response. The flat, dusty miles of central Paraguay flew by. The ground shimmered in the heat of the late spring afternoon. Occasionally the expanses of fields and grazing lands were broken by stands of Quebrachos or axe-breaker trees.

"There are two more things," I said. "First, to the extent you can produce documentary material and specimens of the chemical substances of interest to my client, there will be additional payments. And second, I'll need to cable an answer to my proposal as soon as we reach Concepción."

"That you will have, one way or another," he retorted. "But what makes you think that I have any documents or substances?"

I thought it was time to let him know that he wasn't dealing with amateurs. "You ought to have known better than to use the Parana River as a dumping ground. You just about drove the people downstream in Argentina crazy. Their instruments aren't the latest, but even they can detect the stuff you're dumping in concentrations of only one per million."

He looked a little surprised. "So. I should have been more careful. The material is very dangerous and is deteriorating. I've been trying to get rid of it, but it takes a long time. Evidently I was careless once or twice."

We drove on for some time in silence. The sun beat down on the roof of the car like a great flaming furnace. Clouds of dust rose to mark our passage. There wasn't much to be seen. Only a few farm shanties, and an Indian hut or two. The country through which we were passing grew more varied. Here and there patches of farmland had been cleared. Occasionally the clearings had reverted to pasture in which a few haggard cows were grazing. As we progressed farther north there were more and more patches of scrubby forestland. We had seen very few people.

When we did approach a group of roadside stands, Petersen apparently shared my thoughts about getting something to eat. In any event he pulled over and stopped. There wasn't much of a selection, but finally we found some rather stale corn cakes and some warm soft drinks. We had just started to pull away when Petersen noticed a little Indian boy standing by the side of the road. Next to him was a crudely constructed cage, consisting of wire mesh and boards. Petersen stopped the car and leaned out of the window.

He yelled in a mixture of Spanish and Guarani, "Come here boy, what have you there?"

The youngster trotted around to the driver's side of the car. As he moved away from the cage, I saw what it contained. A half-starved jaguar cub. About the size of a small dog. Petersen was speaking again.

"How much is he, boy?"

"Only 1,000 Guarani, or $5.00 American, please Señor."

One thing about Petersen, he didn't haggle. He immediately handed over the money. Then he surprised me. "Let him go," he ordered.

The boy looked surprised, but did as he was told. At first the cub seemed confused, but it soon got its bearings, scurried across the road, and started to trot off toward the bush. Then I realized Petersen was fumbling in the map pocket of the driver's side door. From its cavernous depths he produced a gigantic Colt .45 automatic pistol. He worked the slide and sighted along it.

"Now for some fun," he said.

The roar of the first shot seemed to shake the car. It must have been a very near miss, but it knocked the cub down, head over heels through the dust. The little cat got up running, bounding and scrambling toward the cover of the bush. Petersen took more careful aim and fired again. It was a headshot. The cub fell and then did a strange, sickening little dance on its head. Hind legs thrashing, then feebly kicking, and then lying still. I didn't look any more.

Petersen seemed to slide the pistol away and start the car at the same time. "I like a little sport," he said, "and I hate those cats. I've killed over 100. That one didn't die well but it was only a baby."

For the rest of the drive there was little conversation. I don't know what Carl Petersen had on his mind. I was thinking of mass graves and gas ovens. Of little Jewish children with their heads dashed against walls and little jaguar kittens kicking their lives out in the dust. I wished Petersen wasn't being so cooperative. Now there was another score to settle.

*   *   *

Colonel Yalinin spoke first. "That criminal Petersen would be entirely suitable for work with the U.S. Government. He'd go well with their other German scientists."

"I agree," replied Major Alex Grusev, "but it appears that their man Prior was having some second thoughts even at this point."

Chapter 13—Further Complications

"I am the doubter and the doubt,"

As the crow flies, it is about 200 miles from Asunción to Concepción. However, the limited roads make it necessary to drive east and then north through San Pedro province. That route, plus the deplorable condition of the roads, the dust, and the heat, meant that it took us all afternoon to make the trip. Concepción is one of the main towns of the Paraguay's Chaco region. This is poor country, wild and quite primitive. The people neither like or understand visitors from the capitol. For this reason, and because of the miserable climate, people from Asunción prefer not to visit the hinterland. Concepción is a simple farming community. Few of the streets are paved and the atmosphere is much like that of an American small town before the turn of the century. (Note: Again, Prior is describing conditions in the mid-1960s.)

There is only one usable hotel, which is named the Primavera. It takes its name from that of the heavily German town farther out in the Chaco. Petersen announced that he would stay at the Primavera. I thought it best to temporarily part company with him, but before I did so I obtained his tentative promise to come with me to the United States to work for what he termed my 'mysterious client'.

I then found lodgings at a little inn several blocks down the street. It was very unpretentious, cheap, and not particularly clean. On the 'plus' side, it looked as if it might be free from disturbances and not a place anyone would look for a free spending ICAL Representative. I had a simple and hopefully ulcer-friendly meal, topping it off with a cup of mat'e, the strong Paraguay tea. Then I retreated to my room to sort things out.

There were several pluses and minuses to be considered. First and most important, I hoped I had separated Carl Petersen from the other people who had designs on him. The Israelis had not appeared since my first contacts with them in Asunción. It seemed very possible that the Germans had shot their bolt. The Paraguayan military police had tolerated our departure. And the other peculiar crosscurrents had not manifested themselves since I had left Buenos Aires.

Then in the second place, I had the tentative commitment from Petersen to be a good boy and go along with me to the U.S. to work on nerve gases. In many ways this was a very questionable result, but it was what I was being paid to do. Of course, getting him to the States was easy to say theoretically, but not so easy to accomplish in practice. The best idea I had was for ICAL to fly an aircraft up from Buenos Aires or over from somewhere in Brazil. This would work if I could find a suitable private airstrip near Concepción and get messages to Pearlman and my ICAL contact in Rio.

The only trouble was that the more I succeeded in the '*Sunlight*' operation, the less I liked it. To the extent that years of ICAL training left me with the ability to view the matter on moral grounds, it seemed that either the Germans or the Israelis deserved a crack at Herr Carl Petersen far more than the U.S. chemical warfare scientists. And thus far, Petersen had certainly done nothing to endear himself to me.

That brought me to a few thoughts of my new friend Kathi von Hausenberg. These did nothing to rededicate me to my mission, and I concluded I had done enough thinking for the day. Then I turned in for the night and slept surprisingly well.

The next morning I was coming out of the inn and, distracted by something, I was not looking where I was going. Consequently, I collided with someone. Even with a brief contact she felt small and rounded and familiar.

Sharon said, "Humboldt darling, how glad I am to see you." I imagined she was. I was overconfident in not realizing that as experienced agents, it would be clear to both Sharon and Hiam Goldson that the abrupt disappearances of Herr Petersen and Mr. Prior were not unconnected. Evidently they had guessed right.

Sharon continued, "Where have you been hiding? I've missed you so much. I've been so busy and there's so much to do. Can't we do some things together?"

I chose to answer her first question. "Things were too quiet back there in Asunción. So I came up here to look around and soak up some local culture."

She laughed. "I thought we agreed you were going to help me. We've traced that filthy Nazi, Petersen. He is hiding somewhere near here in Concepción. And now we think we have him cornered. I put sugar in the gasoline tank of his Mercedes last night and Hiam says that there is no plane out of here until the day after tomorrow." I didn't like the sound of that at all.

"What a surprise. How did you know he'd come here? I just found out myself by accident." I thought I should try to keep up pretenses a little longer.

"We received a message saying Petersen had left the town. It said he would probably go north to this place. For a while I thought you had sent it. But evidently you didn't?" The last was spoken as more of a question.

"No, I was trying to contact him, but failed. But now, as you say, he's pretty well boxed in. What happens next?" I needed to understand what she and Goldson would try to do.

She gave me a long look as though making up her mind. "First," she said, "you buy me something to eat. And maybe a drink to go with it.

That is if we can get something safe to drink in this god-awful town. Then, you'll see."

A block away there was a little café, half open to the street. That is where we went. I had my doubts as to whether or not an ulcer patient would find a suitable breakfast there, but there didn't seem to be much choice. The eating area was very small, with scarcely room for two or three tables outside of the low serving counter. Even early in the morning it was hot and stuffy. Many years of smoke, grease, and heavily spiced foods had left their marks on walls, furniture, and atmosphere. Still, nothing would do, but that Sharon had to drag me in to one of the tables.

After a considerable wait someone came to see what we wanted. Sharon ordered rolls and mat'e, all the while exclaiming how glad she was to see me, and how nice it was to be away from Asunción and really doing something. Interspersed in these thoughts were comments about the weather, and "did I like mat'e as well as she did?" I didn't have to say very much in reply, but I had my thinking cap on.

The prompt reappearance of the Israelis just didn't seem to check out. I was pretty sure that Major Anadon had not sent them after us. Yet nothing else seemed possible. I finally ordered some breakfast rolls and, much to Sharon's surprise, a bottle of wine. I did this solely because I didn't care to drink their water or their milk. But Sharon thought it was a wonderful idea and had two glasses of wine with me. After I finally got her quieted down from raptures about how wonderful it was to have wine for breakfast, I thought I'd try a question or two.

"Tell me more about this message you received concerning Petersen's leaving the capitol city. What did it look like and who did you think it was from?"

She answered, "Well actually I didn't see it myself. Hiam received it, and he didn't really say too much about it."

"By the way," I said, trying to sound casual, "where is my friend Hiam? Did he ever tell you that he almost ran me down back in Buenos Aires?"

Sharon looked surprised. "No. He surely didn't. What happened?"

I felt that had unsettled her enough. "It was just one of those funny coincidences. I was stepping across the street and his car came around the corner. He had to stop very quickly and just brushed me. He apologized of course. Are you sure he didn't mention it?"

She didn't answer. We sat there for some time chatting and looking at the sporadic foot traffic on the street outside. It was getting warmer and warmer and I was perspiring. I was just about to take off my suit coat when I remembered the Mauser pistol in its shoulder holster. Up to this time I had done most of my ICAL work in temperate climates. I didn't know how lucky I was.

Then Sharon rose. "Let's go," she said. "It's not far from here."

It? That could mean almost anything. There was only one way to find out, so I tagged along. She seemed to expect that. We walked two blocks down the main street, and then turned left which meant east. We then proceeded along a dirt road toward the east edge of Concepción. About half a mile away was a little hill, and on the hill was an odd looking small cement structure, or more specifically a sort of blockhouse. One or two scrubby trees provided some shade. The yard was mostly dirt. From a distance, the building looked much like most houses in the better parts of Concepción. A little larger perhaps, but just as placid and lackadaisical looking. As most buildings in that part of Paraguay, it seemed to be in a state of almost permanent siesta, dozing in the hot dusty sunlight. Except that there was a very businesslike, six-foot high, barbed wire fence all the way around the building. Sharon walked straight up to the gate and pressed a button on a small metal box that was attached to the fence. Even at a distance you could hear the alarm bell ringing inside the building. A moment later a small, dark, active-looking individual opened the door and ran across the yard to open the gate. He looked askance at me, but Sharon spoke to him in Hebrew and he let me pass also. I should say I presumed it was Hebrew, for I do not understand that language.

It was a relief to be inside the house, out of the scorching sun. It was even more of a relief to find, surprisingly, that the building was air-conditioned.

I turned to Sharon, "I don't know what we're here for, but even if it was just to get out of the heat, I'll always be in your debt."

She laughed. "No Humboldt, this is our field office. Much of the work that we do in Latin America is directed from within these four walls. And we're awfully busy. Most of our people are out on assignment. Only Yigael, the radio operator, is here." While she spoke, Yigael had opened the door leading into the next room and disappeared through it. When we followed I could see why they needed air conditioning. It was for the heat from a very impressive battery of radio equipment. That surprised me for I had seen no antenna on the building and we are trained to always look for such things.

Yigael seemed to sense my question for he said, this time in English, "Usually we send and receive only at night. Then we use an aerial held up by a balloon. Today we're going to have to take a chance and send it up in the daytime. However, as usual, most everybody is resting indoors so we should get away with it."

Sharon had evidently decided to trust me and got right down to business. I didn't catch all that she said to Yigael because she spoke in Hebrew and sometimes in German. The gist of it was a message to persons unknown to me, but doubtless in Tel Aviv, to the affect that Petersen would be fixed in Concepción for at least the next 24 hours. Bearing in mind the Eichmann kidnapping, and piecing together the bits that I could understand I got a pretty good idea of what was being planned. When she finished giving the instructions, Yigael got busy with his codebook. I had the Minox camera in my pocket and would certainly have liked to take a picture of that codebook, but Sharon didn't let me get very close to where Yigael was working. Finally, when my attempts to get a look at it became too obvious, she pulled me into the other room and slammed the door.

This room of the ImEx headquarters was set up as a sitting and eating room. The furniture wasn't fancy, but it looked comfortable after our long walk. Sharon pointed me to an old sofa and stepped into a small kitchen from which she quickly returned with a couple of tall glasses in which ice cubes tinkled pleasantly. This was doubtless supposed to make me forget about the codebook.

Sharon was happy as a schoolgirl who has just been elected homecoming queen. "Humboldt we've got him," she exclaimed. "After years of effort. And a lot of worry, frustration and even some casualties. We've been watching him for years, you know. And now we've got him cornered and you helped us do it." She leaned over and kissed me.

"I'm very glad for you, Sharon," I said. "I just hope you won't be disappointed."

"No," she answered confidently, "we won't be. The arrangements are all in place. Within 12 hours, Yigael's broadcast will bring all the resources and people we need. This is an ideal place. Even the local police are somewhat sympathetic to us. Of course we have to pay them to be." Then she laughed.

That didn't sound very good to me. It began to look as though I was the one who was going to be disappointed. And I dislike disappointments almost as much as my boss does. There seemed no way for me make new arrangements with Pearlman, and then contact and move Petersen in the short time available. I was just trying to dream up some other counter ploy out of my sizable reservoir of cleverness and trickery when the front door opened.

Evidently Hiam Goldson had a key to the front gate or someone else had let him in. In any event, there he was. He seemed unusually displeased to see me.

"What the hell are you two up to now?" he growled.

Sharon answered quickly. "There's wonderful news, Hiam. We've found the Nazi criminal Petersen. He's at the hotel. And I've sabotaged his car and Mr. Prior is helping us. Yigael is broadcasting right now. In 12 hours Petersen will be in the bag. And we can go home. Home to Israel."

Sharon was so happy and enthusiastic that I don't believe she caught the particularly nasty expression that flickered across Hiam's dark face.

"What a break," he said, "but please excuse me for a moment. I've got to make one business call." Although I couldn't see him in the kitchen where the telephone was, I alone was sitting close enough to hear him quite clearly. He picked up the phone and rang for the central exchange. Then he asked for number 503. He was quickly connected to his party.

Then he spoke, "This is Goldson. I have a rush order. That shipment we discussed must leave tonight as soon as it gets dark. I mean as soon as you've closed for the day. Remember this is urgent."

When Hiam came back into the room he was smiling. He said, "Now that the necessary cover business is taken care of, I can concentrate on the real operation. We'll do it at dawn tomorrow while he's still sleeping, and before anyone else is up and about either."

Sharon seemed agreeable, but said nothing. It looked like everybody was going to be busy so I thought I'd better clear out before they put me to work or rethought their decision to involve me in their planning. It was a two-mile walk back to the little inn in which I was staying. With time to ponder, I found certainty growing. I wasn't completely sure at first, but I thought that the number Goldson had called was one of the numbers assigned to the hotel where Petersen was staying. That seemed to reinforce some other ideas which had been percolating in my suspicious mind.

I made certain arrangements, and then a good hour before sundown I found a seat in a little café across the street from the Hotel Primavera. There I waited. I ordered tea and hoped that a large tip would earn me the right to stay for hours if I had to. The day was cooling and low clouds on the western horizon seemed to hold a promise of rain. The time passed slowly and I was beginning to think I'd made a mistake. This was a bothersome thought too, because if I had and Sharon's operation went off properly the next day, I would be in a mess of trouble.

Then finally, when there was just enough light to see the first drops of rain scattering and then darkening the dust of the street, Carl Petersen emerged from the hotel. I was seated in a corner of the café, half behind a pillar and was pretty certain he couldn't see me. Anyway, he was obviously waiting for someone. He paced nervously up and down, suitcase in hand. He was carrying something else in the other hand. I couldn't make out what it was at first, until I saw one of the lights of the hotel flicker and flash off the blade. I had never actually seen a jaguar spear before and I hadn't imagined it could be such a vicious looking weapon. The shaft was a good four feet long and as thick as the handle of a baseball bat. The blade added another 10 to 12 inches to the overall length. Right where the shaft joined the blade there was a large cross member. Probably there to keep the speared cat from sliding down the shaft and slashing the hunter with its last dying strength. Petersen seemed to be getting impatient and so was I.

I probably looked away for a minute because when I turned back to where Petersen was standing, the BMW 1600 sedan was just coasting to a stop opposite him. Petersen moved quickly across the street and I ducked further back behind the sheltering pillar. He was distracted by the task of fitting the jaguar spear into the car and as he got in I chanced another look. For just a second the courtesy light still illuminated the face of the driver. It was Hiam Goldson. Again my suspicious nature and training had done their jobs.

The car started to move off down the street, gathering speed. When it got about a half block away, I ran out and beckoned to one of Concepción's few taxis. I had reserved it hours before. The driver had an easy time waiting and had a good big fare already on his ancient meter. I hoped ICAL wouldn't mind.

I didn't know Guarani for 'follow that car' so I said it in Spanish as I jumped into the cab. I hoped the Indian driver would understand. He got the idea at once, for we roared off after the fleeing BMW. After about two miles the pair of red taillights which we were following slowed and then stopped. We did also and I bailed out, while tossing the driver what I hoped was not too much money. It was a dark night with the rain still spattering down in big heavy drops, punishing the dirt surface of the road. The car ahead was pointed east on the road which would ultimately take it to the Brazilian frontier. Apparently Hiam didn't want to walk much, for we were not far from the Israeli headquarters. He was obviously turning the car over to Petersen for his getaway. I feeling a bit proud of myself as the BMW started to pull away. After all, Petersen was still free to come to the United States, and I had collected the first Jewish Nazi sympathizer in ICAL history.

At that moment my cab driver decided to switch on his high beams. I suppose he was trying to help me see better. Unfortunately, I was standing almost in front of the cab, and so Goldson saw me. He didn't waste any time, but ducked down in a crouch at the side of the road and snapped off a revolver shot. This produced at least one good result, for my cab driver switched off his lights, turned the taxi around, and fled. Relying on the darkness, I stood very still, but slipped the Mauser out of its shoulder holster. I couldn't see Goldson very clearly, but the training trick of using one's peripheral night vision helped. I turned my head, looked out of the corners of my eyes, and spotted him.

He was crouching about 50 yards down the road and was obscured by darkness and rain. He had missed once and I didn't want to give him another chance. Since I couldn't see him clearly enough, I aimed low. That way if I missed I'd still have a chance of a ricochet hitting the target in the leg or groin. I fired three rounds as fast as the semi-automatic pistol would operate and then threw myself sideways to the ground. I heard a scream and someone staggered off, crashing through the underbrush.

Then I hiked back to town. I didn't mind the rain. There was more than a chance that it saved my life.

*   *   *

Neither Colonel Yalinin nor Major Alex Grusev had anything to say. Both were reflecting on the unimaginable inducements which were necessary to make an Israeli intelligence agent betray his cause in to order to permit a fleeing Nazi war criminal to escape the retribution he so richly deserved.

Chapter 14—Rio Parana

"And I the hymn the Brahmin sings."

I had taken a note of the telephone number of the ImEx field headquarters, and used it the next morning when I called Sharon Sharen. I thought she might like to confide in someone.

"Good morning, Sharon," I said. "This is Humboldt Prior. I have found out some very confidential information that will be of interest to you. May we get together to discuss it, as soon as possible this morning?" This sounded stuffy to me, but I hoped it would fit her image of me as a business recruiter.

"Oh," she answered. "I've wanted to talk to you too. There have been new developments. And Hiam has been hurt."

We made arrangements to meet 45 minutes later in the restaurant of the Primavera Hotel. I got there first and ordered tea and coffee. When she arrived Sharon looked fine but flustered. Also in a hurry. It didn't look as if there was going to be much time for socializing.

I thought I'd better get my words in first. I began "Petersen is gone. He's checked out of the hotel. I can't find a trace of him anywhere. Apparently you didn't fix his car well enough, or he found another one or someone gave him a lift."

"Oh, we know all that," she answered rather shortly. "There was some action last night. It's a good thing you missed it. Things got rough. Hiam told me about it this morning, after he returned from seeing the doctor.

He was watching Petersen last night. Petersen ambushed him, shot him and stole his car." Hiam had evidently told a pretty convincing story.

I asked a natural question. "Do you know where he has gone? Back to Asunción?"

"No," Sharon said, "our car was seen heading east. As if to drive to Brazilian frontier. It's not a long direct distance in kilometers, but to drive there is quite circuitous and takes time. We've got to catch him or he'll totally escape. And we may never have another chance." Then she asked, "Do you possibly have a Brazilian address for him? Or could you obtain one?"

"No I'm sorry I don't. I only met him in Argentina."

She was obviously very determined. And, once she found I was of no immediate help, not very interested in anything else I might have to say or suggest. Evidently I had served her purposes for the time being.

Sharon continued, "Hiam has had me out this morning looking for a car. I've just found one. It's an old Ford. You can see it parked outside on the street. I just hope it will hold up." She was right about its age. From the boxy lines the car had to be at least 10 years old, maybe more. And it looked as though it had 200,000 miles on the odometer. One of the door windows was badly cracked and one side of the front end seemed to sag. I didn't envy her a long, cross-country trip in such a vehicle.

"Is there anything I can do for you?" I asked cautiously. And then as an afterthought, "How is Hiam? I don't think he likes me very well, but all the same I'm sorry to hear he's hurt."

Sharon answered offhandedly. "He has just a slight flesh wound in the leg. No bones were broken, but another inch and the bullet would have severed the main artery. But as it is, it's just an inconvenience."

"Hiam was very lucky to get away." That's what I really thought.

Then Sharon abruptly concluded the conversation and something more. "We don't need you any more. Go back home, Humboldt Prior. If you stay around here you may be hurt. And I'd be sincerely sorry if that had to happen." She didn't even bother to finish her coffee, but instead rose and left the room. Sharon didn't look back. I could see her getting into the old car. After some delay, it started and pulled out into the road. As it did, I waved. I don't know whether or not she saw me.

I didn't warn Sharon about Hiam Goldson's treachery. Perhaps I should have, but I couldn't see how to do it without endangering my own mission. That's one of the many troubles with my job. You hurt people or put them at risk, and there's nothing else you can do. No alternatives. I wished her luck, mentally, because she was going to need it. Chasing after a killer like Carl Petersen in the company of one of his own henchmen. For that's what Hiam Goldson was revealed to be. It was easy now to understand how Petersen got word to decamp from Buenos Aires. I remembered how I last saw him. Standing strong there in the darkening evening with the rain spattering down, and the light flickering on the savage looking jaguar spear. I can be pretty tough myself, but in some ways I hoped that would be my last look at him.

After giving Sharon time to get clear, I paid the restaurant and left the hotel. The bare ground, which was all that the surface of the road amounted to, was already dry and dusty. But as I trudged back to my inn, I could see a darkening bank of clouds that promised more rain. All in all, it had been a depressing start for the morning. And it matched my mood.

I had just unlocked the door to my room and was starting to push it open when something hit me from behind. Instantly there was a second stinging blow as my nose and forehead smashed into the door. I toppled forward into the room with my assailant on top of me. He already had my arms pinned behind me when another person hit me expertly on the head with the barrel of his revolver. I felt myself sinking down into a gray haze, but with a strange feeling of movement. Then everything was dark.

I awakened in what looked to be a room in the Primavera Hotel. At first I didn't move a muscle and just cracked open one eye. This takes self-control, but sometimes will save your neck. Not however when you are dealing with professionals like Staff Major Anadon. He saw immediately that I was awake.

"Well, well, Mr. Prior," said the Major. "Are you still enjoying your visit to our country? Not very successful so far, I'm afraid. That's unfortunate too. Because I quite like you and you are not going to be able to remain with us much longer. I understand that you have decided to return home to the U.S."

I didn't like the sound of that, but there wasn't a good response to a remark of that kind. I just went on listening.

"It seems that trouble follows you everywhere. In Asunción we had bombings. Also machinegun fire. And here in Concepción, midnight shootings. I think our country is not healthy for you."

"Quite the contrary, I find Paraguay both healthful and most interesting." I thought at least I should be courteous.

Major Anadon didn't seem very appreciative. "Nonetheless you are going to have to leave. You and all these others. My men are going out to get those Jews now."

I thought to myself that I would lay odds that his men would be too late.

Then Major Anadon continued. "And we will soon have the remaining Germans in custody as well. We picked up the girl on the way here. She'd been dropped off to try some sort of foolish delaying action. We knew where to find her. And the man, von Hausenberg will also soon be in our hands. Already we have him under observation.

"With you," the Major grinned, "we are going to be more friendly. We cannot, of course, too greatly annoy your mighty employer. We will simply put you on a plane tomorrow morning. It will take you back to the capitol. There, if you are fortunate you will just catch the flight to Buenos Aires. But don't stop there Señor Prior, please continue your travels northward. You don't seem to function very well down here."

The good Major was becoming a little tiresome. I said sarcastically, "I'm sorry to put you to all this trouble. Couldn't we simplify things? Suppose I just take a car and drive east across the border."

Staff Major Anadon's thin smile told me that ploy wasn't going to work. "The roads east to the Parana River are long, tiresome and dangerous. We would fail in our duty to important guests such as yourself if we permitted them to inconvenience themselves in that way."

This was getting us nowhere and it looked as if I was going to have to try something more drastic. Probably involving danger and large amounts of money. Then I heard the shooting. Several harsh snapping explosions of sound. Not far away. Major Anadon looked startled, which was unusual for him. Then we heard a car drive past in rapid acceleration, engine screeching, and gears rasping as it increased speed.

A blond, heavyset, military police sergeant burst into the room. "Major Anadon sir," he yelled, "the German is escaping. He is getting away in his car. A black Volkswagen."

"Swine," Major Anadon spat out the word. "Why didn't you stop him, you fool, you miserable, incompetent, bumbling swine!" Clearly, Major Anadon was much less at ease away from his headquarters at Asunción.

The police sergeant threw out his arms apologetically. "We were watching the house where he was staying. But he must have got out by a back entrance or a window. Anyway he was at his car before we saw him. Then he fired upon us without warning, jumped into his car, and got away. I'm very sorry Major, but there was absolutely nothing we could do." There are many Paraguayans of German descent, so I wondered about that.

Then Major Anadon surprised me. "All right, then we return to Asunción. We'd never catch him along those roads to the eastern border. And if we can't arrest them all, I don't want any of these people in my custody." He turned to me, "And that includes you, Señor Prior. We'll have to let you go too, damn it. You see there are some limits to what we can do as a small weak country. We either succeed completely and uniformly or nothing. We dare not seem to show favor to one side over another." He even returned my pistol.

I didn't waste any time leaving the hotel room. My head was still ringing from the blow that knocked me out, but fighting off the pain, I hurried down the first flight of stairs. I saw them as I rounded the landing. They were coming up. The girl Kathi, and a military policeman. She looked at a brief glimpse to be worried and frightened. Probably Paraguayan police detention was none too pleasant and I wondered if the Major's generosity was going to extend to attractive young women.

Before I had decided what to do about that, the police officer saw me and must have thought I was escaping. He started to unholster his big revolver. I didn't think that there'd be time for explanations, so I kicked out at him from my place two or three steps above. The toe of my shoe drove into his throat and he went down in a choking heap. I hit him again and rolled him out of the way.

And then I got a surprise. Kathi Hausenberg had retrieved the police revolver from the step on which it had fallen and was standing there pointing it. And she was pointing it at me.

"Really, Miss von Hausenberg," I said quietly, "that's no way to say thank you."

"I know it isn't," she answered, "but I've no choice. Please continue down the stairs. And hurry. I'll be right behind you."

When we reached the street there were no police to be seen. Evidently the scuffle and commotion on the stairs had passed without notice. However, there was a sleek, new looking Mercedes Benz 190 parked nearby.

Kathi had more surprises in store. "It was arranged that this auto would be left here for me," she explained, not saying who had done the arranging. "Get into the car please, I need you. I have to have your help. I'm sorry it has to be this way, because I like you and wish I had time to persuade you to come voluntarily. But my father can't carry on by himself. I'll have to reach him right away, and I can't do it alone."

Kathi's small traveling case was already in the car. She seemed to want to trust me, so she willingly stopped at the inn long enough for me to retrieve my backpack and attaché case. I was pleased to discover that the Paraguayan police were not infallible. Confronted with a locked attaché case they have failed to discover and confiscate (or steal) the machinegun inside. I was glad of that for I thought that where we were going I would need something more than the Mauser pistol. Then we started with Kathi at the wheel. And driving very fast.

Neither of us said much for the first twenty miles or so. Then she spoke. "I'm really sorry Humboldt, really I am. And I hope in spite of this that we can be friends. I'm sure you are not accustomed to being ordered into cars, especially by women with pistols in their hands. And I'm not used to doing that sort of thing either."

"I might not mind at all," I said. "I was planning to go this way myself. At least it was one of my ideas. However, I sent most of my luggage back to Buenos Aires and I'm not sure I have all the documents I need to enter Brazil."

Kathi looked relieved and a little happier. The beginnings of a smile started to return to her face. "You see," she said, "there wasn't time to talk things over with you. I was so afraid the police would try to stop us. Father said that Mr. Petersen would probably drive toward Brazil. It's said to be wild country there. I'm told a lot of strange things happen along the Parana River. Awful, terrible things. I guess I didn't think about your intentions, I just wanted you along."

She changed her driving position slightly and half turned toward me. It seems to me now that at that moment I first realized how lovely she was. The laughing eyes were serious now, but still they sparkled. She was wearing a simple brown dress with a little white, lace collar piece, and a light cardigan sweater. The rather conservative and slightly out-of-date appearance only made the picture all the more attractive.

The Mercedes Benz continued to fly over the dusty roads to the east and south. To reach Brazil by any reasonably passable road, we had to trend south to a point almost due east of Asunción. There we would find the main road leading to the Parana River and the Parana and Santa Catarina provinces of Brazil.

After some time Kathi spoke again. "What is the best thing for us to do when we reach the river? Neither of us have the right papers. I don't know how to cross secretly into Brazil, and yet that is what I am supposed to do. I don't know how we will pick up the trail of the man, Petersen. And I really don't know exactly what has happened to my father or where to meet him. We planned for him to evade the police and travel together. And then I heard shooting."

I answered some of her questions. "The police sergeant told Major Anadon that your father had escaped toward the frontier. Driving a black Volkswagen. He shouldn't be too far ahead of us. If you want to try it, perhaps we can catch up with him. This car should be faster."

Then she surprised me again. She smiled and said, "No, I don't think so. I don't think he'd like to see you with me, and he might do something silly. I'd rather stay behind him, at least until we reach the Brazilian border."

The car continued to eat up the miles. After two hours of driving we exchanged places and I did the driving. Apparently this changed our luck for it was not more than 15 minutes before the left rear tire blew out. The car pulled violently to the left and I fought to keep control of the car on the rough surface. Then I eased it over to the side of the road and stopped.

"I hope you managed to get hold of a car with a good spare tire," I said. That seemed to worry her and I was sorry I said it.

"Do you think we shall be long delayed?" The look of concern crept back into he eyes.

I leaned over and patted her shoulder. "No, don't worry, Kathi, I'll have it replaced quickly." Things went quite easily. Daimler Benz goes to some lengths to make running repairs practical. There are little sockets for the jacks and plenty of tools and other timesaving devices. I had the tire changed in 20 minutes or so and we were on our way. I hoped we didn't have a second flat tire before the first could be repaired.

By late afternoon we reached a little village with the impressive name of 'Doctor Juan Frutos.' The name was practically bigger than the town. However, I was getting tired and hungry and suspected that Kathi was also. So I suggested that we stop. She looked worried for a moment.

"Look Kathi," I said, "trust me. I'll get you as far as you have to go and maybe a little farther. But now I think we had better stop and rest. Also it might be best to give our various fellow motorists at little more time on the road ahead. That will get us to the border later in the evening too, when things are more quiet there."

"All right Herr Humboldt Prior." And she smiled at me which was very nice to see. I found a garage that claimed to be able to repair our tire. Then, after a leisurely and very late little luncheon of tea, bread, and reasonably fresh fruit, we continued on. The car seemed to go even faster, although the high pitched whir of its small four-cylinder engine always seemed to deny the possibility of more speed.

As we progressed, I found myself talking to Kathi Hausenberg on a more casual basis and without the gulf of mutual distrust and suspicion which normally separates the intelligence operative from all with whom he comes in contact. She was a good listener and seemed content to let me ramble on. That was a distinct pleasure, for I had had little opportunity in recent weeks, or in recent years for that matter, to talk freely with someone who seemed in sympathy with me. This smiling, brown-haired young woman had that effect.

Kathi talked well too, simply and directly. Among other things I found that it was she who had, anonymously, called Colonel Manzano to interrupt my evening with Sharon a few nights before. I decided that I liked her for it, and hoped that I made the right guess about her reasons for doing it.

Anyway, I was more than a little sorry when we began to near the border. That required more concentration on the business at hand. The country surrounding the Parana River is among the least known in all of South America. In this region, the country of Paraguay comes together with its larger neighbors Argentina and Brazil. A great deal of extra-curricular and often-illegal traffic passes back and forth across the river. The area is like a sort of back door to all three countries. It gets a lot of use from smugglers, intelligence people, and others whose travel documents or purposes or luggage cannot pass much customs scrutiny. It is a lonely, but quite beautiful place. The river flows quietly between marshy banks, as yet unfettered by long-proposed hydroelectric dams. Low trees and bushes add to the air of wildness, remoteness, and solitude.

A full moon was just beginning to rise when we saw the car. The old Ford automobile, which was to have carried Sharon Sharen and Hiam Goldson to their destination in Brazil, was unmistakable. It was standing by the side of the road partly behind a clump of trees, with one wheel nosed deeper into the underbrush. The minute I saw it, I slowed down and flicked off our headlights. Kathi looked at me questioningly, but I reassured her and edged the car to the roadside and stopped.

"That car needs to be investigated," I said. "You know you have some competition from an Israeli group. That is their car. It looks as if it's abandoned, but we'd better be sure." I got out of the car. She signified assent by following my example. I slipped the Mauser from its shoulder holster, checked to be sure a round was in the firing chamber, and, for good measure, cocked the hammer. I didn't want to waste any time if I had to use the gun. I think this was the first time that Kathi knew I was armed, but she didn't seem to object.

The car was empty. It didn't take much work with a pencil flashlight to identify two trails leading away from the old Ford. In different directions. One was a trail of crumpled tangled grass and underbrush leading toward the river, which was only a few yards away. The other was the unmistakable tire track of an automobile which had continued down the road to the frontier. I motioned to Kathi to follow me, and moved carefully down the trail of broken vegetation toward the riverbank. I was afraid of what I was going to find. One or two patches of dark wetness on the grass looked too much like blood for comfort.

As we came out on the bank of the Parana River we both stopped at the same moment. The moon had turned the river to silver. All but in one place. That was the place in which the body of a woman was floating.

Sharon lay there on her back, the way that womens' bodies usually float, peacefully, dreamily, as though she'd been there not for just a short time, but forever and ever. A part of the river and the night. I was sure she was dead, but I waded out into the water and pulled her to shore. Up the riverbank, I dragged the limp body, which had been not long before, so lively and happy, so enthusiastic and so determined. It rolled over. The spear wound in her back was horrible.

Kathi shuddered, sobbed, and spoke proverb-like words. "Humboldt, we need not always keep memories of so much, much sorrow. God's gift to us is forgetfulness when we need it. Let God and time take this from you."

I slipped my arm around her shoulder and pressed her to me. Then we turned and walked back to the car. Two ideas now burned in my mind. One was that Operation *Sunlight* was going to fail and Carl Petersen would never live to reach the United States. I also knew I would always remember my new traveling companion, this lovely young German woman whose eyes laughed and whose wise words seemed to sing.

* * *

Colonel Yalinin turned to Major Grusev and asked, "Are you familiar with the area which they are now entering?"

"Yes, Comrade Colonel, I am. Except for the great Iguacu waterfall, which Prior evidently did not see, it is just as he describes it. The body of the Israeli agent, Sharon Sharen, was found two days later by the joint frontier patrol. They didn't make much of it. Unfortunately such an occurrence is not unusual."

Chapter 15—Ongoing Project

"The strong Gods pine for my abode,"

The night was so bright that I scarcely needed the headlights. I just let the Mercedes 190 drift quietly through the night. On we rolled, at medium speed, down the road over the few miles that were left before we reached the last town before the Brazilian frontier. Neither of us spoke. Kathi seemed lost in thought, as though trying to reach a perplexing decision. I kept seeing Sharon's poor torn little body. Why in God's name did he have to do it with a jaguar spear? The killing might, according to his history, have been necessary. But not that way.

Then I began thinking more about Carl Petersen. I was searching for a way out, for reasons not to return him to the United States. I was remembering my second option. This was to cause his liquidation so that his knowledge of germ warfare couldn't be used by anyone else. In my concentration on this, I must have been gradually accelerating the car.

Kathi seemed to sense my mood. She slid closer to me on the front seat and, just for a moment ever so lightly rested her head on my shoulder. "Gently, gently Humboldt," she said softly. "We don't want to interest any watchers or listeners."

I nodded in agreement. "No, we don't. Things are going to be difficult enough as it is. I have to make a stop in the next town. Right on the frontier. You'll have to come with me. I hope you won't be too disappointed in what you hear."

We were coming into Hernandaras, the last Paraguayan village before the border with Brazil. The little place consisted of only one principal street, actually the highway. There were small clusters of buildings on each side. Almost all were dark. In one or two flickered the yellow flames of lanterns. Another, obviously a café, was more brightly lighted. This was my contact point.

I hoped Abel Zavaleta had received my last message from Concepción. It had been sent in the clear, because I had no time to code it while Kathi waited in the car. The telegram simply said: 'Urgent. Coming your way via Hernandaras. With another. Hope you can provide tickets. Ralph.' This meant I was hoping to enter Brazil, but that I needed the proper papers to cross the frontier from Paraguay. I hoped Zavaleta would have a solution.

I braked the Mercedes to a halt a few yards from the café. Then I got out. Kathi did likewise, with a worried expression on her face. We locked the car carefully. I also took time to be sure the Mauser pistol was ready for use. I didn't want or expect any trouble. But if there were troublemakers about they might try to do their business near the border.

The little café was almost deserted. A small record player's feeble attempts at music making only accentuated the silence. The room was well lighted only in front. Stretching back into the gloom was a series of small tables. I could see a shape sitting at one of them. It looked like Abel Zavaleta.

Kathi seemed apprehensive, slowing her steps. I tried to reassure her. "I don't have many friends in high places, but I do in low ones. That man there is supposedly such a friend. He may be able to get us across the border, but it may involve your hearing some things I wish I'd told you sooner. Please bear with me." Then I took her arm and steered her back to the table where Zavaleta was sitting. He didn't look happy to see us.

"Well now, Ralph," was his officious greeting, "what ever have you been doing? They are very angry back in Washington. They say you have missed several opportunities to do what you were sent here for. Now you come here and make me identify myself to the Paraguayans. And worst of all," and here he glared at Kathi, "you seem to have picked up a traveling companion. What is Mr. Pearlman going to say about that?"

I didn't like Zavaleta's manner or his choice of words, but I didn't have any good excuses to offer. I had to say something, so I tried the truth, or something like it. "This lady is Señorita Hausenberg, a senior employee of a West German security organization. Her government's claims to extradite Petersen are being adjudicated." Kathi looked startled, but then smiled and nodded vigorously. "Therefore we are working together for the moment. We will locate Petersen first, and then sort out the question of who gets him. That is if anyone does. That way we can best defeat the opposition forces, so don't do anything to make me think you are part of those forces." Fear showed on Zavaleta's face. I continued, "Did you receive my messages?"

"Yes, I received your messages," he answered, "Pearlman is coming down to handle things from the Buenos Aires end, and I am to do the same from Brazil. It is your task to locate Petersen and deliver him to one or the other of us. That is if you can do that, which I begin, with all respect, to doubt."

There's nothing like working for an organization that has confidence in you, but I didn't have time to argue about my capabilities. I asked, "Has anyone else been over the frontier this evening?"

Kathi interrupted, "Such as a black Volkswagen carrying one man?"

Zavaleta answered us in turn. "Two automobiles. At dusk came a BMW with two men in it. They had correct papers and crossed without incident. I didn't see them myself, but from the descriptions, one of them was probably the man we want. The black Volkswagen crossed an hour later. I was at the Brazilian customs office at that time. There seemed to be some question when he first made application. But then a senior customs officer entered the room and they spoke to one another. The officer made a telephone call and then the Volkswagen was allowed through." I saw Kathi frown.

"Do you have the necessary documents for me?"

Zavaleta answered in an angry voice. "I can't do miracles and produce new papers for two people on 12 hours notice. And now it's the middle of the night. You'll be the only ones going through. The guards will be extra careful. They'll have plenty of time to examine your papers."

Kathi interjected, "But he doesn't have the correct papers."

Abel Zavaleta was tired and impatient. "I understand that perfectly well young lady. You are going to have wait here. Your friend Ralph, as I'm still to call him, is showing his usual want of consideration for the other people in our organization. If he had informed me of his needs two days ago, all could have been handled with ease. Now as I see it you're both going to be delayed. I'll do what I can, but its going to take a day or two. By that time also, Mr. Pearlman will be nearby and able to make personal decisions about these matters." I didn't like the sound of that and evidently neither did Kathi von Hausenberg. For she then spoke in a different tone of voice, one that I'd not heard before.

"It will not be possible to wait," she said with great determination. "We must enter Brazil at once. Herr Petersen cannot be given time to hide himself again." She rose to leave the café.

"I agree," I said emphatically. "You may not know it Abel, but there already have been several people killed on this operation. And there are other complications. Now that Carl Petersen is gone, the Paraguayans will throw us out of the country if they get the chance. I want to get him before he conceals himself or does any more killing."

"Well then," Zavaleta concluded as he too got to his feet, "you two had better get ready to swim the Parana River, because that is exactly what you are going to have to do."

Kathi then said politely but very firmly, "Let us proceed, Mr. Ralph, perhaps we will find another way."

Zavaleta retorted, "You may do as you wish, young lady. Ralph is specifically ordered to remain here." I gave him a withering look and followed Kathi out of the café.

When we reached the car she puzzled me by getting into the back seat. Apparently I showed my surprise and she answered my unspoken question. "I'm not angry with you or being unfriendly," she said with a shy smile, "it's just that the people we are going to be seeing will understand things better this way. I don't like what I'm going have to do because it reminds me of circumstances and situations from which I'm trying to grow away. But it is the only way left. And furthermore," she smiled again, "I've just become a senior official of West German intelligence. So please be my driver."

"With great pleasure," I said.

"Good. Drive straight to the frontier, Humboldt."

"Yes ma'am." I did as she ordered. The frontier post was perhaps a mile or two from the village. Only two buildings, one for the Paraguayans, one for the Brazilians. Each with a roadblock. And between them the river bridge, and a series of thick barbed wire entanglements starting from alternate sides of the pavement, each extending more than half way across. Viewed from a straight line down the road, they interlocked. This type of barrier is intended to permit low speed traffic but to prevent anyone from crashing through the border at high speed. This of course also gives the guards time to machinegun any car that attempts to pass without permission.

We drove up to the Paraguayan customs station. As far as they were concerned our papers were in perfect order. Indeed the guard scarcely glanced at them. It was no concern of his where we were going after we left Paraguay or how we would enter the neighboring country. I started the Mercedes again and snaked it through the barbed wire barriers.

Then I stopped at the Brazilian frontier post. It was a modest rectangular concrete block building. On the sides, which were perpendicular to the road and therefore commanded it, were small low windows. From each of these protruded the barrel of a heavy machinegun. Evidently the Brazilians had no time for unwelcome guests. A smartly uniformed customs policeman stepped out of the building. He came around to my side of the car. As he did so, I rolled down the window.

"Let me have your entry papers and please leave the car so that we may examine it. The lady may be seated in the building. You will remain outside to answer questions."

Then Kathi spoke words in German from her place in the back of the car. I hardly recognized her voice. It was harsh and steely with practiced command. "You will return to the guard building at once. There you will tell your superior officer that the niece of Colonel General Count Litzingen, and her driver, require admittance to the country of Brazil. The Countess goes for a visit to the General in the state of Parana."

I was not at all surprised when the policeman snapped to attention, then turned on his heel, and double-timed back into the building. I would have done the same thing. I turned to Kathi and looked at her questioningly.

"You see I too have secrets," she said. "Sometimes we must return to our past. I don't like to remember it, or to show it off, but there it is. It will get us through." She smiled a little sadly.

I couldn't think of anything to say, so I just returned her smile. As she had leaned forward to speak to the policeman, her right hand rested lightly on the back of the front seat. It remained there, and I turned my head toward it and kissed it gently. Then I faced the police captain who was hurrying busily out of the Brazilian frontier post.

"A thousand apologies Señorita von Hausenberg. We did not expect you. You and your driver may pass instantly, of course. Again my greatest apologies. Enjoy your visit." At the same time, the policeman was hurriedly raising the barrier gate.

Neither of us spoke as I accelerated the car and left the two Brazilians standing there in the moonlight. Five hundred yards down the road I stopped the car and Kathi, obviously now quite pleased with herself, rejoined me in the front seat. In fact, I let her take the wheel since I thought, especially in view of the events of the last five minutes, that she would be more likely to know where we were going. We reached the little town of Laranjeiras do Sul at about 2:00 in the morning. She seemed to know it from previous visits. There were two small inns.

Kathi had me drop her at the first one, saying, "I will never forget this night and all your help to me, but we had better separate here."

I answered, "I too will remember this night. I'm so sorry to leave you now, but I expect you know best. I hope our two paths will be close together." I was already thinking of how much I would miss her.

She answered with another of her fine old German based expressions; "We'll be going to the same ending and let us promise that the one who reaches it first will wait for the other."

I promised.

Then she got out of the car. I lifted her case out of the trunk and placed it before the entrance of the inn. A sleepy young Indian servant boy was already stumbling out to get it. She gestured to him to take it inside. She was standing very close to me and then leaned forward to again rest her head on my shoulder. I put my arms around her and we stood there, saying nothing, for a few moments. Then I let her go and drove off down the dark road to the other little inn.

I made them awaken me at 6:30 in the morning. This meant I had only about four hours of sleep. I was bone weary but had to be up and doing. When I left Kathi Hausenberg I had seen, out of the corner of my eye, a black Volkswagen parked on a side street next to her inn. I ate a simple breakfast and then checked out of the inn. Kathi had generously left the Mercedes Benz in my care. After some false starts, I found my way to the street on which her father's car had been parked. Yes, it was still there. I stopped behind a large farm truck and waited.

Within an hour, her father, Bill von Hausenberg came out of the inn, got into the Volkswagen, and drove off. I followed wondering how much Kathi had told him. It seemed to me that here he would know how to find Petersen far better than I did. He drove out into the farming country, which in this part of Brazil includes many large coffee plantations. I followed him for an hour or so. I was pretty sure that he would see me, but I didn't see what else I could do. I was also pretty sure that his fanatic pursuit of Carl Petersen would not admit to the diversions needed to put me off his trail.

It was during this drive that I began to do some serious thinking about my position with ICAL. I knew that it was impossible or at least extremely difficult to break away from them. You either had to make them release you or go underground. The former had to be done very carefully, because under certain circumstances their method of releasing an agent from ICAL service was simply to eliminate him. If however I could get free of ICAL, I knew of more than one company in the computer industry that was ready to pay a lot of money for my services.

Another thought that kept going through mind my was that, whether or not my mission was successful, I really wasn't going to see Kathi von Hausenberg again. As I now defined it, success meant Peterson would be dead, and for some reason or other I still felt that would happen. Even if I failed in that and had to merely persuade or force Petersen to do as ICAL wanted, all I could foresee was a trip back to Arizona to resume my dreary existence there. Either way, Kathi would have to return to Germany. After the last few days and particularly after our parting of the previous night, being alone in Arizona without her was not going to be much fun.

Lost in thought, I had apparently slowed down and when I rounded a curve I saw that Bill Hausenberg's Volkswagen had opened up quite a distance in front of me. It was really flying down the dusty road. What was more disturbing was that between me and the Volkswagen was a roadblock. There were men there. With rifles! I drew up to a stop about a hundred yards away from the roadblock. Then I got out of my car and stood there. I had my machinegun out of its case so that I could reach it in a hurry if anyone became unpleasant. One of guards trudged down the road toward me. When he arrived he wasted no time on friendly greetings.

"I am sorry Señor, but from here the roadway is located on private land. No one is admitted. You must turn around." He gestured with his rifle.

I was afraid of something like that. "But what of the other car," I asked. "A friend of mine or at least an acquaintance, is driving that Volkswagen. We were traveling together so to speak."

"What other car?" said the guard. He turned abruptly and walked away. He had me there. I got back into the Mercedes, turned it about carefully, and drove away. It seemed the only thing to do. However, when I reached the curve I slowed, then stopped and looked back. Bill Hausenberg was out of sight, but a distant cloud of dust above the trees betrayed the direction in which he was driving. He had turned and was following another parallel dirt road about two thousand yards away from the one on which I was forced to return.

I drove on perhaps for a quarter of a mile. Then I observed on my left, in a gap in the trees, the beginning of a narrow, cobble-paved road leading off through the plantations. Where the road started, there were ancient looking stone pillars. From one, a rusty iron gate was hanging, almost hidden amidst the weeds. I thought this might warrant some further investigation, but I also thought I'd better do it on foot. I parked the Mercedes in a little grove of trees. In an attempt at camouflage, I spent several minutes piling some branches and grasses around it. Then I set off walking along the paved drive.

The sun was now fairly high in the sky and the day was warm. However, a light breeze made it a pleasant day for a stroll. There was no one to be seen on either side of the little road. Just open farm fields, coffee trees, and patches of scrubby forest. The paved drive showed signs of deterioration and decay, giving the impression of having been little used for many years.

Then to my surprise, at evenly spaced intervals, larger trees began to line the roadside. These had obviously been planted, long years before, to provide an arbor of shade over the drive. Here and there were breaks in the orderly procession of trees. Some had, in later years, fallen victim to storms or woodsmen's axes. However, by the time I'd walked most of a mile down the drive the gaps in the ranks of trees disappeared. It was a though I was progressing along a great hallway, bordered by lofty, overarching columns of green and brown. Still there was no sign of human habitation.

I was trudging up a low hill and beginning to kick myself for embarking in a fruitless walk under the hot sun. Then much to my surprise when I reached the top of the hill I found I had run out of road. The paved track turned sharply to the left and then ended. Beyond that was nothing but a wall of dense scrub and underbrush. There I stood under the heat of Brazilian summer, sweat pouring down my face. I wiped my forehead, facing nothing but a jolly walk back to the car and a tiresome drive back to Laranjeiras, there to try to pick up a new trail. Then, fortunately, I looked forward again. While the road, after its abrupt turn, came to an end, the lines of great shade trees neither turned nor terminated. There they still marched. Just as regular as ever. Stretching off at regular intervals, rising from the lower brush, on either side of a weed-grown avenue.

I thought if they can do it, so can I. So I pushed through the wall of scrub bushes, and kept on walking. After another 15 minutes the shade trees, although still recognizable, were nothing more than the outposts of a dense patch of forest. This forest then ended rather abruptly about 100 yards ahead. When I reached that point I stopped in surprise. Off to my left in the distance were large buildings. Many of them. Some were visibly dilapidated. Others were clearly well maintained and in current use. An enormous gray-brick manor house, much run down, glowered from a little rise nearest to me. A stone forest of chimneys and turrets rose above the building. Behind it in the distance stood other buildings. Some were farm warehouses, stables, and storage barns. Two or three large farmhouses rose beyond. One of these, bigger than the others, was surrounded by a stone wall. I walked on toward it.

It appeared that I had entered by what formerly had been the main entrance to a very large estate, following the original drive leading to the manor house. That original entrance had been abandoned years before as newer construction on the other side of the estate made access from the far road an advantage. The fields between me and the old manor house were low rolling hills so I did not see, at first, the black Volkswagen parked near one of the farmhouses. Just about the time I reached the crest of the next hill and did see the car, I also saw a man standing beside a tree. That fact that he was covering me with his machinegun probably influenced me in my decision to obey the other two men when they drove up in a jeep and ordered me to get in it with them.

*   *   *

Colonel Yalinin said with a yawn, "So it would seem that the stories of long-term German penetration in Southwestern Brazil are still true."

Major Grusev agreed. "Yes Colonel Stepan. It's been going on for a hundred years. They own huge coffee plantations and many other agri-businesses. There have been German families settled there for generations who still don't speak a word of Portuguese."

Chapter 16—Family Friends

"And pine in vain the sacred seven,"

As the jeep bounced over the rough farm track, I took a good look at my captors or, hopefully, escorts. They were dark skinned young men, wearing khaki uniforms, high work boots, and broad straw hats. Just like any three workmen you would find on any one of thousands of farms in the Southwestern United States. Except for the minor matter that all three were armed. My original captor still carried his submachinegun, crooked under one arm, ready for action. The other two had big, vicious looking revolvers in belt holsters. The more I saw of these the greater became my inclination to go along with them to the farm house, like a good boy.

When we got close to it I could see that it was far more than the usual farmhouse. It turned out to be a large, rambling, frequently enlarged three-story building, part frame, and part stone. A tower rose on one side and ornate decoration encrusted the roofline. A Latin version of the Queen Anne. The guards were taking no chances. The one with the machinegun covered me, while the other two marched me up the walk and into the front door. At least I was arriving in style.

The large entrance hallway was plain and business-like. It was in fact fitted out as a sort of waiting room. There were pegs on the walls for hats and coats. A few plain chairs, a long wooden bench, and some aerial photos of coffee plantations completed the décor. I would have been glad to wait longer, but apparently I was expected. They ushered me into the first room to the left of the front door, saluted and departed, closing the door behind me. I was left alone in a sort of office, with an older man.

He was short and stocky, but not fat, and still muscular although he looked over 60 years old. His white hair was cut very short. His demeanor was studious and matched his conservative, slightly out-of-date business suit. He seemed to be a person of some importance. I waited for him start the conversation.

"Kindly state your business," he began with a formal tone. His English was careful and heavily accented. "We are not accustomed to receiving visitors across the rear fields. And I am also informed that we turned you away when you approached us on the new road." There didn't seem much that I could add to that summary of my iniquities, so I let him continue. "If you have business here, you are presumably welcome. If you are just adventuring or looking for land to buy, you will leave at once."

This seemed like an opening. "I'm looking for an acquaintance of mine," I answered. "I was trying to catch up with him on the road. I thought I saw his car outside."

"There is no one that you know who is here," he responded decidedly. "Suppose you tell me who you are and who your friend is and perhaps I may give you directions to go elsewhere."

Under the circumstances I had little to lose. Foreign as it was to all my training, I thought I might catch him off guard by again telling most of the truth. "My name is Prior. I am a representative on a North American organization called ICAL. We specialize in finding people and in certain other things. Really though, I'm not actually looking for the man in the car. I became acquainted with his daughter a few days ago. I like her very much. I was hoping to get in touch with her through him." I hoped that was near enough to the truth to sound convincing. It wasn't.

He looked annoyed. "My name is Litzingen. This is my estate. There are no persons such as you describe to be found here or in this area. I have heard something of your ICAL. There is nothing for you to do here. And now that we have finished with your business, you may leave. I suggest that you not linger in this region. The climate is unhealthy and our people do not understand strangers. Even someone representing ICAL might well find danger."

He yanked at a bell pull on the wall behind him. This instantly produced my two friends from the jeep. They took me back out of the building and drove me to the main road. No one spoke until I was out of the jeep and standing by my not so well concealed Mercedes.

Then one of the men yelled at me, "Go away Señor. If you come back, you get hurt."

I drove back to the town in a distinctly discouraged frame of mind. It seemed that here in Brazil; the deck was stacked against me. For assistance I had only my friend Abel Zavaleta, the petty bureaucrat, and he was opposed to my plans. The Kreisau people clearly had friends. I was sure that it was von Hausenberg's car that had been parked next to the farmhouse. And Petersen, beside being very deadly in his own right, had Goldson the traitor along for assistance. All in all, things didn't look promising. I wondered if I needed help of some kind.

When I reached to outskirts of Laranjeiras, I received another surprise. An unpleasant one at first. There was a reception committee waiting for me. It consisted of two police cars, parked crossways in the road completely blocking it. They had chosen their spot well, for when I rounded a curve and came upon them, I was too close to turn around and get away. Even had I known of any place to go!

I decided to muddle through, as the British say. I drove up close to the cars, stopped, and got out. I attempted to give the impression on an innocent motorist. A Brazilian officer, police or army I was not sure which at the time, strode forward to meet me.

"Good day Señor Prior." Scratch the innocent motorist bit. He continued in passable English, "I am Prefect da Rosa at your service. We have received an air-post letter from the Argentine. It is from a friend of yours and of mine, a Colonel Manzano. He says that he understands that you have crossed into our country from Paraguay. He indicates that you might have forgotten some personal papers. He has sent them on to me, and has asked me to give them to you. I do so with great pleasure" With much formality he handed me a large envelope which proved to contain Brazilian funds, a passport and other papers needed for a stay in Brazil.

"Thank you," I said. "I may have need of these. And Prefect da Rosa, I am most pleased to have made your acquaintance."

"I too, am most honored," da Rosa replied, "and now as to a totally unrelated matter, my superiors have instructed me to examine your papers. These persons have somehow been led to believe that they are not in order. Ah, I see that you have them ready for inspection." With that he took back the passport from me. He examined it with exaggerated care. Just as though he had not had it in his hand a moment before. Then he grinned. "Splendid, everything is in perfect order. My superiors have been for once mistaken."

It was good to be among friends again. I suggested to the Prefect that we continue on into the town and that he join me there for some refreshments. This we did. A bottle of excellent bourbon was soon produced. I rather thought that my new acquaintance would enjoy this sort of thing. After all he evidently was a good friend of Manzano's.

"And how is my dear friend the Colonel," I asked. "I had many pleasant times with him in Buenos Aires."

"I understand that Colonel Manzano is in good health. Indeed, his letter indicates that he is flying here tonight. He asked me to have you wait here for him." This answer of da Rosa's was not particularly welcome. The Colonel's arrival here, away from what seemed to be his usual ICAL territory, could only indicate that they were not happy with the way the *Sunlight* operation was going. Manzano would be a placeholder until Pearlman could reach the scene. But apparently the Brazilians were disposed to be broadminded. I thought I'd presume on their good natures just a little more.

"I am most pleased to hear of the Colonel's arrival. However there are one or two loose ends I would like to tie up before he gets here. Perhaps you or one of your men would be kind enough to assist me."

This request appeared to startle da Rosa a little, but he answered, "With much pleasure." Then he winked at me.

"I would like a discrete watch put on the Litzingen estate. There is a black Volkswagen parked there. When it leaves I want to know it. And also who is in it and where they go."

Da Rosa was most cooperative. "We have anticipated your interest in the matter. Even now one of our light aircraft is circling over the estate. We have some notion of your reasons for being in our country. While we cannot assist you openly we will do everything we can. Our population is changing and is not as enthusiastic about immigrants of certain nationalities and war experiences as was once the case. Most of their former countrymen share our view."

"I am very grateful," I said.

"However," da Rosa continued, "we would like to help you complete your business here quickly, and for you to leave before there is any unpleasantness." Obviously there were limits.

The conversation continued on somewhat aimlessly for a few more minutes. Then we parted. The understanding was that I was to be contacted at the inn when there was any news. I returned there and asked for the same room. I had had enough new experiences.

It was a long afternoon. My small room was poorly ventilated and there were no books and no radio. The sun was hot and seemed to burn right through the walls and roof of the little inn. I was lying on the bed, mostly undressed, when the telephone buzzed. Prefect da Rosa's voice was excited and agitated.

"There is trouble. We may be in time, if I can immediately pick you up in front of the inn. I recommend you bring whatever firearms you have with you. I hope you have something with real firepower because we may not participate or supply you with arms. Please hurry."

I said, "Yes," and slammed down the receiver without waiting to hear any more. I pulled on my outer clothing, then kicked my feet into my shoes, and ran out of the building, machinegun case in one hand and my Mauser pistol in its shoulder holster flapping under the other arm. It seemed I was going to war. Not for the first time, but still very frightening if I took time to think about it.

My feet landed on the plank sidewalk in front of the inn, just as da Rosa's car pulled up in front. It had hardly stopped moving before I was into it and we were on our way.

Da Rosa yelled over the roar of the speeding engine, "The black Volkswagen left 45 minutes ago. Our pilot had radio trouble. He couldn't contact us until he could see where the car was going, land the airplane and then telephone."

"Who was in the car?"

"We think only one man," he answered, "but when he reached the edge of the village he met another car. They both drove on toward a little brick house on the extreme north border of Laranjeiras. Our local men don't know very much about the place. It's always seemed innocent enough, but they have heard that two men arrived there yesterday. The residence is quite isolated and surrounded by heavy brush. My men haven't been able to get close enough to have a good look at it."

"Who was in the other car," I demanded. I was very afraid of what I was going to hear.

"Only the driver. A woman, fairly young. She seemed to be waiting for the Volkswagen."

It had to be Kathi von Hausenberg, naturally still trying to help her father. My eyes began to feel funny, almost as tears, and my fear grew. But that wasn't going to stop me.

Our car roared on down the road. Then I thought I heard another sound off in the distance. Prefect da Rosa stiffened. Without being ordered, his driver accelerated to very top speed. The noise was that of gunfire. Occasional shots and once or twice the staccato burst of a light machinegun. We swerved sharply off the road onto a narrow track and followed it toward the sound of the firing. As we neared the building, the Brazilian police driver expertly spun the car broadside on the track and stopped. We tumbled out on the protected side.

Somewhere over to the left in the thick undergrowth, two people were firing into the windows of the building. We could hear the repeated high-pitched crack of an automatic rifle and the lower popping of a small handgun. The smell of gunpowder was already in the air and dust flew as shots hit the brick walls. Only an occasional shot from the windows answered their fire. Our arrival seemed to accelerate the course of events. Bill von Hausenberg rose from his hiding place, hurled an old German army hand grenade at the building, and then began to run, zigzagging, across the space between the trees and the wall of the building. He ran low like an experienced soldier, changing direction every few steps. Suddenly he dropped to the ground.

There was a violent explosion near the building. Hausenberg leaped up and ran through the dust and smoke toward the door of the building. Then from inside someone fired four or five roaring shots from a Colt .45 automatic. With terrible and recognizable accuracy. The first shot knocked Hausenberg over backwards. There was a scream from the left. The second and third shots seemed to strike him before he hit the ground. Colt .45 slugs hit very hard. His body was tossed first one way and then another, as a leaf in a fall wind. Then his body landed in a heap and lay still.

I shouted to Prefect da Rosa, "Stay here and stay the hell out of it." Then I sprinted from behind the car and dodged through the underbrush. In a moment I could see Kathi, huddled behind the trunk of a fallen tree. She was sobbing uncontrollably and seemed oblivious to the awful danger still within the building. Now, however, it was my turn to be dangerous. Normally, I like to avoid armed combat at close quarters, but I thought I'd enjoy this one.

I had to assume they'd seen me, but I didn't think that was going to help them. Not against what I had in my battered attaché case, which I'd managed to keep with me just for this moment. I threw it and myself down on the ground next to Kathi. I paused to press her arm, and she turned with an amazed look through her tears. Then the shortened AK-47 machinegun came easily out of its case. I flipped the selector to semiautomatic and fired two or three shots into the shattered window. That was the first surprise for them and would keep them low, just where I wanted them.

Then I provided the second surprise. The selector went back to full automatic and I fired a long burst of the special ICAL armor piercing bullets right through the mud-brick walls of the building. I could almost hear the armored bullets humming like angry bees inside, and I did hear a scream of pain. Then a door crashed open on the far side of the building. A car door slammed and an engine roared to life. The familiar BMW shot round the corner of the house, dodged past the police car in a cloud of flying dirt, and hurtled off down the narrow road. Two pistol shots came back at us and I fired a short burst from the AK-47, but hit nothing.

Kathi hadn't moved during the whole performance. When she got to her feet her dress was covered with dirt and her face was smudged with dust and tears. I felt waves of sympathy and tenderness. One part of me dearly wanted to express these feelings, but another said to be careful.

She gasped and cried, "Oh God, Humboldt, it's over. It's all over. And we've lost. I'll never be able to…And my father and I…" Then she fainted and collapsed to the ground.

By this time a second carload of Brazilian police had arrived behind the Prefect's car. They would be able to take charge of what was left of Bill von Hausenberg. They would also be able to diligently search the battered brick building, although they wouldn't find anything. The shots fired from the escaping BMW had come from the passenger side. There had been two men, Petersen and Goldson, in the car.

I carefully carried Kathi to da Rosa's car, then collected my machinegun and attaché case, and asked for some more help. Da Rosa agreed and the driver turned the car and headed back toward the Litzingen estate. When

I reentered the Count's private office 30 minutes later, still covered with dust and dirt, I was particularly cold and unusually grim, even for me.

"Colonel General," I said without waiting for him to protest my reappearance, "I have need of your assistance. Your guest von Hausenberg, who, according to you, wasn't here earlier today, was killed in a gun battle not long after he left you. Your niece Kathi is outside in the police car in a dead faint. I told you a bit about myself before. Now I'll add that the organization called ICAL which I represent, and of which you say you've heard, is a clandestine arm of the United States Government. A very hard arm. If we have to, we can be extremely unfriendly."

The Colonel General stood up quickly. He looked worried. "Go on please," he asked.

"I have some advice for you," I said threateningly, "I don't know what you do here in South America or whether anyone else cares that you are here. You aren't in danger from me for the moment. But you may be at risk from others and your niece is certainly in grave danger. I want her taken away from here, just as fast as possible. Prefect da Rosa tells me you have an aircraft. Fly Kathi back to Argentina or where ever she wishes to go."

Litzingen looked even more alarmed when I mentioned da Rosa's name, but he didn't hesitate. "I warned Herr Bill that it was useless to pursue these dead dreams of vengeance. Now he will not need any more advice. I, for my part, will take your advice and your warning. I will send my assistant and my maid out to the car to collect my niece. She will be protected. We will fly her south and look after her as long as she is in danger."

"Do so," I ordered. Then I turned sharply on my heel, in my best remembered parade ground manner, and left his office.

I watched sadly as Kathi von Hausenberg was half helped and half carried from the car and into the big house. The chances of my ever seeing her again did not look good. Then Prefect da Rosa drove me back to town. On the way I got a question answered.

"Where," I demanded, "would that car have gone?"

"Nowhere distant on the road it was using," he answered. "That way just loops around a few estates and farms and then returns to Laranjeiras."

Sure enough as we approached the edge of the village I saw the familiar outlines of the BMW 1600 half-concealed behind the very inn at which Kathi had been staying. Evidently Petersen and Goldson were trying to be thorough. That would only make what I had in mind for them a little more interesting.

Prefect da Rosa disappointed me. There were limits to what he could, or would do to help me. "We have to let you out here," he said firmly, "but without the AK-47. Our first duty is to our people. There will be no machine-gunning here in the village. And we cannot help you actively. There are too many tongues, loose ones, here."

I argued, but finally lost, got out and walked. I didn't want to exhaust my welcome. I moved cautiously through gathering dusk toward the parked BMW. It looked deserted. I kept close to the wall of the last outbuilding and came around the corner slowly. Yes, the BMW was empty. There was no telling where its recent occupants had gone or when they would return.

After watching for 45 minutes or so, I decided to take a chance that a search of the interior of the car would tell me something. I had the Mauser pistol in my pocket ready for instant use, so as I got into the unlocked BMW I slid the pistol onto the parcel shelf under the dash, ready but out of the way. I was just starting to go through the contents of the glove box when I felt the pressure of cold metal behind my ear.

That's what happens when you are excited and have just saved the life of the girl with whom you think you've fallen in love. You forget about watching your surroundings carefully enough. Obviously, Hiam Goldson had been watching from the doorway of the inn. His voice was just as menacing as the barrel of the pistol which he had pressed against my neck.

"Well then, Mr. Prior, you are overly persistent. That gets people in bad trouble. That's what you are now in, big trouble and dead trouble. Now we'll see how quietly you can start the car and get it going along that road over there. Drive carefully out of the town. If you try anything, the accident you that you are going to have, will come even more quickly."

I've always been inclined to follow the orders of people who have pistols pointed at my head. So I did what he told me to do. The road was dark and it wasn't likely that Prefect da Rosa had seen the car leave. That is if he had even bothered to stay and watch.

The Goldson was talking again in an oily voice. "Señor Petersen is very angry. He's catching a plane back to Buenos Aires. Brazil isn't going to be healthy for him anymore. And especially he didn't like having to stop at the clinic to have a chunk of one of your damn machinegun bullets picked out of his backside. He has told me to cancel you. And I follow orders. At least orders from someone who pays as well as Petersen does."

"What if I paid more?" It didn't hurt to ask.

"I doubt that you can," he snarled, "but even if you could, I like my chances better this way."

He was right, but his conclusion didn't do anything to improve my disposition. The road was gravelly and winding. Imperceptibly I was letting the BMW pick up speed. I scared stiff, but I had an idea about reaching under the dash for my pistol and at the same moment turning the car very sharply. This might just give me a chance to shoot him before he did the same to me. It was a slight chance, but I didn't think I'd have any better opportunity. There'd be no way to surprise him, once he had me out of the car at his killing place. Even now it was going to be tough to do for he was sitting next to me and could see everything I did.

I wondered about another distraction. "Why let him kill Sharon? Why in God's name was that necessary?"

"Shit, yes," he spat out with a snarl. "No more questions. Drive."

Then I saw headlights on the dark road behind us. Coming fast. I slowed a little, allowing the following car to approach as close as I dared. Then I gave an exaggerated glance to the rearview mirror. Goldson turned and looked back. This was as good a time as any for my little driving trick, so I swerved the car wildly to the left, and at the same time made a grab for the Mauser. But things don't always work exactly as planned.

Much faster than it can be told, I was surrounded by violent movement, noise, a great rush of air and sound, a scream, a squeal of brakes and a sickening, splashing thud! Then all was quiet, except for the banging of the open right hand door of the BMW as the car bumped and rattled, half out of control, over the rough ground at the left side of the road.

BMW automobiles have a grab bar on the right hand side door. When I swerved, Goldson had reached for it. By my very lucky chance, his clutching hand instead found the door handle. The door opened and my sharp, high-speed, left turn provided the force to hurl him from the car. There, as I learned immediately afterwards, he was hit in mid air by the speeding car in which Prefect da Rosa was pursuing us. Goldson was killed instantly. Sometimes things just seem to happen for the best!

It was not, however, da Rosa who told me all of this as I stood, still shaken, by the side of the road. The words came instead from the rotund and affable countenance of the early arriving Colonel Manzano. "I had just started to watch the BMW," he explained. "And now Ralph, we don't have any time to waste. You and I are going back to Buenos Aires, under Pearlman's direct orders. There he will consider and evaluate the *Sunlight* operation and your future role, if any."

"As you say," I agreed. "But understand this, Goldson got his 'eye for an eye' here. And Carl Petersen will get the 'tooth for a tooth' in Buenos Aires."

*   *   *

Colonel Yalinin yawned and stretched. The clock on the wall said that it was four o'clock in the morning.

Alex Grusev had been just about to make a sneering remark about the habitual viciousness of American espionage operations, when he remembered stories concerning the viciousness of which his own tired superior officer had been capable.

Chapter 17—Avenido 9 de Julio

"But thou, meek lover of the good,"

South America is a very big place. The first leg of the trip back to Buenos Aires was a flight by light aircraft from Laranjeiras do Sul. Prefect da Rosa provided the aircraft and Colonel Manzano and I provided the three plus hours it required to fly almost directly south to the major airport at Porto Alegre. From there, including a long wait for the first available flight, it took another six hours to reach Buenos Aires, even by a fine Varig 707 jet. All this gave Colonel Manzano time to ask plenty of questions. For most of these, I had no really satisfactory answers or wasn't sure I should give them. For one thing, it was getting difficult to figure out the Colonel's real position within ICAL. He could be anything from a part-time contract operative to a quite senior official. His current attitude seemed to indicate the latter.

One line of his queries began, "Why, really, did you ever permit Petersen to leave Asunción? You had the chance to take him or cancel him there. Or at any time enroute when you were traveling together. And if even yesterday you had been more careful, the Brazilian police could have taken him. Ralph, things are changing as to Carl Petersen. You should know that even the Paraguayans now want him arrested for ordering the killing of old Cornitz." I wondered how much of that I should believe.

I answered, "My orders for the *Sunlight* operation require that I persuade or force Petersen to return with me to the United States. That's a lot more difficult than just shooting him. But I'll get him now one way or another. He's more of a murderer than you know him to be." Then I told Manzano about the death of the Israeli agent Sharon Sharen, all alone there on the border, floating in the Parana River. I expected that this would make more of an impression, but Colonel Manzano took it easily in stride. He didn't seem to have much feeling for people, particularly for those in my line of work.

"That's the chance you people take," he said. "Especially you North Americans. Everything you have to do must be a crusade. That's why you are sometimes so very successful, but also why you fail often. And that's why you, Ralph, have an ulcer. Here we don't try to succeed in a big way. If we just barely make it that's fine. The results, the real ones, are the same. And we get them more often, or at least we think we do."

I didn't have any good response for that, so I offered to buy him another drink. As in the past that was effective in changing the course of the conversation. By the time we finally reached Buenos Aires, the good Colonel had lapsed back into character.

I didn't look very presentable and my papers didn't really provide support for a second entry into Argentina. However, one of the advantages of traveling with senior military intelligence personnel is that customs inspectors don't bother you. Colonel Manzano dropped me off back at the City Hotel. Here I was again. It almost seemed as though the *Sunlight* operation was starting over again. In spite of all that had happened, I guess it was.

Once in my room, exhausted and not caring much for the time of day, I sank quickly into much needed sleep. Later in the day however, I was rudely awakened by the telephone. Colonel Manzano called to say that he had just heard from my boss, Walter Pearlman. Things didn't sound good. Pearlman had said he was arriving in Buenos Aires that evening and would want to see me the next morning. I was to meet him in a little café next to the Claridge Hotel. Evidently a popular ICAL meeting place. I didn't look forward to my session with Pearlman.

I thought that before seeing my boss I 'd better try to get the *Sunlight* operation started again. I wanted it to stay mine to the end. So, later in the afternoon, I again took a bus to the Plaza Britannica. Little had changed. Still the same hot sun, the groups of people strolling somewhat aimlessly about the square, and the same small shops. I asked a few hopefully discrete questions, but no one seemed to know anything new. Petersen's flat was still vacant. The front windows, which had been shattered by gunfire the night of my rooftop acrobatics, were carefully boarded up. I didn't exactly know what to do next. Carl Petersen was sure to either try to kill me on sight or at least give me a wide berth. And all of my contacts were gone.

Finally, I decided to try a new tack. I took another bus ride, this time down to the Boca. This is the wharf-side district of Buenos Aires. It's not a pretty place, but it attracts many interesting people. Interesting anyway to someone in my line of work. People in that kind of an area have to know things to survive. I thought that maybe someone would know something of interest to me.

Petersen had said, what seemed a century ago, that he sold paintings in the Boca. I had drinks, in spite of my ulcer, in one or two of the little dark bars that teem in the area. Then I just sat and worried for a while. Keeping the *Sunlight* operation active seemed my only chance for another contact with Kathi von Hausenberg.

Next, I tried to start up conversations with more questions about hunting, old paintings, or strangers in the vicinity. This did no good, and in fact most of the replies I did get, were more than a little hostile.

At last, I wandered down a side street and blundered into a street carnival. These are pretty much the same the world over, featuring gambling games, target shooting, test-your-strength machines and the like. Also a few displays of curios and a few freaks, both animal and human. The tawdry sameness of it all didn't serve to improve my mood.

Then I saw something that interested me. Off in one corner was a booth offering handwriting analysis. The center of attraction was a tired, old and very obsolete, computer punch-card sorting machine. Someone had removed its outer sheet metal casing so that the mechanical workings could be seen by credulous onlookers. The effect was that of a once beautiful actress, now reduced to performing in some cheap show in an abbreviated costume.

I stepped up to the counter and handed the operator my 100 pesos. He had me write my name on three or four cards, with holes already punched in them. Then he took a good look at me and asked a few simple questions. Next he punched some more holes in the card which evidently already contained information most nearly matching my description. This card, the others containing my signatures and a handful of dummy cards, were placed in the machine. He turned the switch, the card sorter whirred, and it was all very impressive. At least it would have been for someone who had not spent most of his adult life working with computers and data processing. Just as I expected, one of the cards on which I'd written my name came out in the master pocket of the sorter. Then the man read it carefully, or pretended to, and told me all about myself. I was suitably impressed.

"That machine there really does a job," I said. "I don't understand how it reads the handwriting so well, but it has me pretty well figured." Then I laughed. "I hope it doesn't know everything. I've got some secrets that I need to keep."

The attendant replied, "Yes Señor, it's very proficient. Of course only as to your main characteristics." I suppose this was said to reassure a suspicious customer.

"Nonetheless it's very impressive. You must see a lot of people pass by here. Do many of them stop?"

He answered, "Unfortunately not. Most are too busy."

"Actually," I continued, hoping to have made a friend, "I have been in this vicinity looking for an acquaintance of mine. He once told me he sometimes does business in the Boca selling old paintings. Perhaps you have analyzed his writing? He's a famous hunter, also. Of the tigres. (That is what many in South America call the jaguar.) I thought I might be able to purchase some of the hides from him." I looked at the attendant inquiringly. For only a moment, his expression changed.

Then he said shortly and with scowl, "I know no one like that, Señor. Such people are not interested in handwriting games."

I didn't like the way he said that. Petersen was a well-known, respected and powerful man, and yet all the people down in the Boca had seemed peculiarly ill informed. But I let it go. You have to, for in such circumstances it is a mistake to force things. Anyway, I didn't want to spend the evening in such a neighborhood, so I returned to the hotel. Once or twice I had the feeling that I was being followed, but I couldn't pin it down. Probably I was getting too accustomed to that type of thing and losing my sensitivity. Or, I was just tired of it all.

The next morning I had to face the music. It seemed to me that I had gotten off to an early start. However, my boss, Walter Pearlman, was already in the small café, waiting impatiently for me.

He didn't waste any time. "I'm glad to see you are still as prompt as ever," he snarled. "You've certainly made a nice mess of things down here. My newest field representative could have done better. All you had to do was introduce yourself to '*Sunlight*', get to know the man a bit, and make him an offer of employment. But no, you had to go chasing all over the map. Leaving a trail of bodies and missed opportunities. You've got the authorities here, and in Paraguay, and in Southwestern Brazil so stirred up that it will be many months before our good people here will be able to function properly." There was an unpleasant emphasis on the word 'good.'

"No one told me there was an exact set time for this meeting," I answered crossly. "Manzano just said 'to see you here in the morning concerning Petersen'." That was all I could think of to say. But as soon as I said the words, they sounded defensive and stupid, and I could see they were a mistake.

"That's so typical of you, Prior. Our target, '*Sunlight*', in case you've forgotten the code word too, gets clean away and all you have to say for yourself is that you didn't know what time it was!"

"I still have some good ideas I want to try," I said evenly. I really didn't have much confidence in them, but I desperately wanted to stay on the operation. Also I thought saying that might calm Pearlman down. I knew perfectly well that a lot of the bluster was just his way of reestablishing his authority, after having been out of contact with me for some time. I knew it, but I didn't like it.

"What ideas?" Pearlman sounded more businesslike. Underneath his thick veneer of nastiness he was a competent professional. And he wanted to get the job done as much as I did.

"Well, I've been making some inquiries down on the Boca. I've learned Petersen sells his stolen artwork somewhere in the waterfront district. People there aren't acting naturally. He is a familiar figure in Buenos Aires, but no one will admit to any knowledge of him. That makes me think he is known to be in hiding and that's where I'd hide if I was Petersen. I think we should watch the ship departures, if we can. And I'll keep turning over the ground there. It should lead us to a new contact. Also it would help if you could keep Manzano busy among the foreign colony. We might have some luck there too."

Pearlman answered sourly, "I suppose that's all we can do. I'll give you one week. Then we'll pull you off the case and start over. If we can," he added sarcastically.

That ended the interview, which was fine with me. Pearlman left immediately, and after waiting the prescribed time, I walked off in the opposite direction back to my hotel. The sun was warm and the streets of downtown Buenos Aires were crowded. I didn't mind that because I still had the feeling of being followed. Crowds are nice when you want to be alone.

I hadn't told Pearlman about Staff Major Anadon's extraordinary fund of inside information about ICAL. It was still hard to believe, but it was increasingly obvious that there had been a serious security penetration of our organization. The fact that this had been accomplished by the Paraguayan National Police was also obvious, but even less believable. Still, although it probably put me in more danger, I didn't feel like telling Pearlman about it. I might need a bargaining chip if the *Sunlight* operation wasn't ultimately successful. Thinking about what 'successful' meant, I had one thing to be happy about. Pearlman still left me my two options. I could either recruit Pearlman for germ-warfare work in the United States or eliminate him. With Kathi von Hausenberg always in my mind, I had an idea that from then on my attention would best be directed to the latter.

I spent the rest of the day in the hotel, either lobby sitting or, later in the afternoon in my room resting. I thought that I had better let things cool down before probing further into the dangerous mazes of the Boca. I also felt in need of a little rest and quiet. After the events of the past few days I was bone weary. My stomach was tight and my ulcer was burning almost continuously. Finally, at about 3:00 in the afternoon, I took a tranquilizer. The air in the hotel room was hot and almost stifling, but I dozed off anyway. Once or twice the telephone rang, but each time it was a wrong number. At the time I attached no significance to that. Later I did.

I awakened at 7:00 in the evening, quite rested and relaxed, but very hungry. I realized that I had not eaten since early morning, so I went down to the hotel dining room to attend to that. The story of my life. Waiting, tranquilizers, sleep at odd hours and meals in hotel dining rooms. As usual in Argentina they featured numerous selections, but of beef only. However, my choice of steak was excellent.

Dinner didn't take long. As I had nowhere to go, I headed back to my room. As I got off the elevator on my floor, the floor clerk called to me. "Good evening, Señor Prior. A message came while you were out. The caller asked me to write it down and hand it to you. It is in this envelope."

I thanked him, gave him a few pesos, took the envelope, and returned to the privacy of my room. The message was brief. It read: 'Believe I now have particulars needed to close the deal. Meet me in the underground parking garage below Avenida 9 de Julio at 10:00 this evening. I will have my car waiting. M.'

That sounded more like it. The 'M' could only stand for Colonel Manzano. Just as Pearlman and I hoped might happen, he had apparently turned up some vital information somewhere among Buenos Aires' extensive foreign colony. The meeting place sounded more professional too. Evidently the Colonel was starting to shape up. I set my travel alarm clock for 9:30 and made myself take another nap. You can never tell when you will need some sleep reserves to draw on.

When awakened, I left the hotel immediately, taking the Mauser pistol with me as another 'reserve.' You can never tell about that need either. The underground garage below 9 de Julio is an enormous affair. It occupies almost the entire length of the wide street. You enter it either from the basements of the adjoining buildings or from little entrance kiosks and stairways at street level. By 10:00 PM it was dark and beginning to rain slightly. Before I walked down into the garage, I spent five or ten minutes pacing back and forth along the Avenida. I still had the feeling of being followed. It was nothing specific, but it was there. Unfortunately the meeting time with the Colonel was definite, so I couldn't take the time to find and lose the tail. I just had to chance it.

There are heavy steel fire doors at each entrance to the immense garage. One of these clanged closed behind me as I entered. It was dark, indeed very dark, and the scattered ceiling lamps only created little pools of grayness on the greasy concrete floor. I didn't see any sign of Colonel Manzano, or anyone else for that matter, so I walked cautiously out into the center of the garage and stood under one of the lights. The meeting place didn't seem so damn professional now. Manzano could be almost a block away, but I hoped since he had his car he would see me and drive to where I was standing.

The garage was deathly still. Then suddenly I heard off in the distance, two or three more of the steel doors slam shut. A car at the far end of the garage started its engine with a roar. It rolled toward me in the darkness, and then, just as its lights flashed on, it accelerated to a terrific speed. The lights seemed to grow to giant size and momentarily stunned and blinded me. But I had training enough and sense enough to wait until the last second before I threw myself to one side. I ducked behind a support pillar as the car roared past and turned at the far end of the garage with a screech of brakes and the smell of burning rubber.

The back of my mouth felt dry and there was a scared, sick feeling in the pit of my stomach. Someone, obviously not Colonel Manzano, had put me just where they wanted me to be. Then another car engine roared to life behind me. I heard it and at the same instant saw the two headlight spots on the wall ahead of me. This time I didn't wait so long, but leaped to one side and sprinted toward the side of the dark garage, dodging around parked cars as I ran. I had my Mauser out of its shoulder holster and ready for use, but I only had one spare clip of ammunition, so I couldn't start wasting shells.

My move to escape was a signal for someone to turn off the overhead lights! The darkness was complete now, except for the four pools of light where automobile headlights were swinging around the walls as the two cars turned to find me again. I felt a stinging shock as my right shoulder slammed into a support pillar. That must have made noise, because a spotlight, mounted on one of the cars, caught me for a moment. I knew better than to duck, but threw myself backwards. A pistol shot reverberated through the blackness and the slug whistled and whined as it glanced off the pillar where I had been standing. Trying to catch my breath, I moved more carefully and quietly until I reached the wall. I had to find one of the doors. The spotlight chased itself across the garage walls trying to catch me for another shot. The cars circled about like great metal beasts hunting for their trapped and frightened prey. The smell of exhaust gas began to fill the air, and my fear grew. I had to find the best way out.

I was really lucky that they turned off the overhead lights. Superficially it must have seemed smart to have me blinded in the dark, but actually it evened the odds a little. It also told me that my opponents were amateurs, or at best semi-pros in the art of assassination. As I felt my way along the wall, I thought I might have a chance to survive. I wanted badly to fight back, to show them I was at least their equal. However, reason told me not to fire at them. The muzzle flash would show my position and if they had a machinegun they would hose the whole area with bullets and probably kill me. Finally, my hand felt the metal of one of the entrance doors. For what seemed an eternity I groped for the knob. I found it and gave it a turn. Locked!

I had to give them credit for their thoroughness. This door was far across the entire width of the garage from the one at which I'd entered. The cars prowled menacingly about the garage searching for me. Trying to listen over the roar of the engines, I thought I could hear a distant banging on the far door. Hearing this, I decided it was time to give my assailants something to worry about. Steadying my arm on the hood of a parked pickup truck, I took a good two-handed grip on the pistol, waiting for one of the cars to stop for a moment. When that happened, I first targeted the headlight and then let off a shot at about where I thought the front tire would be. The shot followed by its echo, rattled through the garage. Missed.

Then I sprinted 30 yards along the wall, keeping one hand out in front of me to avoid more pillar collisions. Then I aimed and fired again. This time one headlight disappeared in a crash of broken glass. The cars seemed to hesitate as if sensing a more dangerous opponent, and then converged toward the spot from which the second shot was fired. Indeed they were working toward a position ahead of me, apparently thinking I was running forward along the wall.

The trick had worked. After the second shot I turned and ran back toward my original position and then turned again and darted across the wide central bay of the garage. Damn. My leg slammed into the bumper of a parked car. The pain was bad, but the noise was worse. They must have heard it over the sound of their engines, for the cars screeched to a halt and the spotlight played fitfully over the floor. Once it caught me and two or three shots rang out. I threw myself to the floor and skidded to a stop next to one of the cement columns on the far side. The palm of my right hand was scraped raw as I broke my fall, but I had no time to think of the new source of pain. I scrambled up and at last found myself at the far wall. Then I heard two more shots.

Amazingly, these seemed to come from outside the nearby door. Someone, I hoped, was shooting to force the lock. The occupants of the pursuing cars must have heard the shots too, because the searching headlights seemed to pause. When I reached the door and found the knob loose and lifeless. I threw my shoulder against it and the door swung open. Free.

The cool night air bathed my face as I heard the two cars drifting away to the far end of the garage. I gasped with pain as someone grabbed my right hand to drag me up the stairs, and out onto the dark but safer street. I turned and there was Frauline Katherin von Hausenberg, excited but very pleased with herself. She had a small, still smoking Browning automatic pistol in her other hand. She was smiling and actually laughing a little as she pulled me toward a big, black Mercedes 300 sedan which was waiting on the street. I didn't need to be asked to jump in as Kathi took the driver's seat. We sped away into the night.

"Are you glad to see me," she asked. Then she giggled.

"Am I ever," I said as I reached across the center console and pressed her hand as it rested on the steering wheel.

"Yes I know you are, and I missed you so much, and I'm glad, so terribly glad to find you. Those were Herr Petersen's hired killers down there. I've been following you and when I saw you go into the garage I thought something might be wrong. So I waited and when I heard shots I had to get the door open. They've killed people down there before. Thank God I could find you."

There is not enough you can really say to a lovely, young woman whom you like so much, and who has just saved your life. However I tried a few things which she seemed to appreciate.

Then I said, "Do you mean that Petersen wasn't with them in one of the cars? I was hoping that at least I'd know he was still in Buenos Aires."

"No Humboldt," Kathi replied. "In fact I learned this afternoon that he has returned to Asunción."

"Shall we go get him together," I suggested.

"We are doing that now," she answered, "together!"

*   *   *

Major Grusev spoke first. "That underground garage is a bad place. A year ago, two of our own men were machine-gunned to death down there."

Colonel Yalinin agreed. "Yes, Prior was very lucky they sent second rate people against him." However, Colonel Yalinin was secretly pleased that Prior had escaped.

Chapter 18—The Second Option

"Find me and turn thy back on heaven."

It is almost 800 miles from Buenos Aires by road to Paraguay and Asunción, its capitol, so we didn't waste much time getting started. Kathi seemed absolutely determined to start driving at once. However, I did insist on collecting our things at my hotel and at the block of very expensive condominiums where she'd been staying. Then we started in earnest.

The big, black Mercedes 300 limousine fairly ate up the miles and was a superb car for such a long drive. I very glad to see Kathi again and to be working with her to finish with Carl Petersen once and for all. About two hours had passed before I thought to ask her about the car.

"Kathi, where did you get this wonderful car," I asked. "It's just what we need for what we have to do here."

"It belongs to my uncle, General Count Litzingen. It goes with his Argentine residence in Buenos Aires. I believe he has a great deal of money. I never knew him at all until we came here ten days ago. I understand from my father," and here she paused and seemed to shiver, "that Hitler sacked the General early in the war. Then he escaped to South America, taking with him a lot of the family money. At least that is how the story goes."

I didn't press the subject. I had uncovered enough skeletons in family closets as it was. However, I did say, "Anyway, I'm deeply grateful to the General. I'm afraid I was a bit rough in my last meeting with him. I hope he got over it."

Kathi laughed. "Yes, indeed. He now refers to you as 'that old time Prussian officer from America'. That's a great compliment. I also told him more about Herr Petersen. Things my father wouldn't talk about. My uncle wants to help us if he can."

After two hours we changed places and I did the driving. It was much like our last trip together, from Paraguay into Brazil. However, a lot had happened since then, which neither of us seemed anxious to replay. The Mercedes 300 was great on the smooth highways near Buenos Aires and even better as we reached the roads farther in the hinterland. There it simply devoured the bumps and cracks and smoothed them out behind. Kathi slept much of the way.

At about six o'clock in the morning, I pulled over to the side of the road, stopped, and awakened her. She was especially sweet when just awakened. She smiled sleepily and stretched a little, something like a young cat awakening. But kittens don't lean over and kiss you. At least none I'd seen recently. I returned the favor and this kept us busy for a few minutes. Then I drove on with Kathi assigned to find us a place to eat. She did this expertly, and then we traded places so that she could drive and I could rest. We were nearly halfway to Paraguay.

Generally following the northward course of the ever-present Parana River, we had already passed through the larger cities of Rosario and Santa Fe. After lunch and through the afternoon we faced the long stretch north to Resistencia. When we finally reached that place, we parted company with the Parana and continued north to the city of Formosa and then on to the border. We got there, dead tired, late in the day. The Argentine border patrol let us pass with hardly a second look, and Paraguayan customs did the same. They seemed to know of the car and its owner. And to fear both.

Once in Paraguay, we were close to Asunción and had to begin making plans. Kathi's assurance seemed far greater than in days past and I let her speak first.

"I suppose, Humboldt," she began "that it will be best to start by watching his house and asking some questions nearby. And also I could call my uncle or wire him. I think from what he has said, that he will send us some of his men so we can get finish this affair. I don't want you yourself in more danger, I couldn't even think of that."

I didn't want to think of it either, but I had another idea. "Kathi, please do call your uncle and bring him up to date, and we'll do those other things if we have to. First, though, I think we should go straight to the top. We'll have a little rest tonight somewhere and then tomorrow we'll call on Major Anadon. I just have an idea that he's going to help us this time." I couldn't exactly have said why I thought this. Somehow, however, I didn't think that even Staff Major Anadon would continue to swallow all the killing that Petersen had been doing. And somewhere deep in my mind was brewing the idea that I could turn his knowledge of ICAL against the Major.

We rolled into Asunción very late in the afternoon, having driven about 800 miles in about 18 hours. I knew only of the Grande Hotel, but wanted to avoid familiar places. Anyway, Kathi seemed to have heard of the Terraza Caballero, and found it without too much difficulty. Looking like exhausted and battered immigrants, we trudged into the lobby, and I was polishing my Spanish for room negotiations, when Kathi simply told the dubious looking manager on duty that she needed to call her uncle, Colonel General Count von Litzingen. The call was to be made to enlist his aid in obtaining accommodations. This produced a significant change in hotel staff attitude. The call was put through instantly, and it quickly developed that the General indeed maintained an apartment in the hotel. Home at last.

We were both dead tired and after something to eat and much-needed showers, fell asleep almost instantly, decorously in separate bedrooms. I for one am very good at going to sleep after 18-hour automobile drives. At some time late at night I heard my door open, smelled a wonderful combination of powder and bath soap, and heard the rustle of something silky. At once I was wide-awake and...

* * *

(Soviet Translator's Note: 'Comrade Major. At this point several sentences on the tape were undecipherable. You can imagine I did my best to listen. I apologize for this anti-socialist failure.')

* * *

The travel alarm woke us again at seven o'clock the next morning. It was a pleasant awakening, for I found Kathi snuggled next to me, sleeping peacefully with her head nestled on my shoulder. I let myself drift back into the warm pool of drowsiness and pleasure. But not for long. Then I kissed her awake and we parted to get ready for our visit to the local specialist in police brutality.

On previous visits, I had not gone willingly to Major Anadon's office, but I remembered the way. The low, plain building which housed police headquarters looked just the same. We parked the Mercedes limousine directly in front and told the sergeant at the desk that we wanted to see Staff Major Anadon. This seemed to be an unheard-of request. The policeman regarded us with much surprise, told us to wait, and hurried off. He returned at once.

"Staff Major Anadon is a superior official dealing with confidential matters," he told us importantly. "He does not see people without appointments. You are to state your business to me."

We thought we had answers for that. I handed Kathi one of my ICAL business cards and she wrote 're Count von Litzingen' on it. "Kindly give this to the Herr Major at once," she ordered. As the sergeant trotted off to do our bidding, Kathi grinned and whispered, "I find I'm getting quite good at giving orders."

The policeman returned very rapidly with a very different look on his face. "You are to enter at once," he said, "and would you please tell me again the name of your organization? I'm supposed to remember it." I didn't bother to answer.

Staff Major Anadon seemed more friendly than when we'd last been together. Perhaps the fact that someone came willingly to see him put him off his guard. Or, more likely, the influence of Kathi's uncle pervaded even to Paraguayan police headquarters.

"Well now, this is a delightful surprise. Señor Prior and Señorita von Hausenberg. Have you two joined forces at last? And what brings you here?" he said with irony. "Usually people do not come calling on me. And if I remember correctly, you both seemed most anxious to leave the last time we were together." Here he laughed and showered us with the smell of garlic, which seemed to be a feature of his meals whatever the time of day.

Kathi winced noticeably. Then she said passionately, "We are the only ones who are left. The old Hasso Cornitz was killed here by Petersen. The Jewish girl was killed on your territory by Petersen. My father was killed over in Brazil by Petersen. And Herr Prior was almost killed in Buenos Aires on Petersen's orders. Hasn't this gone on long enough? How much longer are you going to permit this to continue? What worse does he have to do? He has already committed every crime that can be imagined. And now he has added fresh killings to his record."

Staff Major Anadon smiled thinly. I could never tell what his expressions meant. This one showed worry, but with a vicious cast. But on his dark face that could still mean anything.

I thought I could give him more to consider. "Those I represent would still be willing to solve your concerns by removing him from your vicinity. However, I propose an even easier alternative. All we ask is that you direct us to him and then let us alone for 24 hours. If we can't do what is necessary in that time, you can do whatever you want with us."

Kathi added angrily, "And we won't care, because we'll both be dead if Herr Petersen is not!"

Major Anadon seemed impressed and more worried. He licked his lips and fumbled momentarily with a gold pencil which rested on the otherwise bare surface of his desk. Then he spoke. "With respect, it is very difficult to know what answer to give to your requests. What you ask is most dangerous. Señor Petersen is deadly and is still not without powerful friends. On the other hand, you two," and here he looked particularly at Kathi, "also prove to have very strong arguments. We cannot ignore the Count's wishes or have his niece placed in any danger. We must address your proposal Señor Prior, for we are after all a small, poor country. We cannot afford to offend, and we are, as I said, poor, ever so poor."

I had thought that something like this might arise. I removed a thick envelope from my suit coat pocket. "That reminds me," I said blandly, "ICAL is extremely dedicated to the development of internal security and police departments in the countries of this region. Especially those poorer ones."

"Are you indeed?" he responded.

"Yes, there is a special foundation for such purposes. I have been authorized to make a contribution to the security services of your country. Curiously enough, I happen to have it here in this envelope. Five thousand American dollars. Cash. I am sure that you, Major Anadon, would be willing to accept it on behalf of your country."

"With much pleasure," he answered. "At last I think we are beginning to understand one another." He turned to Kathi. "Do you think, Señorita, that your esteemed uncle would as well be gratified by such an understanding?"

Kathi said firmly, "Ja. However the Herr Colonel General has always valued most the final results of such understandings."

A look of resignation passed over the Major's dark face. Then his features wrinkled in a broad smile. "I will not be telling you anything directly or as you say 'for the record', but I suggest you be my guests at a dinner to which I am invited this evening. This is the sort of thing to cement a cooperative enterprise. I will call for you in my official car, at eight o'clock. We will be dining in San Bernardino. It is a suburb north of here. Very pleasant, cosmopolitan and private. You will meet all sorts of interesting people." He added emphasis to the last few words.

Kathi and I both caught his meaning. With little further conversation we bid Major Anadon a temporary adieu, and returned to the Terraza Caballero. Now all we had to do was wait. Kathi looked tense and worried. I suggested she call her uncle again to report progress. She retorted that we'd made no real progress yet, but agreed to do so. For what I hoped was the last time, I struggled through the coding procedure and sent a message to Pearlman. I was purposefully indefinite. Even in Kathi's company the day dragged. We both felt withdrawn, conserving nervous energy for what we hoped would be our final effort.

As promised, Major Anadon called for us promptly at 8:00 in the evening. His big, black Cadillac limousine looked pretty old, but it got us to San Bernardino in good time, just before the dinner hour.

A Paraguayan formal dinner party is quite an affair. Ninety-five percent of the population of the country is dirt poor, but those who are not, really are not. Many of the guests were still entertaining themselves in the reception rooms of the immense private residence. The host, a retired army general, greeted us affably and after a few private words with Major Anadon, conducted us by a circuitous route to the main dining room of the mansion. Evidently we weren't supposed to mingle.

Our host seated us with care and immediately called the remainder of the guests in to dinner. Staff Major Anadon was seated at the center of one side of large white linened table. A central position befitting his real importance in the country. Kathi was seated on his right and I was on his left. As usual Kathi looked wonderful. Conservatively dressed in black, but for that the more distinguished. I was my usual rumpled self.

The other guests filed in and after the usual confusion found their places at the immense table, surrounding nearly 500 square feet of white linen, silver, antique glassware and fine porcelain. Dress uniforms and formal clothing predominated. Medals and jewelry gleamed in the light of the crystal chandeliers. Chairs scraped on the antique hardwood floor and everyone looked around to assess their relative seating positions and the importance of their tablemates. I was somehow not surprised to find, directly opposite the Major, the familiar but now odious features of Carl Petersen.

He, on the contrary, was extremely surprised. His eyes darted about. He reddened noticeably, even under his ever-present tan, but finally regained his composure. Then his near-yellow eyes grew cold. The meal proceeded. Course after course, wine after wine. Menus and dinner guests may change as you go over the world, but gluttony does not. It is no wonder that man descends from his parents not from his head or his heart, but by way of a spot on his belly. At our part of the table conversation was stilted and sparse. Thinking of one of the secret ICAL files I'd read, I thought it was my duty as an added guest to liven up the proceedings.

I turned to Major Anadon and said in a loud voice, "Major, do you find the study of names to be of use in your profession?"

The Major looked surprised, but said, "Yes, Señor Prior, because so many names seek to conceal more than they reveal."

I continued, "I was studying some old files at my home office. It had not occurred to me that, for example, the name 'Petersen,' which is usually thought to be of Norwegian or Danish origin, may just as well come from a Russian name such as 'Petrovoff'." Out of the corner of my eye I could see Petersen start with alarm.

"How interesting," Major Anadon answered, now looking at me intently. I could see that Kathi also had turned away from another conversation and was watching and listening as well.

Next I said, again louder than necessary, "But Major perhaps we are excluding others by speaking of matters of technical interest only, probably the study of linguistics does not interest Herr Petersen. Indeed he is uncharacteristically silent this evening. Perhaps something does not agree with him or some business arrangements have gone wrong?"

The word 'Petrovoff' had told Petersen that I knew his real identity and history as a traitorous Soviet agent, posing for decades as a German. He responded with real venom. "Ah no, my North American friend, my very persistent North American friend. Quite to the contrary. I am still just as I was. There have just been the usual difficulties to attend to. Foolish people who interfere in my affairs for equally foolish reasons. It is most unfortunate that they are all so ineffectual. In Buenos Aires they try to spy on me. Here they try to blow up my house, but suffer for it. They dog my footsteps while I'm traveling, but to no avail. In Brazil there are more difficulties, but they too are overcome. Most satisfactorily overcome. The people who try to do these things to me are fools. But most of them are a cowardly sort of swine anyway, so we're better off with them dead." Here he glared straight at Kathi von Hausenberg.

I saw her wince as though she had been slapped. She said nothing, but took a big gulp from the wineglass which was in her hand. Then she put it down and moved her hand to her lap as though to take up her dinner napkin.

Carl Petersen started to say something else, but the words never came. Instead Kathi's hand came up from her lap with her little Browning pistol pointed straight at Petersen's chest. A woman across the table screamed and farther down someone jumped up and a wineglass was upset. Chairs crashed to the floor, as Petersen hurled himself to his feet and away from the table. Major Anadon grabbed for Kathi's hand, knocking the pistol upwards. A single shot rang out. There were more screams and Petersen raced from the room. Major Anadon still had a hand on Kathi's arm when I hit him from behind. It was my best imitation of a karate blow, delivered into his neck at his 'brachial plexus,' as hard as I could hit. He released her and, slumping in his chair, clutched at his arm, his black features contorted with pain.

Petersen disappeared through a far door and, as if by magic, police officers began to filter into the room. Jostling the other guests as little as possible, two of the officers grabbed me from behind and dragged me from the table. Out of the corner of my eye I saw Kathi being marched away between two others, with Major Anadon, either fortunately or by design, accompanying her, not me.

Apparently the dinner was to continue, for I heard no more disruptions as I was conducted through a pantry and a china kitchen, then through the main kitchen and out through a sort of annex at the rear of the mansion.

"What about the other man," I shouted at the policemen, "he's the one you want, not me. He's an escaping Nazi war criminal. If he gets away, the Major will be angry."

They stared at me impassively and I found myself outside before I could do anything to prevent it. However, in their haste they'd failed to disarm me. I still had the Mauser. Out-of-doors, they halted, fumbling with the door of the waiting police van. I had to make something happen, and looking wildly about, thought I saw the answer. On the wall behind us was one of those glass-covered central electric meters. It controlled the main circuit for the entire building.

While the policeman in front of me was still busy getting the van's doors open, I drove my right elbow backwards into the pit of his comrade's stomach. The man doubled up, retching and gasping. Without waiting even a second, I then kicked out and caught the second officer with a terrible blow behind his right knee. That's a vital spot if you can kick hard enough, and I could feel his ligaments give way. The man howled and collapsed to the ground. The Mauser pistol fairly leaped out of its shoulder holster and with it I clubbed the first man on the side of his head. He too went down. Then I used the pistol in another way. Two rapid shots into the main electric meter shattered it into a hundred pieces and plunged the house and surrounding grounds into instant darkness.

I returned to the mansion at a dead run through the annex. Luckily and by training I'd absorbed a good understanding of the layout from my previous walks through the building. The door by which Petersen had escaped looked like it should lead down a broad hallway and to a library and trophy room which I'd glimpsed upon entering. The hall was dark, so I moved along it very carefully. I was pretty sure Petersen would be hiding in that trophy room. He had to realize Major Anadon had put us onto him. With all the police around, I didn't think he would chance leaving the house. He would have to wait for things to quiet down.

The door to the library was ajar. Inside, it was inky black, with only the barest outlines of the furniture and decorations to be seen. Here a huge lounge chair loomed up. Over there a desk or large table. Above the fireplace I could dimly see the head and tusks of the trophy mount of a gigantic African elephant.

I don't like blundering into dark rooms. That is a good way to become dead, so I slipped low through the door and crept, crouching along the wall. I felt my way very cautiously, hoping to catch Petersen silhouetted against the lighter gloom near the windows. Then I stopped and froze. There was a soft thump far on the other side of the immense room. Something wooden, bumping against something else of the same material. Then it was deathly still, but I thought I could hear a heavy breathing. I moved again very slowly and quietly, easing my body between the wall and a large chair. When I reached the corner of the room, I paused and carefully moved my hand on the next wall. It contacted a peculiar object fixed to paneling. Just a small and empty metal clip. Then I moved further and found the wooden shaft of a weapon.

I rose slightly, allowing my hand to reach slowly up the thick smooth handle. After about four feet I felt a heavy steel crosspiece. I didn't need to explore further nor would it have been safe. The razor sharp blade of the jaguar spear would have ripped open my hand. Now the empty clip on the wall made sense. There had been a display of two such spears. Once again, Petersen had equipped himself with his favorite weapon.

Suddenly there was a crash against the wall behind me. Someone had thrown something from the far end of the huge dark room, at least 40 feet away. I kept very still. Then came another crash and something slid off a table making a third crashing noise as it hit the floor. I profited from the distraction to shift my pistol into the other hand and remove the second spear from the wall. Then I moved further along the wall, searching for something to give me more advantage. My pistol might not be enough in the dark against such a deadly fighter. The cool brick of a fireplace stopped my progress, but also gave me an idea. In such a household, a fireplace should always be ready for use. My hand closed on a match holder and a can of kerosene fire-starter, both standing on the hearth.

I listened carefully. The room was deathly still, but I could just hear breathing and slight movements at the far end. Petersen was listening for me, but I was quieter. He was probably a bit frightened, and not sure he knew what to do next. But I knew.

First, I laid the jaguar spear as backup, full length on the floor pointing in the direction of my enemy. Next, I opened the kerosene can and poured its entire contents on the hearth. Finally, cupping the matches in my hand I struck one, ignited the entire pack, and hurled it into the widening pool of kerosene. The flame shot up, filling the room with an eerie flickering light.

In an instant, Carl Petersen leaped up and charged me with his spear held high. I shot him twice as fast as I could fire, but that didn't stop him. Though wounded, he came on staggering and screeching at me in German and Russian. His relentless spear attacks had killed many jaguars, but I remembered reading that the Spanish infantry of Cordoba had defeated the Swiss spearmen by rushing in under their pikes. Unfortunately jaguars don't read. At the last moment, I threw myself flat on the floor, at the same instant raising the point of my waiting spear. I felt a lighting-like stab of pain as Petersen's spear slashed at my shoulder. But at the same instant heard an awful scream. Petersen caught the blade of my spear low in his belly, head on, and impaled himself on it down to the cross guard. He stumbled back, groaning, clutching the heavy spear, and weakly trying to drag it from the wound. Blood was running along the shaft, and also gushing blackly from his mouth. Then he toppled forward, screaming again as though the spear wrenched in the wound, and fell dead at full length across the burning hearth.

My improvised kerosene flare was just burning down when the lights went on again. Then, drawn by the shots and screams, Major Anadon, our enraged host and several other excited looking Paraguayan civilians rushed into the room. The Major took in the remains of the situation with one dark look, and ordered the others out. He was really quite considerate. He even helped me tie a rag over the flesh wound in my shoulder. Then he arrested me.

*   *   *

"So," said Colonel Yalinin in a tone which combined resignation with some satisfaction, "the Red Slayer of the SS, Carl Petersen or Karol Petrovoff, met his deserved end."

"Yes, Comrade Stephan," answered Major Grusev, "an unpleasant death but singularly suitable."

Termination

CHAPTER 19—PENETRATION

"Brahma."

I spent the night in jail. There's a first time for everything. I'd been an active ICAL Field Representative for years and had participated in a number of pretty dicey operations, but this was the first time I'd been so thoroughly caught. I wondered how long it would take before Pearlman or, more hopefully Kathi's uncle, Count Litzingen, could get me out. The jail cell was small and stuffy, and none too clean. Other than a distinct minimum of plumbing facilities, the only furniture was an old army cot. There was a mattress which was dirty and a few blankets which, fortunately, were clean. The wound in my shoulder was aching badly and I felt drawn dry of physical and mental energy. However, I did manage to sleep a little.

They woke me up the next morning. Bright and early by their standards, which meant at about 9:00 o'clock. A dour police officer brought in a few pieces of bread and a mug of weak tea. I was hungry, even after the large dinner I'd eaten the previous evening, but was cautious about jailhouse food, especially in Paraguay. I had eaten only a little when they brought in the doctor.

My shoulder was pretty well numb by this time so it was absolutely no fun having him examine the wound. It wasn't serious, but from what I could see, it was ugly. A three-inch gash slanted through the meaty part of my right shoulder. The doctor roughly pulled the wound open, let it bleed, and doused it with disinfectant. Then he stitched it up. That's easy to describe, but it was barely possible to endure the pain. Red lights danced in my eyes, and I found myself pounding the bed with my left hand. I have a low pain threshold.

Next, and more encouragingly, another jailer brought in a bowl of hot water, soap, a towel and some primitive shaving materials. He said nothing, but I drew the inference that I was to get cleaned up for something. This didn't take long. Then, feeling about a hundred years old and with my shoulder aching at every step, I was led down a hall, up a flight of stairs and into Major Anadon's office.

It still looked about the same. Modern, businesslike metal office furniture, light carpeting, and the same abstract painting on the wall. There had, however, been some additions. Against one wall two jaguar spears, crossed, were displayed. The blade of one was mostly shiny and clean. The other blade was a dull reddish brown. I didn't care for the Major's newest taste in décor.

The other and much nicer addition was that Kathi von Hausenberg was already seated in one of the two chairs facing Major Anadon's desk. I lowered myself gingerly into the other chair. It's surprising the amount of shoulder movement there is in the simplest action. Major Anadon was apparently lost in his contemplation of some papers, so I didn't interrupt him. I just reached over and gave Kathi's hand a squeeze. She was already looking me over and smiling. That was the best thing so far.

She whispered, "Are you all right? The police told me there had been a fight and that someone was killed, but that it wasn't you. Is it all over now?"

"Yes, Kathi, it's over. All over. Now we just have to see what music the Major wants to play, and then face it."

She mouthed the German words, "My uncle" and "don't worry."

Major Anadon looked up from his papers. He gave us his usual toothy, garlicky smirk, and called for someone over the intercom. A young police sergeant entered the room, removed some of the papers, and left some more. The Major glanced briefly at these, and then threw them aside.

Then he spoke. "When you consider their reactions, the citizens here are really amazing. I expected to have all the best people in Asunción down on my neck this morning. Yet here we are less than 12 hours after a shooting, an act of vandalistic destruction of property, and a bizarre assassination and no one has said anything! Can either of you imagine why?" He paused. We said nothing.

Not really expecting an answer, the Major continued. "Pistol fire interrupts an exclusive dinner party. A house full of guests is plunged into darkness. One of the city's leading residents is skewered with a jaguar spear in the country home of another of our best people. And those present are all too proper to complain!"

"Maybe they are afraid of you," I said pointedly.

"Or Señor Prior, they are afraid of someone else. Of Uncle Sam or Uncle the General, or both" he said grimly. "Of course the story will eventually seep out. But our good people here are sensitive. I suspect several of them knew a good deal more about your late friend Petersen or Petrovoff than they are now willing to admit. They will just want to sweep the whole thing under the rug. If our ordinary people, the poor people of this country carried on in your manner there would be headlines in all of the newspapers. You are indeed fortunate," he said sarcastically, "that you decided to spear a rich man. Here that's much more private."

"I agree," I said. Kathi looked encouraged, beginning to understand the Major's disposition.

"I thought you would," he responded. "Well, now we have had five deaths in this affair. Don't you also agree that is about enough?"

Kathi spoke suddenly. "It is all over now. There were very many dead souls which were crying out for vengeance. They now, I suppose, are still. At least that is what I was always told would be." Then she continued, speaking much more positively, using what I'd come to think of as her German aristocrat tone. "What are you going to do with us? Surely you can't be thinking of charging us with a crime. That would be most unwise."

Staff Major Anadon looked quizzically at her. "This is a very complicated affair. More so than either of you yet imagine. Complicated even considering, Señorita von Hausenberg, the issues raised by your most powerful family and Señor Prior's most powerful employer." And again he smiled in his own peculiar way.

We waited.

Then the Major continued. "You, Señorita, are free to go. It may surprise you, but a mere pistol shot at one of our exclusive dinner parties is not too unusual. No charges have been brought against you. You may leave now if you wish. Or remain to listen."

Kathi didn't move.

Major Anadon continued. "The case of Brother Prior here, is more complex. The matter of his having caused violent death to one of our important citizens is relatively inconsequential. I am more concerned about his previous activities and those in which he might engage in the future."

I didn't know exactly what this was leading up to, but guessed and thought I ought to get a word in. "Kathi, I expect the Major may be going to tell you some unusual things. I hope to have a chance to give you my version of events."

She answered simply, "Whenever and wherever possible, I shall look forward to it."

Somehow those words made me feel very glad. "Well then Major," I said, "let's hear what you have to say about my 'activities'."

"It develops, Señorita von Hausenberg, that your friend Señor Humboldt Prior is quite a fellow. He has a certain history and usually has a lot to say. Just now, however, he is unusually quiet because he has about twenty stitches in his shoulder."

Kathi was on her feet in an instant and leaned close to me. "You didn't tell me you were hurt. Which shoulder is it? You shouldn't be sitting up. I want to…"

Major Anadon waved her back to her chair. "There is no need to be alarmed Señorita. Señor Prior has always been pretty durable. The late Herr Petersen just cut him a little. Just before your clever friend speared him through the guts."

Kathi winced. Even I didn't like to remember the look on Petersen's face as he fell forward onto the spear.

Staff Major Anadon continued, "You see we know a good deal about Señor Prior. More almost than we would like to know. It is really quite a story. About three years ago, my country began to think its economic difficulties were even worse than usual. We are a poor country at best and our exports were declining. At first, we simply sought to learn more about the world in which we must compete for trade. Therefore we employed some experts in North America, paying them large sums. One thing seemed to lead to another.

"Then we began to focus on what we thought was a large international consulting firm. We were lead to believe, after further payments, that the firm, called ICAL of course, had information on some secret international marketing arrangements. Arrangements that effectively froze out small countries such as Paraguay. The firm proved to be quite unusual, with a very limited clientele. They receive large fees from a few large organizations and agencies of the U.S. Government. But no one from these generous payers can tell you anything at all about this ICAL. The payments actually seem to be made in care of the United States Army as a sort of fiscal agent. Most unusual! Except that, strangely, our modest payments went directly to an official of this ICAL. A man called Pearlman." I stored that fact very carefully.

"We wondered about this, so we infiltrated a person into this so-called consulting organization." The knowledge that I'd been right about his audacious penetration of my organization was little consolation next to the enormity of the implications both for ICAL and perhaps for me.

Major Anadon went on. "This ICAL is so large, so efficient and so professional that it was really quite simple. They weren't on guard against the modest activities of obscure police intelligence officers from small countries. So you see we've known about our friend Prior, or as he is known 'ICAL Field Representative Prior' for several years. We have direct access to ICAL's central files. However much he may have served a good cause or have been required to serve as he has, your friend has a history of intrigue and mayhem all around the world.

"On this particular operation, he was sent first to Israel to gather information. He was indirectly involved in two deaths there. Then he received orders and a final briefing and was sent to Buenos Aires via Chicago and New Orleans. En route he effectively disabled our Washington agent who was following him. Left him standing without money or papers in some small American town. After that experience, our man still has not recovered his full composure.

"Fortunately we had another man on the plane which brought Prior here to South America. Regrettably we lost him at the airport. However we knew all about his assignment with regard to Señor Petersen and hoped he would complete it before he reached Paraguay. We were most sorry that he wasn't lucky enough to do so.

"So then we became directly involved and more killings began. Believe it or not we abhor this type of violence in our country. And we don't want any more of it. For all we know you both may be assigned other targets here. You have become too proficient, particularly as a team. With all due respect Señorita, to your uncle the General, and Señor Prior, to your friend Pearlman, you have each been declared an undesirable alien and are being deported at once." Inwardly I sighed in relief. I also quickly pondered the implications of Major Anadon actually knowing my boss.

Then he added almost as an afterthought. "And Brother Prior, we have concluded that you are just a little too effective. We don't want to see you again anywhere in this region, under any circumstances or disguises that ICAL may devise. Also you know a little too much now about our own Paraguayan affairs. Therefore I've issued certain instructions to our agent within ICAL. Steps have already been taken. ICAL has experienced serious administrative difficulties. Certain papers and computer files, in fact the entire set of data pertaining to one Humboldt S. Prior, have mysteriously vanished. Your record has been wiped clean. Like it or not, they can no longer use you."

With that he thrust a bulky envelope into my hand, and gestured toward the door. I could see the envelope contained our papers and a pair of airline tickets. "Now," the Major said, "you may go and go quickly. Your baggage is in my car. We will take you to the airport. There you will be watched and put on the next flight, forcibly if required. Although I doubt that will be necessary." Here I thought I saw the suggestion of a wink. "And one more thing, Señor Prior, I've decided to accept your farewell gift to me. It was kindly forwarded here by certain neighbors. It is that interesting Kalashnikov model attaché case which you carry. That, you will not find in the car. I will add it to my new display of jaguar spears as a little remembrance of this affair."

As we walked out of his office I glanced back. Major Anadon's dark face was again smiling with that peculiar pursed-lips smile. I wished him well.

The airplane flight down to Buenos Aires passed much more quickly, but no less pleasantly than our long automobile drive of two days before. There was time for sharing most of my history with Kathi. She seemed to value knowing it very highly. We were held in the international travel section of the airport and so did not officially enter Argentina. I hoped that kept Colonel Manzano out of the picture. At my suggestion Kathi did put in a call to her uncle, Colonel General Count Litzingen, who was waiting at his residence in Rio de Janeiro. At first I just stood close to her, listening. Count Litzingen was pleased to hear directly that Herr Carl Petersen or Karol Petrovoff had been permanently removed, and that the orders the Count had evidently given the Paraguayans had been followed.

Then I intervened. I quietly suggested to the Colonel General that he recover the remainder of the stolen art works and assert claims against the rest of Petersen's estates on Kathi's behalf. Indeed I said it would be very wise for him to do so. He instantly agreed, in fact I thought I could hear, over the telephone, the click of Prussian heels obeying orders. Petersen's money would make Kathi a very wealthy young woman. She deserved it.

Then to my great, great regret I had to part from Kathi von Hausenberg. Her Uncle's plane was coming to take her to Rio and I had to return to Washington, D.C. Staff Major Anadon had proved highly competent, but I explained to Kathi that I'd better test the waters at ICAL headquarters just to be sure I was free. We hoped to meet again soon either in Washington or West Germany, and to telephone each other still sooner.

I reached Washington, D.C., the next morning and stowed my gear in an inexpensive motel near the airport. Then I went directly to ICAL's offices on Vermont Avenue. Pearlman and his associates could be unpredictable when angry or confused and my 'disappearance' from all their records would cause both. I hoped there wasn't going to be any trouble. It was only a short taxi ride from the airport. I got out of the cab a block away and walked casually down the chilly street toward the familiar stone and brick building. There was no sense in making too spectacular an arrival.

It was about 11:30 AM when I arrived. The first wave of noon-bound staff people was already starting to flow out of the front door. I pushed past them and identified myself at the lobby desk of the duty officer. I presented my pass and asked to see either Walter Pearlman or Mrs. Lesky. That is normal procedure if you are not expected. The duty officer examined a computer printout, frowned, and handed my pass to an assistant who disappeared with it. I stood waiting in the non-welcoming, sterile, marble-lined lobby. My shoulder ached and there was no place to sit.

Finally the duty officer's assistant returned with another man. I had never seen this person before, but he seemed from his dress and manner to be a higher-ranking ICAL official. He thanked the duty officer and conducted me into a visitors' meeting room just off the lobby. There he seated himself behind a small desk and invited me to take a chair. I did so.

The official spoke in a bland, businesslike manner. "Now then sir, if you'll give me your name and some identification, and tell me why you are here, I'll see what we may do for you." Since he'd already seen my pass, it appeared that Major Anadon's attack on my ICAL records might have been successful.

I said, "My name is Humboldt Prior and I'd like to see Walter Pearlman."

He scarcely waited to hear my answer. He replied, "We have no one here named Pearlman and your name does not appear in our authorization files." The first was almost certainly a lie, but the second might hopefully now be the truth.

Still probing, I said, "But I just gave my ICAL pass to the duty officer."

The man's face seemed even more expressionless. "That is not the manner in which it was reported to me," he answered with an air of patient toleration. "I simply understand that you wanted to see one of our staff people. No reason was given and nothing was said about any form of identification. I can only repeat that we have no record of you here, and that under those circumstances we cannot permit you to have contact with anyone here except our public affairs officer. And then, of course, we will have to establish your need for any information about this organization or its employees." The man was a good actor and a better liar. He finished the conversation with a courteous nod. I nodded back.

I walked out of the ICAL building into the gray noon-hour. It was a peculiar feeling. One minute you belong and the next minute they've never heard of you. For years I'd been praying for the day when ICAL would release me. Now that had happened and it would take some time to get used to. There was a slight feeling of regret, but only a slight one.

There was also a feeling of fear. Walter Pearlman could be very ruthless and very dangerous, and might not be through with me. I could feel the weight of the Mauser pistol under my arm, but surely couldn't rely on that sort of thing for the rest of my life, whatever that was going to be.

Then I thought of the Government Computer Center basking in the warmth of Arizona. There reposed its huge computers with their vast expanses of memory and mass storage waiting for use in the far distant future. Just the place to record and store a form of insurance policy. I would send Mr. Pearlman a warning about what could happen if I was not available to keep certain secrets, including those concerning his personal cash flows from his friend in Paraguay. That should do it, I thought, feeling better. A computer program would protect me, and I had in mind one or two related steps that I could take once back in Arizona.

The sidewalk outside the ICAL building was now crowded with people leaving it and the neighboring offices. A few flakes of snow drifted down. I stood watching, beginning to realize I'd never be called there again. I was a free man.

In a few minutes two familiar figures came out of the front entrance and walked past me. Walter Pearlman's face froze, but he walked by without even a trace of recognition or greeting. Farewell, Mr. Pearlman I thought. Mrs. Lesky also ignored me but as I watched them disappear into the crowd I might have seen her wave. I turned and walked the other way.

* * *

Major Grusev started noticeably as the substance of the report came to an end. The monotonous voice of the translator droned on, but now the words simply terminated the file of information received from the Soviet intelligence agent who was hidden in Arizona's U. S Government Computer Center.

It was a another bright spring morning in Kuybyshev. Sunlight was streaming into the windows of Colonel Yalinin's office. The Colonel wearily turned off the tape player. Major Alex Grusev walked stiffly across the room to remove the last tape.

Then he turned to face his superior officer. "That's it, Comrade Colonel, the complete report. What are we to do with it? There's a good deal of information about this ICAL organization, some of which has been little known. Also some potentially useful information about some personalities in Latin America. Finally there is the matter of the man Prior. Perhaps he can be located. Under the circumstances I think he could be made to work for us.

Colonel Yalinin didn't answer immediately. Instead he began fumbling through the papers in his 'IN' tray. Most looked routine. There was among them however, one envelope marked 'Urgent'. He had noticed it the previous day, but with his age and experience he knew that urgent matters are seldom handled by correspondence. Simply to further delay the necessary response to Grusev's request for instructions, the Colonel opened the envelope and began to read its contents.

First a severe frown and then, slowly, a grim smile spread over his normally impassive features. "Listen to this Grusev," he said. "It's a supplementary report from the same agent. Newly received. It concerns the taped report we have just heard. I'll dispense with the background material. It reads 'You have received a lengthy report from this station under File 30745PCDP4. I have just ascertained the following additional information which may influence your subsequent use of the original report.

'I have learned of secret experiments recently carried out by a special team of civilian specialists in artificial intelligence. These experiments involve trials of computer generated literature. I'm not competent to appraise the exact nature or significance of these experiments.' Here Major Grusev snorted with annoyance.

Colonel Yalinin ignored the interruption and continued to read aloud. 'I understand they basically provide a very sophisticated series of computer programs with known historical circumstances, a set of described characters, and a wide array of plot forms and possible events and activities. The first computer program combines these and follows steps in the program to produce a set of sequential literary constructions. Additional programs receive these and repeatedly improve them by applying literary criteria developed from analysis of existing popular works of fiction.

Where necessary, random numbers are used to provide alternate outcomes, sometimes completely unexpected by the programmers. The newest computers at the Center are said to be so much more rapid in their execution of the programs, that these repeated processes may be accomplished in a few days, producing ever-longer sequences. In effect, the computer programs are writing a sort fictional literature. I have not been able to learn the present status of this project or its real results. Reportedly it has been suspended for lack of funding.

'I wish to report further that most thorough inquiries reveal absolutely no record to the effect that any person such as Humboldt Prior was ever employed at U.S. Government Comp Cen, Arizona. In view of this circumstance it is with sincere regret and apologies that I must suggest that the material previously forwarded concerning the so-called *'Sunlight Operation'* ought to be regarded as coming from the artificial intelligence experiments and not as relating to actual events.'

Major Grusev simply stared at Colonel Yalinin in amazement. For once he had nothing to say. Colonel Yalinin concluded his consideration of the report. He said firmly, "In view of this second report, there is nothing further to be done. Instruct our agent to cease wasting his time and our funds on this matter. Send the reports to the archives. Maximum security. To be released only on my personal orders. The whole thing may just be a false electronic fantasy. Or yet it may be true." Colonel Yalinin secretly hoped it was.